OCT 0 6 2021

After the Ink Dries

CASSIE GUSTAFSON

SIMON & SCHUSTER BFYR

New York London Toronto Sydney New Delhi

An imprint of Simon & Schuster Children's Publishing Division
1230 Avenue of the Americas, New York, New York 10020
Text © 2021 by Cassie Gustafson
Jacket photography by Anthony Paz/Essentials/iStock
Jacket design by Sarah Creech © 2021 by Simon & Schuster, Inc.
Interior illustrations © 2021 by Emma Vieceli
For information about special discounts for bulk purchases, please contact Simon & Schuster Special Sales at 1-866-506-1949 or business@simonandschuster.com.
The Simon & Schuster Speakers Bureau can bring authors to your live event. For more information or to book an event contact the Simon & Schuster Speakers Bureau at 1-866-248-3049 or visit our website at www.simonspeakers.com.
Interior designed by Mike Rosamilia
The text of this book was set in Adobe Garamond Pro.
Manufactured in the United States of America
First Edition
2 4 6 8 10 9 7 5 3 1
CIP data for this book is available from the Library of Congress.
ISBN 978-1-5344-7369-0 (hc)
ISBN 978-1-5344-7371-3 (eBook)

For anyone who's ever been stripped of choice, who's needed to borrow strength to survive. This book is for you.

And for Carl, my ceaseless champion.
Thank you for always believing.

CONTENT WARNING

My Dear Reader,

This book contains material that some may find potentially triggering or traumatizing, including:

- sexual assault and abuse
- suicide ideation, self-harm, and attempted suicide
- bullying and victim-shaming

If you need to take breaks while reading this book, please do. Also, please consult the resources list on page 399 should you feel the need.

All my best,
Cassie

PART ONE

SUNDAY

ERICA

I DON'T SEE THEM AT FIRST—THE NAMES—BECAUSE MY eyes are closed, and my eyes don't seem to want to open.

A groan escapes me as I lie here, overheating in my own sweat. Then the nausea hits. Not a wave, like some people would describe. This is a semitruck of vomit hurtling downhill, brake lines cut. I try to peel my eyelids apart, but my lashes feel glued together.

Unease scratches at me. Something about . . .

The party.

What happened last night? With me, with Thomas? I don't even remember making it back to Caylee's house. Actually, I don't remember much past . . . what, the fireworks? Yeah, there were definitely fireworks in Zac's backyard. Thomas and me. A bonfire. *Did we . . . kiss again?*

Pressing my palms to my eyes, I try to force answers, but the effort drives splinters through my brain. I flip the pillow over and ease my cheek against its cool side. God, why did I drink so much? I can only hope Caylee didn't have to take care of me. Or worse—Thomas.

What did I do?

I sigh. Caylee. She'll have aspirin *and* answers.

When I drag my eyes open, I expect to see the purple walls of Caylee's room. But the gray walls that surround me are a slap in the face.

Terror dawns: This is not Caylee's room.

My eyes rake the space, but no matter where I look, the images don't make sense.

On the far wall, a Lakers basketball player occupies a poster, the top left corner peeling. A flat-screen TV sits on a dresser that spews clothes. Red plastic cups, a deck of playing cards, litter the floor.

My stomach plummets ten stories when I spot what's draped over the desk chair—a guy's blue-and-white varsity jacket, the kind all the jocks wear at Bay City Prep. Like the one Thomas has but never wears that I borrowed once.

The smell of the room hits me. A masculine scent, but somehow wrong, like heavy cologne mixed with something sour. I sit up quickly—too quickly—and tug the sheets closer. My vision blurs as dizzying heat rips through me.

There are bruises on my arm. No, not bruises. I look again, seeing the dark marks running up the inside of both arms for what they are.

Words.

Dozens of them, scrawled out in angry black marker.

The first word to register is **here**. As I stare, trying to find meaning in it, I realize it's part of a sentence. Twisting my arm, I read the phrase stretching from upper elbow to mid-forearm: Ricky was here.

Ricky? From Spanish class? Thomas's lacrosse team? Why would he . . . ?

Something closes in my throat.

Thrashing at the sheets, I scramble to my feet, then sway and have to steady myself against the bed. The need to vomit overwhelms me, but it's shoved down by the horror of what I'm seeing. Covering my arms, from palms to shoulders, are words and graphic pictures scribbled in black marker.

My skirt is gone. Marker spirals down both legs. The words Erica Walker is a sluuut and whore stare up at me— black tattoos inked onto my skin. Next to a sketch of an exploding penis, another name stretches across my right foot: Forest Stevens.

Forest? But he's so nice, so funny. Thomas's best friend.

Why would they do this? Why would anyone do this?

I lift my sweat-soaked shirt. Writing extends across my stomach and all over both thighs. Then I see my underwear. The lace looks faded.

No, they're inside out.

Who took them off? Thomas? Me? Someone else?

Oh my god, Oh My God, OH MY GOD.

Was I . . . ? Did they . . . ? They wouldn't have . . .

Rape.

. . . done that to me, right?

No. Ricky and Forest wouldn't. I know them.

And it doesn't feel like I've been . . . violated like that. Because I would know. I could tell.

Right?

Leave. Now.

Frantic, I kick through cups and clothes until I find my jean skirt in a crumpled pile. I grab then drop it. It's damp. Using my fingernails, I bring the skirt a few inches closer to my face and sniff. The stench of stale beer assaults my nose. Not pee . . . or worse.

Questions hurtle through my mind. *Where the hell is Caylee? Where was she last night? She was supposed to have my back. . . .*

And Thomas.

Where was he while Ricky and Forest—his friends, his teammates—wrote on me? Did they take off my clothes?

Oh my god. I have to get out of here.

Having no choice, I pull on the wet skirt, cringing as the damp fabric clings to my thighs. I tuck in my shirt and notice my bra is missing—the pink push-up I bought, just in case Thomas and I . . . Where is it? I scan the room, but it's nowhere.

And my boots. Where are my boots? I can't leave without them. They're my favorite.

4

Then, from across the room, I see it—an image sliced from a nightmare. My reflection in a mirror.

I once saw a photography art exhibit here in Los Angeles on the life of drug abusers, full of haunted-looking meth addicts. Only this time, the disturbing face is mine. *Erica Walker: Exposed.* Writing dominates every length of my bare arms and full thighs—black insults floating on a sea of pale, milky skin. My boobs hang heavy under a lacy shirt, pink nipples nearly visible without a bra. Matted black curls frizz around my head. My eyes look like a raccoon's, smeared with mascara and eyeliner, the whites bloodshot and dull.

To think I'd felt so sexy last night.

I spot it then, stuck inside the frame of the mirror. The photograph shows two faces I'd recognize anywhere since Caylee has the same picture taped inside her locker. Caylee and Zac—her, blonde and tiny and beautiful; him, a pasty-white Hulk. I find the letterman, flipping it over to reveal the name embroidered on the back: BOYD.

Zac Boyd. I'm in Zac's room.

This can't be happening. This is bad. Worse. Zac and I didn't . . . We couldn't have. I would never do that. He's Caylee's boyfriend. And I'm with Thomas.

At least, I think I am?

I need to talk to Caylee. I need to figure out what the hell happened last night.

My gaze snags on a Sharpie, half-hidden by bedsheets.

They drew on me, hands so close.

My knees buckle. I fall hard against the bed and close my eyes to block out the words, the names, branded across my body, but too late. They're etched on my brain: Ricky.Forest. Erica.Slut.Whore.

This isn't happening.

Panic blooms in my chest.

From downstairs, the sound of male laughter rips through me. My head snaps to the door.

I can't find my boots. My favorite boots.

But I have to leave. Now.

I rush for the door, bare feet avoiding scattered clothes and textbooks. A playing card sticks to my foot—a six of spades. I shake it free.

At the top of the stairs, I pause to listen, taking in the first floor below me. Zac Boyd's living room looks like a massacre. Upended red cups sit in pools of sticky liquid. Jackets, single shoes, and blankets are heaped in mounds. Shoved against the far wall, the glass coffee table rests on its side, a large crack down the middle.

Male voices filter in from the kitchen.

"Ah man. My shit hurts so bad right now, I can't even tell you."

Oh my god. Zac.

"Was it the keg stand or getting dropped on top of it?"

Ricky? His name on my arm.

Laughter erupts, maybe four voices in all, including Forest's distinct guffaw.

Forest's name on my foot. I shift my gaze to the stairs.

"Well, at least I wasn't as drunk as Erica," Zac says.

"You mean 'Mouth'?" Ricky. More laughter.

Did they just call me "Mouth"?

"Her tits were hot, man."

My face scorches. *They saw me topless. They all saw me topless.*

"Like fucking melons, man." Zac. "How'd she manage to keep those things under wraps all this time?"

"Well, they came out to play last night, that's for sure." *Stallion. Chris "Stallion." But he's in love with Jasmine, treats her like a queen. They've been together forever.*

Below, the guys explode in more laughter: Zac, Ricky, Forest, Stallion.

Shame pierces me. *What the hell happened?*

Downstairs, a toilet flushes and a door opens, then footsteps lead toward the kitchen.

"Tommy VanB! He lives!" Ricky shouts. "We thought you'd died in there, man."

"Naw, man," Thomas replies.

My heart stops. *Thomas is still here? Downstairs with them?*

Thomas VanBrackel: the guy I've had a crush on since my first week here, who tripped over his backpack the first time he saw me. Who sits behind me in Spanish class, took me stargazing at the beach. Who played me a song he wrote just for me, bought me the Edward Gorey poster I have in my locker. The guy I watched make the winning save in yesterday's lacrosse match, who kissed me for the first time in the parking lot where anyone could see before asking me to be his girlfriend. His *girlfriend*. Thomas—the very last memory I have of last night.

At the party, we'd stood next to each other by the bonfire, watching as Zac and Stallion and Tina lit off firework after firework. Tina was trying like always to be one of the guys. They'd wanted Thomas to join in, but Thomas had turned them down, choosing to stay with me instead. He'd looked so gorgeous, blue eyes reflecting the firelight, smile bright and playful. Standing that close to him, I could smell his deodorant mixed with fire smoke, feel his body heat radiating through his T-shirt—the silly one with the narwhal he'd worn just to make me smile. Then, laughing, he'd given me a piggyback ride inside Zac's house and we'd . . . gone upstairs, I think . . .

And after that? Blank canvas. A void.

I'd been all jumbled nerves and frantic energy last night, calming myself with every sip from the water bottle in my purse, the one I'd filled with vodka at Caylee's a few days back. I'd wanted Thomas to kiss me in front of his friends again so everyone would know we were official.

And now? What happened between hanging out with Thomas, and his friends seeing me naked? Why would they write their names on me? What if Thomas's name . . . ?

But Thomas wouldn't. He would *never* do that.

Not Thomas.

So where was he when everything happened? And he's in there now, in the kitchen with them.

"We were just discussing your girlfriend, VanBrackel," Zac says. "Wonder when she'll wake up."

"Maybe we should go check on her," Ricky replies.

I clap a hand over my mouth to choke off the sob welling up. I can't let them find me here. But there's nowhere to go!

Clutching the rail for support, I ease down the staircase, but my foot collides with a red cup, knocking it over. I freeze mid-step, watching in terror as the cup bumps down the stairs, splashing pale liquid onto the wall and carpet. The cup comes to rest on the wooden landing below with a tiny *thump*.

Oh god.

I jump at the sound of glass breaking in the kitchen.

"Dude, Thomas. What the hell?"

"Someone's got butterfingers."

Their laughs trail me as I hurry down the stairs and to the front door, avoiding the kitchen at all costs. Trembling, I twist the knob and slip outside.

God, not Thomas. *Not. Thomas.*

Bright sunlight sears my vision. I rush from the house as something inside me cracks and the tears begin to fall.

ERICA

KEEPING MY HEAD DOWN, I HURRY ACROSS ZAC'S FRONT
lawn, the damp grass sticking to the soles of my feet. I shiver
in the cold March air, then swipe at my eyes and scan the street
for my car, ignoring the scattered vehicles still parked in the
driveway, especially Thomas's blue Tacoma.

Don't cry.

There.

Down the street, my beat-up Corolla sits under a massive
eucalyptus, looking obscene on this pristine street. As the only
car Mom could afford on her nurse's salary, it's normally a huge
source of embarrassment. But now, the sight of it brings tears
of relief. Today it looks like a sanctuary.

A strong breeze whips my hair, drying my eyes as I rush
across the street.

I'm almost to my car when a blast of alarm hits. I don't have my purse; no keys, no phone. Glancing back at the five cars filling Zac's driveway—Thomas's truck—I know I can't go back in. They'd see me. I was lucky to have escaped unnoticed the first time. And if I don't sit down soon, I'll pass out right on this pavement.

Please no one come out of Zac's. Please, God.

Squeezing my eyes shut, I'm about to break down in the middle of the road when the thought dings: *Spare key, back fender.*

I could kiss Mom right now for her overly cautious hide-a-key. Bending down near the back tire, I feel inside the wheel hub. I will myself not to look at the marks on my arms, fixing my stare instead on a pitted dent in the rear door.

My fingers close around the tiny rectangle of metal. Popping the magnetic tin free, I plop down on the pavement. Rough asphalt scratches the backs of my legs, and old beer stench wafts from my skirt. With my legs outstretched, I can't ignore the obscene drawings and words staring up.

Ricky.Forest.Erica.Slut.Whore.

Why would they do this?

Was I . . . ? Was I conscious when they . . . ?

And Thomas?

But Thomas wouldn't. I know him. He couldn't have been there when Forest and Ricky wrote their names on me, while Zac watched. Maybe Stallion, too.

Thomas wouldn't have let that happen.

But a tiny voice whispers again: *He's in there now, isn't he? In the kitchen with them.* Maybe he knows what happened last night too. Probably all of Bay City knows by now, and I'm the only one who doesn't.

Eyes closed, I try to swallow down wave after wave of panic rolling up my throat. But it's too much. I scramble to my knees, loose rocks digging into my kneecaps. Warm bile splashes onto my arms and skirt as I heave and heave on the pavement, but I can't even care.

Finally I'm empty. I take a shuddering breath and wipe my mouth with the back of my hand.

Please no one come out and find me.

The sound of crunching gravel shatters my focus, dragging my eyes to the noise.

Thomas's truck?

But no. Two doors down from Zac's, a shiny silver Lexus pulls out of a driveway. I hug my arms to my chest, intently aware of my missing bra and tear-streaked cheeks. The sleek car slows, inching past me. The driver's nearly invisible behind dark tinted windows, but I can feel his hostile glare as he takes me in: a half-clothed girl, graffitied and hungover with a rat's nest of smashed curls and smeared makeup, huddled on the pavement next to a pile of vomit and a clunker of a car.

What have I done?

This moment confirms my worst fears. I've never belonged in Bay City, not since transferring here at the beginning of the semester. Not ever. And now I never will.

The Lexus continues its snail crawl past million-dollar homes and manicured lawns. Even after he turns the corner and speeds away, the driver's stare lingers, sharp and shaming.

Please no one leave Zac's right now. Please.

Inside my car, I search for something to wipe off the vomit spray and find a crumpled paper towel with a smear of jelly from my toast several mornings back. I'm dying of thirst, but all I have is an open can of Diet Coke in the cup holder. The flat soda does little to soothe the burning in my throat or mask the bitter bile taste.

Drive-thru? I squash the idea. Not with these marks.

Home. Now.

My gaze catches on the passenger seat, where my sketchbook lies open. On the upturned page is the last illustration I did of Erica Strange, the caped and masked alter-ego superhero I created. It's obvious I based her on myself, though she's clearly a swifter, braver, more badass version. Even Thomas started calling me "Erica Strange" after catching me doodle her in Spanish class. Plus, I gave her my lucky black boots—boots that Dad bought me before he moved that are now missing.

In my sketch, below the giant words *What Would Erica Strange Do?*, Erica Strange balances on top of a skyscraper, one fist holding the spire, the other at her hip, while her bat sidekick, Sparky, hovers by one shoulder. She stares with determination into the distance as her cape and hair whip around in the wind. One single arched eyebrow is visible above her violet eye mask, portraying unwavering confidence. This confidence is where we differ, she and I.

Last night before the party, I'd sat here and studied this sketch, sipping from my water bottle of vodka and chasing it with Diet Coke while waiting for Caylee to get here. I'd tried to pull strength from Erica Strange, to gather the confidence to go inside and be the girl Thomas thought I was—the Erica Strange I drew on these pages. At least, the version of me who isn't afraid to speak her mind or worried what other people think. She's never overwhelmed with anxiety or struck down by panic attacks. And last night, I'd gotten it in my head that I could be her. Was her. Felt the cape flutter invisibly around me as I'd stepped out of my car. Felt the cool air rustle through the not-quite-there eye mask as I strode across the street to meet Caylee, texting Thomas that I'd arrived.

But now the image hurts to look at. I've never felt so un–Erica Strange as I do right now.

Slamming the sketchbook closed, I chuck it in the backseat alongside the pointless, lingering question *What Would Erica Strange Do?* Because Erica Strange wouldn't have gotten herself into this mess in the first place: clothes missing, wet, inside out. Wouldn't have let herself get written on like some stall door in a public bathroom or gotten so drunk that guys saw her naked— Thomas's teammates.

Think he's going to want you now?

A softer voice: *Erica. Drive home. Now.*

Incredibly, my car starts on the first try. The radio bursts to life, blaring a thumping beat and edgy male vocals. Of course, it just so happens to be one of the songs from the massive playlist Thomas made me that I'd rushed to listen to in the hopes of impressing him even though I'd never paid much attention to rock music before.

Stupid stupid stupid!

I jab at the power button, my heart thundering as the music cuts out.

When I speed past Zac's, I can't help but glance at his front door. My breath catches. Thomas is emerging, keys in hand, throwing an arm up to shield against the blinding glare of daylight. I glue my eyes to the road in front of me and slam down on the accelerator, hoping against hope that he doesn't see me.

THOMAS

I CROUCH DOWN ON THE KITCHEN TILE, MY HEAD POUNDING.
The guys all watch as I mop up the last of the OJ and broken
glass. I made a huge mess, but I've gotta get the hell out of
here. My live audition's in less than two hours. So why am I
still here?

Above me, Forest groans, his eyes closed. He's leaning forward, his tall, gangly body practically bent in half, shaggy hair
a mess. Over jeans, he's still wearing the little-kid shark costume with the crotch cut out so that it fits his long torso.
It rides up, fraying at the seams, the gray shark tail hanging
limply from his butt, while his head's poked through the shark
mouth so the rows of teeth look like a necklace. And he doesn't
seem to notice the wet patches all over his pants where the
glass of OJ I dropped splattered him. Or more likely doesn't
care. He's pinching his lips like he's trying to keep the vomit

in. In a sick way, I'm glad someone else feels as shitty as I do.

Across the island, Ricky keeps lighting the gas burner on the stove, then blowing it out. He reminds me of a little bird with the hood of his red sweatshirt pulled up and small chest puffed out. Next to him, Stallion rests his head against a cupboard and swirls the pulp in his OJ. What with his height, and broad shoulders, and the dark sunglasses he's got on, he looks like a hungover FBI agent. Guess the daylight outside is too much for him.

My socks stick to the floor as I cram the last of the dirty paper towels into a plastic cup. The trash can's overflowing so I make for the sink, but a wave of what can only be puke rises from it. I give up and set the cup on the counter.

I've gotta go, should've already left.

Zac's still watching me, leaning against the fridge looking like a giant—not surprising considering how much time he spends lifting heavy shit. He holds his bad arm that's smothered in a cast and locked at a ninety-degree angle like a Tetris block.

"Make sure that's wiped up good, VanBrackel," Zac says as I grab a dish towel from the rack.

I don't bother responding, which doesn't matter because Zac's started up again, on his third tirade about the keg nozzle getting stuck. At least he's not talking about her anymore. I could hear them all the way from the bathroom. Who says shit like that?

And last night . . .

I push down the memory of Erica as my guts try to revolt. Gripping the edge of the countertop, I blink hard and swallow.

Stallion takes a swig of juice, clearing his throat. "So, Caylee stayed late. Anything we should know about?"

Zac's smirk widens. "She's a firecracker, that little hellcat. It's why I put up with her crazy."

I squeeze my eyes shut, knowing I've gotta get home, tune my guitar, do a final run-through of my songs if there's time. I was supposed to be home last night, and my father's going to kill me. But I can't be late for my audition this morning. My uncle's waiting for me. He flew all the way here just to watch me.

Ricky snickers, and I tear my eyes open. Four gazes train on me. I missed something. "What?"

"Just asking if you're still all pissed off," Zac says, "or if you've had the chance to get over yourself."

I remember being pissed last night. But I'm not anymore. I'm just . . . tired. So damn tired.

"Fuck off," I tell them, though it comes out whiny. I make for the living room and hurl couch pillows, searching for my keys.

"You always have been one righteous motherfucker," Zac calls after me. "Why don't you write a song about it? Call it 'Brooding Music Man'!"

My hands fist.

Leave. Grab your shit and go.

"Who's up for breakfast?" Zac asks.

"Oh, shit yeah," Ricky replies.

Condiments rattle as the fridge door opens.

I overturn furniture, chuck jackets, but no keys. How the hell can they be hungry?

"Good, 'cause you're making it. I gotta call the maid to clean this shit up before the step-monster gets back, you bunch of wild beasts!"

Laughter.

I search around the broken coffee table, rip the blanket off the floor where I'd slept, then freeze.

Erica's boot.

A single black boot sits below the blanket beside my keys. How'd it get down here? Did she leave barefoot, then? Dropping to my knees, I spot the second boot under the couch. My hands shake as I dig it out, then I pull on my Chucks.

I'm turning to leave when I hear "VanB."

Zac leans against the doorframe, holding his casted arm. Behind him, Ricky's at the fridge, pulling out an egg carton and bag of frozen hash browns. Stallion rests against the counter, texting like mad, probably to his girlfriend, Jasmine. Forest braces himself against the sink, and I don't know how he isn't puking at the smell of whatever's in there.

I straighten up, keys in one hand, boots in the other, pushing the hair from my eyes with an elbow. "What?"

Zac walks over, surveying, standing half a foot shorter than me but making up for it in bulk. I must look like hell in last night's clothes, with breath and a hangover that makes me wonder how I ever thought drinking was a good idea. Or coming to this stupid party.

His gaze finds the boots in my hand, but for once, he doesn't comment on her. "You good?" he asks. "You know we're just messing with you."

I don't meet Zac's eye, hating how close he's standing. "Fine. Why?"

"Well, last night got a little crazy, is all."

My fists tighten. "I don't remember last night."

Zac cocks his head. "You don't . . . ?"

A text pings through. Uncle Kurt: **You ready for today?**

Checking the time again, I curse. How the hell am I supposed to do anything when I feel this shitty, let alone make it through a live audition? And my father's going to *murder* me.

"I gotta go."

Zac nods, tongue pressed inside his cheek. "Sure, sure. Well, till practice, then." He claps my shoulder but doesn't turn to go, just keeps on staring.

I grit my teeth. Damn it, our extra practice, too, on top of everything else! Boots and keys in hand, I duck out the front door and suck in lungfuls of fresh air. The sun blinds me as I trip down the steps, standing exactly where I'd stood last night when Erica arrived, looking hotter than I'd ever seen her. I'd tried not to stare too hard but couldn't look away. Then she'd smiled at me, and I'd taken her hand, so stoked just to be near her.

Now, glancing down the street, I half expect to see her running barefoot down the sidewalk. But I see only empty curb and a bunch of trees. I'd given her enough time knocking over that glass of OJ, then. She must be long gone.

But how'd she get here last night? With Caylee, probably. So, was she walking now? Calling someone? Because she doesn't live close by. Still, I picture her on foot, everyone pointing and staring, wondering why she's not wearing any shoes.

My stomach turns, and I'm almost sick next to my truck.

I have to get home, and shower, and make it through my audition, then everything'll be okay.

I'm not angry anymore. I'm not. I'll call her later. Tell her I have her boots. Ask if she wants to do lunch tomorrow. Pizzaz, maybe. Or Junie Bee's. She loves their fries.

Nothing comes up as I dry heave again.

I swipe at my eyes, tossing her boots in my backseat. Pulling my phone from my jeans, I haul myself into the driver's seat. I should call her now. See where she is.

I click on recent calls. In her contact photo, Erica sits in my passenger seat with a neon smile, one hand trying to block the shot. Sunlight filters in, washing out the photo and glinting off the two overlapping W's of her Wonder Woman T-shirt. She looks so happy. That day, we'd gone to Junie Bee's with everyone, and even the guys had acted cool. We'd eaten chili cheese fries, and laughed when Ricky poured soda all over himself, and Erica and I'd slid into a corner booth to chat, just the two of us.

I need to talk to her, check on her.

Before I can think twice, I click "call." But it doesn't even ring, going straight to voicemail. The sound of her upbeat voice kills me.

I hang up and toss my phone. Throwing my truck in reverse, I realize, for the first time ever, I'm relieved she didn't answer.

And—*shit*—I'm going to be late. I can't be late.

ERICA

WHEN I PULL INTO THE PARKING LOT AT OUR APARTMENT, Mom's van isn't in her usual spot. I drag myself out of the car, bare feet stepping around an oil stain, and rush up the stairs to our unit. The sun beats down on me as I tip over the clay pot of rosemary, grab the hidden key, and let myself in before any neighbors spot me. I want nothing more than an ice-cold glass of water and to lie down and sleep for the rest of my life, but first, I need to look, and then I need to call Caylee.

In the entryway, I pull up short and catch my breath. A half-empty pack of Double Stuf Oreos still sits on the coffee table next to two mugs with used tea bags. They're left over from yesterday afternoon when Mom and her best friend, Valerie, binge-watched *Scandal* reruns. As I was leaving, I remember the two of them in heavy debate over how hot the lead actor dude is.

My nausea grows as I take in the peeling Formica counter-tops in the kitchen, the corroded faucets and yellowed grout.

How can the apartment look exactly like it did when I left? God, I need water.

A bright pink Post-it glares up from the counter. Ignoring it, I glance in the dishwasher, which is full of dirty dishes. Reaching into the cupboard, I pull down a shiny red mug emblazoned with *Someone in Seattle loves you!*, a gift from Gramma Anne for my fourteenth birthday and her not-so-subtle reminder that we needed to visit. It was also the last birthday I spent with Dad before he left. And he and I have talked only once since his semester started up again in January. But how can I possibly be thinking about Dad right now? I have much bigger problems.

Filling the mug with cold tap, I drink like a horse, which takes away my nausea for the briefest of seconds. Then the queasy feeling returns like a tidal wave. Tears spring to my eyes as I steel myself and turn to Mom's note:

> Erica,
> Tried your phone all morning—
> no answer. Had to leave to meet
> with caterers. Could have really
> used your help today.
> —Mom
> P.S. Call me to let me know
> you're okay.

Crap, Mom's fundraiser!

The clock on the microwave glows 8:17. I'm already over an hour late. For weeks now, Mom's made a huge deal about the pancake breakfast, her second-ever event at the new hospital. She'd wanted me to help set up and entertain her patients while they ate their weight in pancakes.

Guilt hits when I think of Mom's disappointment, of Mrs. Pensacola's arthritic, blue-veined hands folded neatly in her lap. I know Mrs. Pensacola's been waiting all week to talk to me about her oil paintings or give me more pointers on my figure drawing and composition because I said I'd be there today. But given the condition I'm in, there's no way I can go. And I can't text Mom without my phone. I could use the house phone, but then I'd have to call and Mom'd know right away from my voice alone that something was wrong. She'd ask questions that even I don't have answers to yet.

Panic flutters in my chest as I squeeze my glass into the packed dishwasher. I have to lie down.

But glancing down at my legs, I know I have to look, and I have to call Caylee, though I sure as hell don't want to do either.

I veer right, into the sweltering heat of Mom's room, and flip on the light switch. I don't know what I expected in here either because her room is the same as always. Everything about it screams "old lady," from the glass bowl of potpourri on her dresser to the pastel-flowered bedspread that are both older than I am.

Still, I search the room, trying to find something different, something changed, but everything looks like a museum exhibit, preserved exactly as it was when I left. Except . . .

Hanging halfway out of Mom's hamper are an oversized T-shirt and jeans. Aside from her scrubs, it's all she ever wears. I look down at my own clothes—tiny skirt, skintight top.

Missing bra. Underwear inside out.

Maybe if you'd worn jeans last night instead, covered your skin. . . .

But no, I'd wanted Thomas to see me.

And maybe he really had, naked and all.

No. He wouldn't. Not Thomas.

Maybe there are more names. Thomas's name.

Stop. Call Caylee.

I clench my teeth, then yank the ancient landline phone from its cradle that Mom insists on keeping "for emergencies," and pull against the spiral cord as I plop onto Mom's bed. I'm nearly catatonic with fear thinking about Caylee's possible reactions. Does she know what they did to me? That I slept in her boyfriend's room? Or is it really as bad as I'm thinking? Maybe it's all just a prank, some kind of sick joke. . . .

But my ears still ring with Zac's words from earlier: *"Like fucking melons, man."* Talking about my breasts, that he and everyone else saw—Zac, Ricky, Forest, Stallion, and maybe even Thomas. Then I remember my inside-out underwear because someone took them off me, and I can't remember who.

26

Hot tears leak down my cheeks as I suck in a breath. I don't want to do it. But I have to know.

I've never really searched down there before other than to shave myself after that embarrassing first week in the locker room. Now, avoiding the writing, I set down the phone with its faint dial tone and stand. Opening my legs, I peel my underwear aside, eyes on the stupid bowl of dusty potpourri. I can't make myself look at the writing anymore, so I press two fingers to myself and bring them in front of my face.

There's . . . nothing. No soreness. No blood.

I do it again, harder this time, with the same result.

So, they didn't . . . rape me? Because I should be able to tell? I've had sex before, but only once, on my friend Isabela's couch in a basement that smelled like mildew. Isabela's my childhood friend from my old school, St. Agnes, who I haven't really talked to in over a month, and the guy in question is her older cousin who was staying with her family at the time. He was seventeen, I was thirteen, and I remember feeling so flattered for all the attention. We'd done it just the one time, but it had hurt like hell and gotten blood on the couch. I'd felt sore for several days after, not at all what I would call a "pleasurable" experience, especially since he never talked to me again.

So, I'm pretty sure I'd be able to tell if something like that had happened last night. And that's when you call the cops.

I stare at my arms, legs, covered in writing and disgusting drawings.

But what about this?

The ceiling fan beats down warm air in time to the thudding of my heart. I grab the phone and dial Caylee's number. It's the only number besides Mom's that I've memorized. God, what if I don't ever find my phone? Then I'll have to get a new one, even though I can't afford it. And that's only the beginning of the things I need to do.

The phone begins to ring.

I loop the cord around my finger.

The phone rings again.

Three more loops.

The ringing continues—three, now four rings in all.

By the time Caylee's voicemail starts up, my entire index finger has disappeared inside the coils of the phone cord.

Where are you, Caylee?

I scan my arm, the cramped way Ricky wrote his name.

He was so close to you.

Forest's name on my foot.

They were so close to you.

And Stallion? Zac? Thomas?

Why was Thomas still at Zac's? Does he know what happened?

Thomas is the first guy I've ever really dated. There had been a few guys at St. Agnes in the two years I was there, but nothing like what I have with Thomas. Or . . . had. Thought we had, I guess.

The beeping announcing Caylee's voicemail catches me

off-guard. "Caylee, hey, it's me. Call me, 'kay? On my house phone, not my cell. I can't find . . . It's missing. I don't know where. Listen, I really need to talk to you, 'kay? Like, *really* need to talk to you. Please call me." I slam the phone down, my skin covered in sweat.

For a split second, I consider calling Amber, a redhead in my class who's nearly twice my size with more than double my confidence. Amber's "throat-punch transgressors" attitude and assertiveness have always intimidated me. We've hung out enough over the past few months thanks to the fact that she and Caylee have been friends since elementary, but I don't know Amber's number, and even though I have it in my phone, I've never actually called her. The most we've ever done is group text, with Caylee as our buffer. Plus, if I did call Amber, what would she say? Probably throw out a snarky one-liner or lecture me on "disgusting" high school boys. Or she'd give me the "have some freaking self-respect" spiel she gave Caylee about Zac last week, which was beyond awkward and made me wonder how the two of them have stayed friends so long, especially because Amber was right about Zac.

The one time Amber and I seemed to hit it off was over lunch when we were talking about Frida Kahlo. Amber knew a lot about her activism, but not about the bus accident that nearly killed Frida, which got her to start painting, or the fact that she also did frescos and etchings. Midway through my conversation with Amber, I'd felt like I was finally earning her approval. Then she said something about Frida being an early feminist, and I jokingly responded, "Just another man hater!" even though I knew that had nothing to do with it. I'd only said it to make Caylee laugh, which it had, but when I turned back to Amber, she seemed . . . disappointed somehow.

So how could I possibly reach out to her now about last night if I have no idea what she'd do with the information? No, she's a well-known tattletale. I *know* what she'd do. She'd want to tell someone—an adult—but I can't risk word of this getting out. Calling her isn't an option.

I try to think of someone else I could call, but I've only been at Bay City for a few months and don't have anyone else's number. Caylee and Thomas have been my main friends, and even if I wanted to contact him, I don't know Thomas's number either.

I stumble to my room, where I find my scattered colored pens and the folder on my nightstand filled with sketches I've done, but these aren't of Erica Strange. Since moving here, I started illustrating comics of my real life, too—Thomas and Caylee and all things Bay City. My entire life at this school is in this folder. I'd scan and upload these sketches onto my private website, alongside my Erica Strange ones but in their own thread. Still, if I'm being honest, lately I've done a lot more sketches of Thomas and me than I have of Erica Strange.

Brushing aside my pens, I flip open the folder, knowing what I'll find even as I do—my first-ever Bay City spread. It's a paneled page of Thomas and me from the very first time I saw him. I run my hand across the image of Thomas smiling up at me and can picture that second day at Bay City Prep so clearly in my mind. Mom and I'd just moved to the edge of town, away from my old friends and school. I still hadn't met anyone, and I remember feeling so out of place and so very alone, not to mention lost in the giant hallways. People jostled me as I searched again for my first class, and I tried to summon my inner Erica Strange but didn't get very far. Even the violet pants I had on that'd seemed "Erica Strange" cool in my room now felt "squishy eggplant" cool. Suddenly, everything started to crowd in, and blind panic ran through me. Without warning, I felt on the verge of a full-blown anxiety attack right there in the middle of the hallway. Fighting tears and a flood of pelting thoughts, I rounded yet another corner . . .

And there he was.

He sat on the other side of the hallway glass in the courtyard—a beautiful white-skinned, dark-haired boy with broad shoulders and eyes pressed shut in concentration. Early morning sunlight streamed over him as he leaned against a picnic table, black Converse tapping out a silent beat as he strummed along to whatever music he heard in his head. His eyes flew open, and he scrambled for a notebook and pen, sticking his tongue out as he jotted down the thoughts scurrying through his mind. Something about the way he closed out the world, air-guitaring and journaling like no one was watching, made longing well up in the pit of my stomach. I thought about my suffocating panic from moments ago, broken now only because I'd been wholly distracted, but that more often than not got the better of me. I wanted so badly to be as free as he looked.

He glanced up at me then, startled—dazed, even—to see me staring back at him. I knew I should feel embarrassed, look away, but all I could do was notice how perfectly his sea-blue shirt matched his eyes. He recovered quickly, mouth quirking into a lopsided smile before forming a single word: *Hi.*

Hi, I mouthed back, causing his grin, then my own, to widen.

The warning bell rang, sending both our gazes skyward before snapping back to each other.

He shrugged, resigned: *So it begins.*

I scrunched my face to let him know I shared his agony. We stayed there, suspended in time, before I broke the connection with a little wave. He returned the wave, flashing another smile before scrambling to his feet and tripping over his backpack, which made me laugh.

I bit my lip and turned to head for my locker, but not before throwing a quick glance over my shoulder and catching his eye again. Though he stood with his backpack slung over one shoulder, his eyes stayed tethered to me.

My mind pinged with questions: What was his name? What

did he write in that notebook of his? What music filled his ears that allowed him to lose himself in the middle of the school courtyard? Because whatever it was, I wanted in.

I didn't know it back then, but he would become my first friend at Bay City. He'd transfer to my Spanish class, sit right behind me, and ask me about the Erica Strange drawings that filled my sketchbook. I'd learn his name, that he played guitar and wrote songs. I'd call him Thomas the Rhymer and he'd call me Erica Strange. But in that hallway, all I knew then was, when the boy from the courtyard looked at me through that window, I felt less alone and like maybe Erica Strange wasn't so out-of-reach after all.

Now I drop the folder of drawings back onto my nightstand and all the memories with it. My gaze travels across the room to my bulletin board that's covered in pictures and bits of art inspiration. There's the Disney princess stickers Caylee gave me as a joke next to a photo of her, Amber, and me at Pizzaz Pizza Parlor, with Amber flipping off the camera. This half-covers a picture of Isabela and me, taken at St. Agnes a few weeks before I transferred. Then there's the Lead Paint album cover for Thomas's favorite band, a Los Angeles County Museum of Art ticket stub from our second date, one of Thomas's Spanish worksheets he'd messed up on, the note he'd left on my car after his friends had been jerks, and finally, the grainy photo he'd taken of us at the beach the night of our first real date, his tan face smiling beside mine. *But we're the same! Twin artist souls!*

Thomas the Rhymer and Erica Strange! And then I have to stop looking. The horror of last night's party crashes over me, again and again. Each time feels like the first time.

In blurry images, I replay it all: Zac's backyard, dotted with a few dozen classmates and the blue and white colors of Bay City Panther pride; groups huddled around two perspiring kegs of cheap beer and the roaring bonfire; the snap and sparkle of bottle rockets and fireworks igniting; Thomas's dark hair falling over crystal-blue eyes, his mischievous smile aimed at me.

I glance again at the folder of drawings.

Where were you, Thomas?

I want to collapse onto my bed, but it's heaped with clothes—several rejected outfits from last night. Heat balls in my stomach as I remember yesterday's manic excitement while I got ready for the party, music cranked as I bounced around my room, fretting over stupid details, like if I should wear my hair up or down. Makeup, playful or sultry? Like everything had to be perfect. As if any of that could possibly matter now.

Best friend won't call you back. Thomas's friends wrote on you. God knows what else. You'll never live it down. Never.

My body flushes with heat. I fling the clothes off the bed and kick at them, pummeling the mattress with my fists. I kick and hit until I'm out of breath, despite what it does to my pounding head. As I squeeze my fists to my mouth, a silent shriek tears at my throat. Stupid, stupid, stupid!

I stop short at the sight of gray. On the floor, the arm of

Thomas's sweatshirt drapes over my clothes, the sweatshirt he'd given me to wear after his game. I scoop it up, feeling the soft fabric between my fingers. His audition—it's today. Had he forgotten? No, he definitely wouldn't have. Blood pounds in my temples as I breathe in the scent of him.

But he was there, in the kitchen.

An instant later, I drop the sweatshirt, overwhelmed by heat. When it reaches my stomach, I know I have only seconds to make it to the bathroom. Moving as quickly as my lead body will allow, I sprint to the bathroom, flinging open the toilet lid as vomit erupts. Shaking and spent, I press my clammy forehead against the cool plastic of the toilet seat. Through a blur of tears, my eyes find the shower curtain covered in bulgy-eyed goldfish. I have to shower. I have to get this crap *off* me. But the effort to stay upright is too much.

Pulling the bathroom rug to me, I lie down against its matted, gray fur, tears leaking from my eyes. I'm so embarrassed. Mortified beyond belief. I feel disgusting. *Am* disgusting. Normally the hair and dirt stuck to the rug would appall me, but I only need to glance at the smudged Sharpie covering my skin to realize that I couldn't get any dirtier.

THOMAS

"THOMAS, GET YOUR ASS IN HERE."

Shit. My father.

I'd heard my parents talking in the kitchen but had tried to slip past them and escape up the stairs. My truck must've given me away. Or the front door. Or my guilt. Everything about this morning is going so wrong. But if I don't leave soon, I'll never make my audition in time. I need to get this over with, and fast.

I swallow hard and try to throw myself together in the steps it takes to get to the kitchen—smooth my hair, my damp shirt. Anything to make me look a fraction less shitty than I feel. But I can't erase the evidence of sweaty pits or alcohol breath.

Mom's clearing away breakfast dishes while my father stands at the bar top, holding a steaming mug of coffee. He's got on a pressed gray suit that won't let anyone forget he's a senior partner at McMurray and Associates, even on weekends when he's not in court. Taking one look at me, he jabs a finger in my direction, face filling with disgust. "Where the hell were you? You had your mother worried."

With my father there's never a right answer, so I stay quiet.

His hands death-grip the mug, anger multiplying. "Not going to answer me, huh? So, what then, after finally showing some promise on that lacrosse field last night, you're just going to screw it all up? And you look like hell. Partying all night, I suppose? Wasting your goddamned life?"

"Tyler," Mom whispers from the sink.

"What?" my father spits, and Mom goes quiet, returning to the silverware she's rinsing. "The boy has to realize there's more to life than parties and beer, Sharon. You work hard or you're nothing."

My anger flares. I only made time for Zac's party because Erica was going to be there.

"*Hop on, little croc*", my brain replays.

I yank myself out of that memory so fast, feeling sick to my stomach. I can't think about last night. I need to get my ass out the door ASAP.

But my father rages on, no end in sight, comparing me to my older brother, Michael—ambitious, driven, three years into his premed degree—everything my father wishes he could intimidate me into becoming. I grit my teeth, heart pounding, refusing to say anything for fear he'll keep me longer. Plus, I know what this is. He's still punishing me for spending the winter break with my uncle Kurt. My father had probably hoped letting me go visit Kurt would deglamorize my uncle's lifestyle in my eyes, show me how hard life as a tour manager for a rock band is, and that next summer I'd agree to take some worthless internship at his law office. Of course, my father had been wrong. I knew I'd love it. And I had. Every single hectic, sleep-deprived second of it. And halfway through break, when I'd gotten notice of my callback audition to USC's Thornton School of Music, it'd felt like fate.

But what kind of shitty fate would it be if I missed my audition because my father held me hostage? He has to remember today's the big day.

I breathe a sigh of relief when I hear his favorite threat, the one he works into the end of every conversation: "You place one toe out of line again, Thomas, and you can forget all about that fancy music school of yours. Do you understand me?"

Music school—the rug he'd rip out from under my feet if given the smallest chance. Or, more specifically, Thornton, because it's all come down to them.

Beginning of my junior year, my father had made a crazy deal with me: make first string in lacrosse and keep a 4.0 for the remainder of high school in exchange for him paying my way through a degree in music . . . if I managed to get accepted. He'd probably only agreed to the deal because he wanted to watch me disappoint him yet again, either by failing *or* upholding the deal. Or maybe he just wanted to have something to hold over my head, only to find some lawyerly loophole and wriggle free in the final hour. Or most likely, he never thought I'd actually get this close. Whatever his reasoning, I'd had no choice but to accept his terms.

I nod at him now. Understood.

"Good. Now get out of my sight." He slams his mug on the counter before making for his office, probably to pick up the phone and repeat this conversation of disapproval on someone else.

I let out my breath. From the sink, Mom gives me a small smile, gripping a soapy breakfast plate. Of course she's all smiles now that he's gone. But she looks as small and breakable as the plate in her hands, so I shove down my irritation and give her a quick hug before darting for my room. I call out behind me, "Love you, Mom. Sorry I made you worry."

I barely catch her "Love you too, sweetie. Good luck at your audition," as I pound up the stairs. She did remember, then.

In my room, my eyes fly to my electric-acoustic, Eleanor, resting in her stand. The silver Sharpie scrawled across her glossy mahogany body glints in the light—four autographs signed to me, ink not even three months dry. The names belong to all the members from Lead Paint: Benji Solaris, only the greatest lead guitarist in the world of alternative rock, alongside Chad, Kobe, and Arjun. Eleanor had been a gift to me from Uncle Kurt for helping him over break.

But now I can't see Eleanor without thinking about Erica. My guts clench.

I still need to tune Eleanor, shower, get my ass on the road, but instead I whip out my phone and click into messages, then Erica's name. The final message she sent last night stares up:

Here :)

and my reply:

:D

I'd been stoked to get her text, practically mowed everyone down as I hurried to Zac's front door to meet her. But looking at her text now, everything I want to say evaporates. I pause, then type out: Hey, listen . . .

Too weird. I erase it and start over.

Erica Strange! But I erase that fast. Far too enthused.

I think about her boots in my backseat. Should I tell her I have them so maybe we could meet up today and I could return them?

Erica, can we talk? I erase that for Wanna talk? But what if she doesn't? What if she turned her phone off earlier so I *couldn't* talk to her?

Could I blame her?

I hold down the delete button till that disappears too, cursor flashing. Then my phone pings, startling the shit out of me—another text from Uncle Kurt: You on your way, kid?

Damn it!

Splashing water on my face, I run wet hands through my

hair, then scramble into the clothes I laid out yesterday. I'd planned out today so differently in my head: sleep well, eat breakfast, arrive early, find my uncle, check in, find the practice room, tune Eleanor, calm my nerves . . .

And Erica. Last night . . . I'd planned that so differently too. I swallow hard, fighting the urge to puke again.

But there's no time. I snap Eleanor into her case and sprint from the room.

ERICA

THE TWISTING OF THE BATHROOM DOORKNOB SHATTERS MY
sleep. Two quick knocks follow.

"Erica? You in there?" It's Mom, her tone frantic.

"She has to be," says the voice of Valerie. "Her car's here."

I bolt upright, then remember where I am. *Bathroom floor.*
Disgusting rug.

The knob twists again but the door doesn't open. Locked,
thank god.

What time is it? Fundraiser over already? I rub my face, feeling the scaly imprint the rug made on my cheek.

"Erica, you open this door," Mom commands.

"Yeah, okay," I manage, voice gravel. "Just a minute." I take
in the beer-and-vomit-covered remains of last night's outfit.
Worse, my graffitied limbs are on full display. My head snaps
around the room. *Towel? No, that'll never cover it all. But what?*

Then I spot my fuzzy purple bathrobe hanging on the door and tear it from its hook.

"Erica, I'm not kidding. Open the door this instant!" Mom's voice morphs into straight-up pissed.

"Just a minute!" I call again.

The robe has longish sleeves but only comes to mid-calf. It definitely won't cover my shins, let alone my foot where Forest's name is scrawled next to the exploding penis. But I'm out of options.

Mom and Valerie whisper-argue as I throw on the robe, unlock the door, then plop back on the rug and whip my feet under me.

As the door flies open, I burrow into the fabric, praying neither of them can see through it to my humiliation. Mom flits in like an angry white hornet, hair tossed up in its perpetually messy knot. A two-sizes-too-big St. Joseph's Hospital T-shirt hangs over old jeans. She's everything I'm not: thin to my curvy, tall to my compact, and has smooth chestnut hair that mocks my crazy mop of curls. She's bony, too, like Caylee, though she lacks Caylee's delicate features.

And if Mom's a bee, Valerie's a beetle. Nothing gets past her hard-shell exterior. Valerie stands in the doorway, arms crossed, her dark eyes surveying the scene. I can't remember a time when Valerie hasn't been around. She and Mom did nursing school together back when I was a baby, and ever since she helped Mom land the job at St. Joseph's, they've become even more inseparable. I melt under Valerie's gaze, afraid she'll know—that they both will—just by looking at me. Not that Mom has any experience with catching me drink alcohol. The few times I have, I was a lot more careful.

Sure enough, Mom's stern expression melts in confusion when she sees me hunkered down next to the toilet. "Erica, what's going on? Why are you on the floor?" She kneels, eyes raking over me.

I can't meet her gaze, though I could cry with relief that there's no Sharpie on my face. Still, I pull the robe collar higher. I know I have to answer her questions, but what can I say? And if I open my mouth, she'll smell the alcohol.

"You smell like vomit," Valerie announces, ever blunt like Amber, hands on her wide hips. "And you're lucky your mom didn't call the cops and send out a search party." I try not to look up into her knowing, golden-brown face. She's got two boys who are older than me, so she understands what a hangover looks like. But if she does know what's going on, Valerie doesn't say anything to incriminate me, for which I'm eternally grateful.

Mom eyes me. "You sick, Bug?"

The concern in her voice is too much, coupled with her use of the childhood nickname I earned after becoming obsessed with ladybugs. I feel my face crumple as I nod and start to cry. There's no way I can tell her the truth about what happened. It would be bad enough if she found out I lied to her about spending the night at Caylee's, and her finding out about my drinking would kill her. She'd be so disappointed, which is worse than mad. And to tell her what I woke up to—the writing; gray walls that were supposed to be purple and the varsity jacket that didn't belong to Thomas; Caylee's photo in the mirror; the guys in the kitchen judging my breasts; Thomas still at Zac's; puking in the street in full view of that creepy Lexus driver. What would my mother think of her sweet little Erica if she knew all that? The thought makes me cry harder.

I'm saved from further tortured thoughts when she scoops me into her arms and holds me like I'm a kid, as if I don't have fifteen pounds on her. I try to cinch the robe tighter without drawing attention, then settle against her.

"Give the girl some space, Lydi," Valerie says. "In fact, I'm going to take my own advice and get out of your hair. I'll be in the kitchen if you need me. As for you"—she turns on me—"next time you call your mom and let her know you're okay, understood?"

I nod once into my robe.

As Valerie clears the doorway, Mom slaps a hand to my forehead. "Is it food poisoning? The flu? You do seem warm. Let's get some fluids in you, okay?" She pulls away, eyes searching mine. "Why didn't you call me to come get you? You know I would have." This close up, the lines of fatigue etched across her face stand out. I think of my sketchpad, the few swipes of black pen I'd use to capture years of stress. She's been running herself ragged these past few months, trying to prove herself at her new job by working crazy overtime.

I avoid opening my mouth too wide, knowing my putrid alcohol breath will instantly give me away. "I know, but you had your big fundraiser thing. I didn't want you to worry." My throat tightens around the lie.

"And you thought not texting me and letting me know where you were was a better option?"

From the direction of the kitchen, the coffee grinder whirrs. Mom sighs at my silence. "Erica, promise me you'll let me know the next time something like this happens." I'm already nodding as she finishes, "At least text me that you're alive, okay? You know how I worry when I don't hear from you."

I feel like a dizzy bobblehead. "Okay," I say, though there will never be a next time.

Mom sighs again. "All right. You going to throw up on me?"

I shake my head.

"Come." She rises, holding out her hands for me to grab. "Let's get you into bed."

"I've got it, Mom," I say, knowing she'll see my legs, my feet. "And I want to shower first." It means I'll have to look at the writing, but I can't avoid it any longer.

"But don't you think . . ." She leans down to pull me up.

"Mom, seriously!" It comes out harsher than I mean, and I cringe.

"All right, all right! But I'm taking your temperature before you shower."

I breathe a sigh of relief as she disappears, then lunge for the bottle of mouthwash and swig a blast of minty syrup. It makes me gag. Dragging myself onto the toilet, robe and all, I tuck my feet under me. Though my nausea's lessened, my head still throbs, insides weighted like freshly poured cement.

Mom returns with a sweating jug of purple Pedialyte and a cup of water, flitting around me, doing her Nurse Lydia thing: aspirin, water, temperature.

"Think it's the flu?" Mom asks, even though I have the thermometer in my mouth.

Gray walls, red cups. I shrug so I don't have to lie.

"What are your symptoms?" she asks.

Humiliation. Panic. Dread. "Nausea and headache," I mumble.

"When did the vomiting start?"

Middle of the street. Next to my car. "Um, super early this morning."

"Last time you vomited?"

Tried to call Caylee. No answer. "Depends on what time it is." I *need* to get ahold of Caylee.

She extracts the thermometer. "Nearly noon. Hmm, no temperature."

"Were there any messages for me on the machine?" I ask.

Mom shakes the thermometer. "None that I saw. Why, where's your phone?"

Dang. "At Caylee's." *I hope.* "I left it there." Each small lie tightens the vices on my conscience by another click.

"All right, well, let's hope it's only a stomach bug and that it'll run its course in the next day or two if it hasn't already." Snatching up the bottle of aspirin and the thermometer, she points to the jug of purple Pedialyte. Grape—the worst replicated flavor. "You need to drink that, at least half, before I leave for my shift in thirty minutes."

Right. The pancake breakfast was only the volunteer portion of her day.

"How was the fundraiser?" I blurt out.

Hovering in the doorframe, she gives me a weak smile. "Oh, you know, same as before. Mr. Peters tried to overdo his pancake limit and I nearly had to do the Heimlich on him, but we did raise a good amount of money. And Mrs. Pensacola asked about you. She's really taken a fancy to you and your art." Mom's fists find her hips. "Well, I don't *have* to go to work, you know. Valerie could handle my shift. She already said she wouldn't mind."

Mom never misses her shift, or the opportunity to pick up her coworkers' shifts. "I'll be fine, Mom," I lie. I'm yesterday's party away from fine.

"Are you sure? I could . . ."

"Mom. Seriously, it's fine." I need to find Caylee. I need to shower. To see, to know.

She exhales through her nose. "Okay. Only promise me you'll hydrate and get some rest."

"I will."

"You promise?"

I roll my eyes. Mom's big on promises. "I promise!"

"Good." She turns to leave.

Guilt creeps in. "Sorry I wasn't there. To help out and visit with everyone."

"It's okay. We managed. And besides, you can't help being sick, Bug. So, take your shower, then go straight to bed. And get some rest." The door clicks shut behind her, trapping the guilt inside the tiny bathroom with me.

I listen to Mom's fading footsteps and the TV clicking on, then reach for the cup of water she left, running my thumb over the cartoon onion decal on it. Every time Dad would see this cup he'd say: "Mine eyes smell onions; I shall weep anon." He was always quoting Shakespeare. I remember running to my room as a kid and scribbling down any quote he'd say in my journal. Then I'd recite it back to him later, usually getting it wrong, which would always make him laugh. But that was before Dad decided it was a problem that Mom preferred modern works by feminist women over dead white dudes like Shakespeare. Not that he'd minded back when she was his student, though it definitely seemed like a reason he'd left in the end.

Draining the water in a few rapid gulps, I eye the Pedialyte with suspicion. I attempt a sip but fake grape tastes even worse than I remember, like cough syrup mixed with bathroom cleaner.

Then the black marks on my foot pull my attention, and I'm jolted by the electric shock of remembering. For the space of a fleeting memory about my dad, a passing thought of Pedialyte, I'd forgotten last night.

It all descends on me again in a horrible, heavy panic. There's still no word from Caylee. Did she get my voicemail? Does she know what happened? What don't I know?

Sneaking to the door, I crack it open. Snippets reach me of Valerie's and Mom's murmured voices, interwoven with a TV ad. I tiptoe across the hallway to Mom's room, close the door behind me, then dive for the phone and redial Caylee's number. As the phone rings, I lick my thumb and rub at the "re" from "here" that sticks out of my sleeve, but all it does is bleed the ink and make it look worse.

The phone rings four times, then goes to voicemail. Fear stirs in my stomach. *Where is she? Why isn't she answering?* I hang up without leaving a message and make a decision. Tonight, once Mom leaves for her shift, I'll drive over to Caylee's house and explain everything to her.

Only, how do I explain what I don't know? "Don't worry, Caylee. I only slept in Zac's room with half my clothes gone. Apparently two of Thomas's buddies drew on me, and several saw me naked, including your boyfriend. And I don't remember any of it. But everything's hunky-dory!"

Jesus.

I close my eyes against the mental images flooding in.

Shower, Erica. Before Mom sees.

From the living room, I hear Valerie tell my mother good-bye as I slip back into the bathroom, lock the door, and turn on the shower. Water gushes into the tub. In my periphery, my reflection hovers in the bathroom mirror. I rip my shirt over my head. Beside me, my mirror ghost does the same.

I need to get this Sharpie off me before anyone can see it. But, more important, I need to know if there are other names on me. Because Thomas's won't be one of them. It can't be.

Kicking off my skirt and underwear, I brace myself to turn, to look at my naked body in the mirror, but I can't make myself do it. My heart feels like a trapped bird—all frantic wings and sharp claws. Squeezing my eyes shut, I tell myself to get it over with. To know the truth. So, I turn and face the mirror.

A strangled cry escapes me.

The body reflected in the glass doesn't belong to me; the marks covering her skin are a stranger's curse, someone else's shame.

For years, Mom has refused to let me get the Jack Skellington tattoo I've wanted, saying I'd look dirty with one, but here I am, dirty and marked anyway.

Filling every space between the words are random scribbles, intermixed with more hasty drawings of exploding penises and hanging breasts. Some marks look patchy and faded, like the Sharpie started to dry out.

But the words show up clearly.

Though the mirror reflects them backward, scrawled across both breasts are the words **fat TITTIES!** My vision blurs as I stare at my partially blacked-out nipples. Across my stomach, **EAT ME** and **FINGER FUCK THIS SHIT** are attached to arrows that point at my scribbled-on crotch, the ink smeary and smudged. The front of my thighs still read **Erica Walker is a sluuut** and **whore**, and the top of my foot, **Forest Stevens**. I turn my arm and stare again at the name scratched across it: **Ricky was here.**

But not Thomas.

Forest's and Ricky's names I knew about. But there's more writing. Like giant stitches, sharp points of half-concealed words stick out from between my legs. After several ragged breaths, I'm no closer to being ready. But I need to look, to know if it's there. Planting my feet together, I bend my knees and inch them apart.

Up the inside of one thigh is **Stallion!** *He did this too.*

Stallion's face flashes through my mind, followed by his girlfriend's. I see the two of them together at lunch, him fawning all over her. Why the hell would he do this to Jasmine? To me?

But it doesn't stop there. I have to blink several times to read what's printed on the crease where my thigh joins my pelvis: **Zac B. BITCHES!**

Dear god.

Zac Boyd. Caylee's Zac.

Tears leak from my eyes and run down my face. This is bad.

So bad. Caylee's boyfriend! No wonder she hasn't called. If she knows . . .

Oh, Caylee. I'm so sorry.

I can't even remember how the names got there. I can't. . . .

I think back to Zac, saying all those horrible things about my body in the kitchen because he'd seen. He'd seen me like this. He'd written his name on my inner thigh. Stallion, too. Had I been wearing underwear then, or had they seen everything of mine, between my legs?

They did this to me. Stripped me naked and wrote on me. Every single one of them. Four names on my body. Four names. But Thomas's name isn't anywhere.

I hate myself for the tiny glimmer of hope it feeds my heart as I search again for his name, letters tumbled over themselves like how he writes on his Spanish homework. But it's nowhere.

Get it through your head, Erica. Four guys drew on you. Four guys—from the varsity lacrosse team—wrote their freaking names on your naked body. Four. Guys. And who knows what happened with your underwear!

Did they do this because it was me, or would any girl have done, token scholarship girl or not?

Throwing open the toilet, I gag. The water I drank streams out, tinted purple from the sip of Pedialyte. I heave again and again until there's nothing left, the pounding shower tap muffling the sound. More tears sting my eyes as I stay bent over, panting.

My skin crawls. The blurred words and images take on strange, moving shapes, like shiny cockroaches scuttling all over me.

Willing myself to stay calm, I rip aside the goldfish curtain and scramble into the tub, redirecting the flow from the faucet to the showerhead. Freezing water blasts me while I fill my loofa with body gel, but it warms quickly as I scrub at the words in frantic circles. First my arms—Ricky. Then my feet—Forest. My breasts—Titties. Ribs—Eat. Stomach—Fuck. Legs—Slut. And crotch—Whore. Last, I scrub up the inside of one thigh—Stallion—then the other—Zac.

Ricky. Stallion. Forest. Zac.

But not Thomas.

Does he know what happened? Maybe I could talk to him, if I had my phone . . .

Eat. Fuck. Titties. Slut. Whore.

The heat overwhelms me, and I dry heave into the drain, but then I'm back up and scrubbing over and over each mark until it begins to lift, little by little.

How the hell am I going to tell Caylee?

The soapy water falls away—a murky, bubbly trail of terrible words slithering down the drain. Numbness settles over me like a net as I scrub until my skin stings and I can't take any more. Then I shut off the water and step onto the rug. After clearing away the steam, I stand naked and exposed in front of the mirror, my entire front half glowing red and raw from the scrubbing, the ink partially faded like a splotchy painting.

But now that I've showered, I realize that some of the desperate hope I've harbored has splintered and fallen away. I thought I would feel better. I thought that removing the words would make it go away, at least a little, but now it's somehow worse. Instead of tattoos across my skin, traces of each picture—each name—remain like scars. Stallion's name. Zac's. Ricky's and Forest's. This is worse than I thought. If Caylee knew . . .

Beyond the bathroom door, our doorbell rings. My gaze snaps toward the sound because I know exactly who it is.

Caylee.

THOMAS

HOT LIGHTS BLAZE DOWN ON ME AS I TAKE MY SEAT, CEN-
ter stage. The silver autographed names flash as I lift Eleanor
from her case and pray silently that the faculty—three men and
two women—will like me. From where they sit in the front
row, they have to see me shaking, but I can't steady myself.
Behind them, in the rear of the auditorium, I spot Uncle Kurt
sitting in shadows.

I wonder what he's thinking. Since I was so late, I'd had
to park at the top of the parking structure and sprint down
multiple flights of stairs. Whizzing by a refreshment table, I'd
skipped the donuts but chugged a cup of coffee, trying to wake
myself up. Instead, it made me jittery and threatened to burn
a hole through my gut. I'd barely had time to check in, tune
Eleanor in a side practice room, and run through a few rushed
chords of "Johnny B. Goode" before being ushered in here just

as my uncle found me. He'd looked me up and down, asking where I'd been.

Now I try to study the faculty—or my future professors, if all goes well—as I adjust the mic and pop filter. One of the five is the guitar professor, though I'm hoping it's not the scary-intense woman in yellow. She sits in the middle, studying her notes with a sharp expression, while a bald guy and tiny woman talk on her left. On her right, a guy in a black turtleneck leans in his chair while his neighbor sips coffee, yawning.

As I plug Eleanor into the amp, double-checking it's turned on, the intense woman speaks: "Good morning, Thomas. I'm Professor Kovich. I teach studio guitar here." My stomach drops as she continues, "Would you please open by telling us which program you're applying for and why you chose this school?"

I cough. "Um, sure. Yeah. I'm applying for your guys's"—*your guys's?*—"uh, Popular Music Program, and I'll be playing three songs. Singing and guitar. And, uh, what was the other question?" What the hell did I just say? Where were the lines I'd practiced till I was blue in the face?

They all stare at me, Professor Kovich cocking her head. "Why you want to attend Thornton," she repeats.

Endless reasons. Besides being one of the nation's top music schools, plus what *Rolling Stone* magazine called "cutting-edge" and one of the "most productive new music scenes," it's in the heart of L.A. next to places like Capitol Records and the Walt Disney Concert Hall. I'd give anything to play at Troubadour for the senior showcase in front of a huge audience; for every class to be a potential invite to accompany famous musical artists on live TV or play for Emmy-nominated shows; to work with unbelievably talented professors who care about you. To be someone.

"Why wouldn't I?" *Shit.* I said that out loud, and it oozes "arrogant asshole." That's not at all what I meant, or how I meant it. I had practiced saying something else, something perfect, but what? "I mean, I've heard great things. Really great things." *Really great things?*

Professor Kovich stares hard, clearly not impressed. "How about you tell us what music means to you, then."

It's both a challenge and another chance, and it should be an easy question, one I went over again and again. But my mind is completely blank. Because how do you describe what it feels like to listen to insanely good music that traps itself under your skin where you feel it, just below the surface, humming throughout your whole body? There are suddenly no words, either, for what the time over winter break with Uncle Kurt and the guys from Lead Paint meant to me—all of us crammed in *Shit Show,* the tour van that smelled like feet and pine air freshener, or us all crashing together in tiny hotel suites. The guys had treated me like a kid brother. And when they'd found out I'd made it to live auditions, they'd started coaching me on perfect finger placement or vocal articulation. But how could I tell these professors that the best part of being on the road was how far away it made Bay City feel? That I'd gotten a true taste of what life could be like every single day surrounded by music-passionate people, that going back to regular life had been near impossible? The only good thing about coming back had been meeting Erica.

Erica.

No. Focus on the question—what music means to you. In this program, I could discover who I'm meant to be. I could live and breathe music every day.

Because music means *everything* to me.

And Erica had meant . . .

"Everything," I say into the mic, too loud. The faculty flinch away at the sudden noise.

I recoil, mumbling, "Uh, everything. Music means everything to me."

Such a pathetic answer. I glance over at Uncle Kurt, knowing I'm blowing it while he watches, and after everything he's done to help me with my application. When I'd emailed him my personal statement, he'd made me start over. Twice. "Want it more," he'd said, till I'd gotten it right. And when I'd sent him my prescreen audition video for feedback, without me knowing, he'd sent it to a professional editor friend to add transitions and fix the sound quality. Then, when I'd gotten the email mid–winter break inviting me to live auditions, he'd coached me every single day, making me do mock auditions in the hotel suite, the greenroom, the back of the van, again and again till he was satisfied. "The audition starts the moment you walk in," he'd said.

And it had, the second I took this stage. I try to square my shoulders and smile, shake off my mistakes, knowing posture, body language, confidence—it all matters. Everything matters. But in front of the faculty, in front of my uncle, I've lost all the words I'd rehearsed and am fucking it up royally, which clearly the faculty spokeslady thinks too, because she throws up a dismissive hand. "Why don't you just . . . get started, then?"

Erica, the girl in the boots.

I shake my head hard. That's not the right lyric. Think. What had Benji said in that greenroom after I'd admitted how scared I was about this audition?

"Don't just show them you love music, Tommy. Show them how much. Tie it to an emotion. Play something true."

But I can't. My mind erases like an Etch A Sketch, and I can't remember what song I'm supposed to play first, let alone the melody, the opening line . . .

Girl in the boots. Girl in the boots.

Not. That. One. The clock in the back ticks by another second. Then another. Then another.

I clear my throat, play a chord, stop. That's not the right chord *or* lyrics. That's *her* song.

Fuck. *Think, think, think!*

But I can't. All I see is her, and if I think about her now, I'm *sunk.*

My chest grows hot, flush creeping up my neck. "Sorry," I mumble, stumbling over another chord. "Sorry."

You're blowing it!

Something true. Play something true.

That's . . . Erica. At least, it was. The night at the beach washes over me—Erica beside me as I strum Eleanor. We're huddled on a fleece blanket on a cold sand dune as I play her the song I wrote for her.

"I . . . ," I say to the faculty, my eyes squeezed shut.

Erica's staring at me with her huge eyes, absorbing every lyric: *The girl in the boots.*

But I'm running out of time . . . The songs I'd prepared . . .

My eyes fly open. "Can I . . . can I change songs? To one I wrote?"

Professor Kovich looks beyond exasperated, arms folded tightly. Even in the shadows I can see my uncle shift, annoyed or disappointed maybe, but I can't take the question back. And the song won't leave me alone, pressing into every part of my brain. I see Erica wearing my letterman, hair whipping in the wind, skin smelling like body lotion—freshly baked vanilla cupcakes—mixed with salty ocean and dried seaweed. It'd been the first time she'd ever heard me play, watching me intently and clapping like crazy. She'd kept asking me to play song after song, till finally I'd worked up the courage to play the one I'd written for her. The way Erica'd looked at me, smiling a dazzling smile, I knew she could read on my face how hard I was falling for her. With Erica, I felt like I could be anyone, that I was someone.

Black turtleneck professor gives me a nod. "Sure. Whatever song is fine."

It's from pity, but I don't care. I just play, just need to play. My fingers find the right chords, and suddenly, I'm right there back on the beach, playing Erica the song I'd written about seeing her for the first time.

The Monday I'd returned after winter break, I'd been so bummed out, missing Uncle Kurt and the guys and not at all stoked to hold up a whole lacrosse team till Zac's arm healed. That morning before school, I'd thrown myself onto a patch of mangy grass beside a picnic table, air-guitaring along to a Lead Paint song, thinking about them, about being on the road again. And when I looked up, there she was on the other side of the hallway window, jolting me out of my dark thoughts. People jostled around her, but she didn't turn away, her face perfectly clear through the glass. I remember her green eyes, her smile . . .

A smile so lovely it fills you with fire
One even men drowning would stop to admire

. . . the purple pants she had on that would've made Prince proud. I'd scrambled to my feet, tripping over my backpack and nearly falling like an idiot, which had made her laugh. I'd smiled, tried to look away but couldn't. And she hadn't looked away either. When the bell finally rang, she'd sent me a little wave before disappearing, trailing electric sparks in her wake. I'd watched her go till the courtyard's reflection made it impossible. Pulling out my song journal, I'd scribbled the last line in what was to become her song, this song: *Frozen in place by the loveliest face*, a lyric I sing now . . .

Like a slow-melting spell, the auditorium comes back into focus, the last of the chords fading away. I'm shaking, a tear sliding down my face. Stomach dropping, I come back to myself, remembering I'm onstage, auditioning in front of all these people. I swipe at my cheek, humiliated beyond belief, gaze dropping to Eleanor. Uncle Kurt bought her off Benji, just for me. My uncle has done so much for me. He's the only one who showed up today, believed in me enough to help me make it on this stage. And I just fucked it all up. What a colossal thank-you.

Agonizing seconds later, Professor Kovich speaks. "Thank you, Thomas. That will suffice."

Beside her, Turtleneck Guy is nodding. Clearly he's had enough too.

Based on the clock, I technically have time for at least another song, but the faculty can call the audition at any moment. Honestly though, I'm so relieved it's over. Whenever I've played Erica's song before, it's made me feel ten times lighter, but right now it feels like taking a full-body hit at practice.

The stage is absolutely silent as I exit stage right. I can't even look at my uncle, unable to face how totally disappointed in me he must be.

ERICA

I MET CAYLEE AND AMBER IN ENGLISH CLASS WHEN CAYLEE approached me to work with them on a group project. I remember being surprised how nice Caylee was because she's so pretty—the type of person that everyone notices with a perfect teeny waist and wind-tousled hair, delicate, sun-kissed porcelain features and wide eyes. After we became friends, I secretly called her "Caylee Mermaid" in my head and even started drawing her in my sketchbook with a glittering, scaly tail. And Amber . . . well, it took me zero seconds to learn that she takes absolutely no shit from anyone. The secret alter ego I've been sketching for her is an ivory-white Medusa owing to her death stare that could turn offending souls to stone.

The one time they came over to our apartment was to work on the English project because Caylee's kitchen was mid-remodel and Amber's moms were hosting a poetry slam. Of course, I'd spent that whole morning cleaning *and* most of my allowance on the gourmet foods I'd seen them eat, including the B-Thin bars Caylee practically lives on.

When Caylee and Amber had arrived, I'd invited them in, nervous beyond belief. An awkward silence followed while they took in the place—cracks, stains, and all. Caylee did the polite, barely-move-your-head-while-glancing-from-the-corners-of-your-eyes type of looking. Amber did . . . Amber. She tossed her auburn hair over her shoulder and took in every corner. I only hoped she wouldn't say anything blunt or judgmental like she did about everything else because I really didn't want to cry in front of her and Caylee.

But she didn't. Amber merely asked, "Well, are we going to get started, or what?" then with an "Ooh, cupcakes!" she made a beeline for the food. And Caylee seemed touched that I'd noticed she liked B-Thin bars. She smiled at me then like she approved of me, not even seeming to mind that I'm poor.

And that was the last time Caylee came over. Until today.

Now Mom's footsteps head for the front door, the echo of the doorbell still sounding throughout our apartment.

Leaping from the shower, I pull on my robe and scramble to my room. I snatch up a pair of leggings and a long-sleeved shirt to cover any faint traces of leftover writing. By the time I make it to the living room, Mom has already answered the door and is chatting away. In the entryway, silhouetted against the light outside, stands Caylee, just like I knew she would be.

As I step closer, I'm panicking. *Does she know? Is she mad?* She hasn't been back here since our group project. I'd been so nervous that day, so embarrassed, but now I can conjure up only a trace of that mortification because Caylee witnessing the true state of our crappy apartment is the least of my worries.

Caylee steps inside, slipping off her sandals by the front door, my purse slung over one shoulder. Then she flashes me a smile and a quick wave.

I could cry I'm so relieved, not only for seeing Caylee, but for her smile that says everything's okay. *She's not mad.* So maybe she doesn't know what happened. Or maybe she has answers that will explain it all away: *"Oh, come on, E. Of course it's not like that. What a drama queen you are!"*

I hate myself for even thinking there could be another explanation, especially after everything I overheard from Zac's kitchen. It's not possible, not with the writing I found or where that writing was located. Despite all this, the sight of Caylee smiling calms my breathing.

"It was so crazy," Caylee's saying to my mother, continuing whatever conversation they'd begun. "We were watching a movie one moment and the next . . . Bleeeeeh." Caylee pantomimes vomiting, opening her mouth and sticking out her tongue. She tucks her blonde hair behind her ear, a telltale sign she's lying.

Thankfully, Mom's oblivious to Caylee's giveaways. "Well, thank you so much for taking care of her last night. I was worried when I couldn't get ahold of you both, but it sounds like you had your hands full."

"No problem, Ms. Walker." Turning to me, Caylee holds up my purse like evidence. "You left this at my house." She brushes more hair behind her ear, overemphasizing her lie, but adults never seem to question her innocent-looking face. "How you feeling?" she asks me, slinging my purse over her shoulder.

"Better now," I say, and it's true. I can't shut out the images of the faded writing for even a second, but at least I have my best friend back. Caylee can be a little flaky at times, but she's still my best friend. And now I have to find a way to tell her about everything. Except, how do I bring up that her boyfriend wrote his name inside my thighs? The thought fills me with dread. "Thanks for bringing my purse," I tell her. "Want to . . . ?" I gesture toward my room.

"Yeah." She nods, ready to follow.

"Okay, well, I'm off," Mom says. "Take it easy, Erica. Don't overdo it. And Caylee, thanks again for taking care of my little girl."

I cringe at Mom's "little girl" comment, but Caylee pauses only a half second too long.

"Any time, Ms. Walker," Caylee replies. "Have a great day at work. I mean night!"

Then Mom's off, leaving Caylee and me alone.

Caylee follows me to my room. Even though Mom left, I

close my door for good measure, then turn to face her. "Thanks for coming over, Caylee."

She shrugs from the middle of my messy room, an awkward smile on her face. "Sure thing."

I try not to look at the clothes heaped on the floor, the tangle of bedsheets, the embarrassing collection of Disney princess POP! figures lining my bookshelf. And of course, only now do I notice the stale air that reeks of trapped body sweat.

Tell her about Zac's name. "So, uh, why didn't you call me back? I tried calling you twice." I cross my arms in front of me, attempting to act nonchalant but knowing my tone sounds judgmental.

She mimics my crossed arms. "How was I supposed to know that was you calling on the other end, considering how many times your mother tried to call me this morning? When I heard your message, I drove straight over. And lied to your mom, twice. So, you're welcome." She plops on my bed and holds out my purse to me, both of us aware that this is the closest we have ever come to confrontation and that neither of us is good at it.

"Right. Sorry. Thanks for coming, Cay. Really." Taking the purse from her, I peer inside. "Please tell me my phone is in here?"

She shrugs a shoulder. "I think so?"

"Oh my god, what the hell?" I yank my wet fingers from my purse as a fermented, sour smell hits me.

"It's beer, by the way."

I drop the purse to the floor and rifle through it. "Who the hell spilled beer in my purse?" *Please tell me my phone is okay. Please tell me my phone is okay.* My makeup is completely ruined, my wallet soggy. Thank god I left my sketchbook in the car or that would've been destroyed too.

"Um, that would be you. Remember?" She takes in the worn carpet, eyes lingering on an unidentifiable stain.

I cringe, pulling my wet phone from my purse. "Oh god." I press the side button. The screen stays blank.

She smiles over at me, sympathetic. "Yeah, you were trying to take a picture with Thomas but dumped your beer instead. A full cup from the looks of things."

I throw myself into the desk chair and plug the phone into its charger. I should wait till it dries, let it sit in a bag of rice to pull out any moisture, but I don't have time. I'll have to chance it.

Caylee rushes on, "You were a little party animal last night." She leans in, breaking into a conspiratorial smirk and nudging my knee. "You and Thomas were all over each other by the bonfire!"

My mouth tightens into a smile. So, Caylee doesn't know. Not all the details at least. Because if she did, my relationship with Thomas would be the least of her concerns. Question is, what does she know? "I . . . I don't remember much," I confess.

"Seriously? Well, what part do you remember?" Caylee's eyes are so striking, so burnt-sienna brown, so earnest, that I have to look away.

Staring at my phone, I try to pull memories from the party. "I remember being by the fire. With Thomas. Everyone in the backyard. Zac and his bottle rockets. Tina trying to outdrink the guys. Forest's shark costume. . . ."

This last part earns a snort from Caylee. "Man, Forest is hilarious. Who would even think to wear that? But sorry, keep going."

The charging symbol appears on my phone's screen. *Thank god.* It was dead, but not *dead* dead.

"And . . . then Thomas and I went inside?" I say. It comes out like a question as the details evaporate.

"Well, you tried. He had to carry you. Piggyback, you know? Very romantic." She bounces off the bed and over to my bulletin board, where the beach picture of Thomas and me is tacked. "Speaking of, this is cute."

I sort of remember the piggyback from last night, laughing and tripping in the backyard. "And that's it?"

She pulls the tack from the picture, surveying it. "Pretty much. You two disappeared. I'm assuming to, like, seriously make out in Zac's room and declare your undying love for each other. But you don't remember that part?"

I shake my head no.

"Dang." She frowns, re-pinning the photo. "I was hoping to get the lowdown. But I guess you'll just have to ask him when you talk to him."

My stomach twists in knots. "Think he'll call?"

"Why wouldn't he? You two are *in love*."

I glance to where my phone is charging. Would Thomas call? Or maybe he'd already tried, but my phone was off. Maybe when I had the chance to look, I'd have a message from him, or a text at least. "So, what happened with the rest of the party?" I ask Caylee, trying to stay on task. "Like, after Thomas and I went inside?"

"*Carried* you inside. He had to physically *carry* you." She starts to laugh, then sees my expression. "Not that I'm judging!"

My face falls into my hands. "God, I'm never drinking again."

"Yeah, okay."

I look straight at her. "I'm serious, Caylee."

"Don't be such a drama queen, E. Everyone gets wasted at some point. And I'm sure when you guys talk, you'll just laugh it off together. But if you're worried you two slept together, I mean, it happens. That's how Zac and my first time went down, and look where we are now."

I'd heard from Amber that Caylee had slept with Zac the very first time they'd hung out. Alcohol was involved, of course. And now I can't count the number of calls I've gotten from Caylee, near tears, afraid that Zac's going to leave her for someone else, certain that he doesn't find her attractive anymore. Ignoring this, I say, "I'm not worried Thomas and I slept together. I, like, checked and there wasn't any . . . signs down there. . . ." My face scalds. "But, um, last night, what happened after the two of us went inside?"

73

She shrugs. "Well, the keg got tapped soon after and the party pretty much wound down from there. Zac went inside to grab more booze—and came out tasting like tequila, so that was fun. Meanwhile, I got stuck outside with Julie, who was super drunk. She had a rough night too, if it makes you feel any better. You know how in love she is with Ricky and how he's always flirting with other girls right in front of her?" She waits for my nod. "Well, guess who got to sit through, like, thirty minutes of drunk Julie crying? This girl." Caylee thumbs at herself, then shrugs. "But hey, what are friends for?"

Julie sits in front of me in English and hangs out with us sometimes. And for some unknown reason, she's madly in love with Ricky. At one point, Caylee tried to play matchmaker between Julie and Ricky, but his "she's not that hot" comment had shut that down fast. Of course, Caylee'd never told Julie.

"So, everyone left the party then?" I ask.

Come on, phone. Turn on already!

Caylee picks up my Rapunzel figurine. "Pretty much. I finally got Julie calmed down and sent home with Amber. Amber wasn't stoked to play taxi service, let me tell you, but said it was her 'womanly duty,' or something. And then I found Zac on the stairs. He was coming down with the guys and I asked where you were so I could check on you, but Zac told me you'd passed out in his room and that he'd already made sure you were all good and he'd, like, given you a blanket or something. Which is so sweet of him."

A strange humming starts in my ears. *Tell her now! But how?* "Who else was there?" I ask. "Coming down the stairs, I mean?"

Caylee shakes her head, thinking. "Um, it was Ricky and Stallion. And Thomas, of course."

Heat pools in my chest at his name. Thomas was with them the whole time? Have I been so desperately wrong about him?

"Oh, and Tina. She was so drunk last night, she's probably *still* passed out. Man, what an attention whore."

Whore.

"Tina knows you're with Thomas now, but she just won't let up," Caylee adds. "Not that she even likes him anymore. She just can't stand for the spotlight to be off her. I hate her for you."

So, Tina was upstairs too. Not surprising. I stare blankly at my phone as it powers back on.

"Oh, and Forest, I think," she continues. "Man, Forest is so freaking funny! I still can't believe he jumped in the pool in that shark costume. He's, like, totally stoner chill, unless of course you mess with his little sis, Elle. Then watch out! I mean, have you noticed how adorably overprotective he is of her?"

My phone buzzes in my hand as notifications crowd my home screen—missed voicemails and text alerts from my mom trying to get ahold of me last night. Thinking about her frantic worrying fills me with sadness. And I really had hoped Thomas would've called, or at least texted . . .

Wait, there's a social media alert. I sit up so quickly I almost face-plant. It's from Tina. She tagged me in a photo two minutes ago.

"What's up, E? You look sick."

Caylee's voice startles me. I lock my phone and toss it on the desk. If Tina tagged me in a photo, it can't be good. She *hates* me. I desperately want to look, but I don't want Caylee to see in case it's really bad, which means I'll have to wait for her to leave. I clear my throat. "Just a million messages from my mom. So that's it, then, from last night?"

Caylee shrugs, plopping on the bed. "Yeah, not much else to tell. After that, Zac told everyone to clear out. . . ." Her eyes find mine, a smile spreading across her lips. "But, um, want to hear something really scandalous?"

My stomach fills with rocks at the joy radiating from her. I nod slowly.

"Well, Zac and I had, like, a date in his parents' room since *his* room was occupied." She gives me a mock-accusatory look, though she's all smiles now. "And, oh my god, you should have seen Zac last night! He really wanted me. Like, couldn't keep his hands off me. He hasn't wanted me like that in ages. And in his parents' bed, too!" She starts to laugh.

I stare at the Caylee in front of me and try to match her with the Caylee she is around Zac. The Caylee who sits, silent and still, dwarfed under her boyfriend's massive shoulder. The Caylee who, at Pizzaz, picks at her salads and nibbles on one or two of Zac's discarded pizza crusts. The Caylee who—whenever Zac gets a text—leans forward suspiciously and tries to scan the screen. I hate it, the difference between this ecstatic Caylee and the one buried in her turtle shell when Zac's around. I hate so much that he can buoy or crush her with his mood of the hour.

Zac B. BITCHES! *You have to tell her.*

"It was awesome, E," Caylee continues, face lit up. "Just so great to get his full attention again. But that's not even the best part. Are you ready for this? After we had sex, he was lying on top of me and then . . . he told me he loved me!" She squeals into her fists. "He just looked into my eyes and said it! For the first time! Like, he actually said, 'I love you, Caylee-bear.'" She flings herself back onto my comforter.

I can't breathe, watching her elated expression as I feel Zac's name burning on my inner thigh.

She gushes on, oblivious. "And here I was thinking he was losing interest. Like, ready to break up with me, or something. But how ridiculous is that? Because clearly he's not if he's telling me he loves me!"

Zac doesn't deserve her, but if I told her what happened now, would it break her? I glance over at a drawing of Erica Strange taped to my dresser. She's scaling a stone fortress, her confidence infallible, Sparky at her side. She knows that horrible monsters lurk within, but she doesn't hesitate for even a second. I turn back to Caylee. "And you believe him?"

"Hmm?" She props herself up on one elbow.

"Do you, like, think that he meant it when he said it?"

Hurt flashes across her face. "Of course I think he meant it. Why wouldn't he mean it? I'm his girlfriend."

Tell her. Tell her now!

The office chair squeaks as I wheel closer to her. "Sorry, I didn't mean it like that, Caylee. Seriously, I'm happy for you. I'm . . . so glad he finally said it, is all." *Do it, Erica.* "But . . ."

Her phone buzzes. She tears her eyes from mine, pulling her phone from her hoodie and scanning the screen. "Gotta run. I'm meeting Amber at Juiced." She types a reply as she scoots off the bed. "Girls' date. You want to come with?"

Wait! I want to scream. *I have to tell you something!* But how? Then a horrible thought strikes. Maybe she would think I invited it all somehow. That last night, I'd wanted the attention or was trying to steal Zac in some way. The thought makes my head spin, but Caylee has a vicious jealous streak when it comes to Zac. I clear my throat. "I'd better not."

"Okay, cool." She shrugs, voice lukewarm. "See ya tomorrow, then."

I can't. I can't. But . . .

As she pulls open the door, I call out, "Caylee!"

She turns back, eyebrows raised in question.

"Did Thomas say anything to you?"

"What?" Her face looks annoyed, like she was expecting me to apologize again for questioning Zac's declaration of love.

"When Thomas was coming down the stairs, did he say any-thing to you?"

She frowns in thought. "Um, he looked a little sloshed like everyone else. But no, he didn't say anything. Zac just told me where you were, is all. And speaking of Zac"—she's looking at me now—"it was really nice of him to let you sleep in his room last night, so if you get the chance, maybe you should thank him." The cool edge to her voice surprises me. I must've really upset her; she's halfway out the door already.

"Feel better, E." With a little wave, she disappears.

Zac, Forest, Ricky, Stallion. And Thomas. He was there the whole time—from bringing me upstairs to coming down with the guys. Tina, too.

Two thoughts slip past the numb: *What don't I know yet?* And worse: *Did Thomas watch?*

All I know is I have to find out. And maybe I'm about to.

I scramble for my phone. The notification is eleven minutes old and has since updated. It now reads: **Tina Marcus has tagged you in 5 photos.**

AFTER LEAVING AUDITIONS, I'D BARELY HAD TIME TO THROW on my practice jersey before heading straight to the field, only to get reamed out by Coach for being late.

Now I stand in front of the goal, trying to monitor the ball's whereabouts, but despite the Gatorade I chugged, my head pounds with every movement. The heavy clouds aren't making anything easier, blocking out the sunlight. Plus, it looks like it's going to rain, which it hardly ever does in SoCal. And the wind's insane today, whipping practice plans and empty water bottles around.

Trash from blown-over cans tumbles across the field. I bat a plastic bag out of the air with my goalie stick, chucking it away from the net. My head's too full—everything from cleaning up orange juice in Zac's kitchen while listening to Erica slip out the front, to seeing my uncle in the back of the auditorium during auditions, then afterward, as I'd practically sprinted back to my truck, reading the text from him: Will call this afternoon. I hadn't bothered staying for the Q&A or campus tour. There was no point. Plus, I knew Uncle Kurt was catching up with his buddies in the department. Since he volunteers with the school to give students hands-on experience in the music world, he knows everyone, so he'd definitely hear how badly I botched it all anyway. Not that he didn't see it for himself. I'm already dreading his call.

When I glance up, I catch Stallion's gaze from behind his face mask. He stares a second too long, chucking his chin at me before turning away.

What's that about? I watch him track the ball, then rush Cole down the field. *You're being paranoid,* I tell myself. Of course Stallion looked at me. I'm the goalie.

Zac stalks the sidelines in his Panthers jersey minus the pads, moving like a man who's got a full ride to Syracuse, which he does, so long as his elbow heals properly. His good hand holds a clipboard with practice plans, but Zac's oddly subdued. Normally he's shouting orders across the field like he owns the team, which, considering who his father is, he practically does. Zac catches me staring and flashes a grin, like we're in on some secret together. Heat balls in my stomach when I turn away, and I get an eyeful of dirt from the wind.

Blinking hard, I watch Forest as he backpedals and side-steps, trying to thwart Mario's attempts to near the goal. I can tell he's moving a little slower than usual, but at least he's not acting weird.

I spot Ricky in the thick of things, but he doesn't glance my way. And there's Cole and Matt. They were at Zac's last night too but left early because of their curfews.

Mario sprints by, and I catch sight of his shorts. They're the dark blue mesh kind, with a small crocodile patch on them.

And I see Erica from last night standing by a roaring bonfire, biting her lip and smiling, holding my hat over the flames.

"Hop on, little croc," I tell her.

"Trying to get me alone, Thomas the Rhymer?" she asks.

I shake my head so hard my helmet rattles. *No.* I don't remember what happened. I don't.

I know I should text Erica. Not that I had much time before or after my audition, but that's not an excuse, and I'm sure she's wondering why I haven't reached out. Or maybe her phone's still off. Regardless, I could've sent her a message earlier that she'd get when she turns her phone back on.

I watch a loose paper flap against a chain-link fence in the distance, promising myself I'll text her as soon as we hit the locker rooms.

"The hell was that, VanBrackel?"

Coach's shout startles me, and I spin, caught off-guard. Coach Mac has thrown up his hands, the other coaches mirroring his exasperation. Sure enough, the ball's sitting in the net, Mario having just scored. The whole team's staring at me.

I didn't even know the ball was close, let alone whizzing past, and I'd made zero effort to block the shot.

Next to Coach, Zac's holding his elbows, arms crossed and head shaking.

"Sorry, Coach," I mumble through my face mask, feeling everyone's eyes burn into me.

Coach beckons. "Thomas, a word."

I shake off my helmet, tuck it under an arm, and jog into the wind.

Coach Mac stares me down, crushing his hat in his hands. He looks crazed, wind blasting his hair in all directions. "What the hell's going on out there, Thomas? Yesterday you were on fire, and now this crap?"

Zac laughs, slapping the clipboard against his thigh. "Girl troubles, I'm afraid."

I stare at Zac, both shocked and willing him not to say any more. Zac joking around out here is unheard of. Normally within a thousand yards of the lax field, Zac gets worked up to no end, shouting orders. He lives and breathes lacrosse. But I guess we're all off our game today.

Coach's face goes purple at Zac's indifference. "I don't give a rat's ass what's going on. We can't afford this inconsistency, especially with the PV game bearing down on us."

Today, I can't find it in me to care, but I say, "Sorry, Coach. I lost focus. It won't happen again."

Coach glares at me, then at Zac. "As for you. Just because

you're not on that field right now doesn't mean you get to dick around, especially if you want to come back next month. We have some lacrosse to play, and if neither of you can remember that, then I have ten guys who would be happy to replace you. Understood?"

Under the heat of his glare, Zac and I both bark out a "Yes, Coach."

Coach jams his hat back on his head, crazy hair puffing out the sides. "Good. Now get the hell back out there, Thomas, and let's see some goddamn focus, okay?"

As I jog back to my post, Forest's stick slaps my shoulder pad. "You good, my man?"

I wonder if he means more than this field, this game. But I shove my helmet on and huff out a "Fine."

"*Girl troubles*", Zac had called it, like that sums it up.

Retrieving the ball from the net, I fling it to Stallion. He catches and cradles it, readying the players for another toss-up. The scrimmage resumes, and I throw myself fully into the game. Not only for Coach, but because I'd do anything to get the hell out of my head today.

ERICA

IN THE FRACTION OF A SECOND IT TAKES TO REREAD THE
notification on my phone, I realize my world has imploded.

A part of me knew it was coming. It was only a matter of
time. That's how these things work, don't they? Everyone finds
out, shares the gruesome details, and delights in someone else's
misery? I'm completely screwed.

Screwed. A disgusting word. The point of a rusty nail driving
into the arch of a foot.

Tina Marcus tagged you in 5 photos.

Tina's hated me since the moment she saw me with Thomas
at Pizzaz Pizza Parlor. Apparently, Tina also despised Thomas's

ex-girlfriend Angie, who he dated freshman year, so much so that Tina allegedly threatened to kick Angie's ass on multiple occasions. And that was before it'd come out that Angie had been cheating on Thomas the whole time.

Guess I'm about to find out just how much Tina hates me, too.

Clicking takes me to my profile, where the images go front and center.

Squinting into my phone, breathless, I stare at the photos. They're all from Zac's backyard, Thomas and me.

I click the first one.

In it, I've got a red cup in one hand and Thomas's hat in the other, held over a fire pit. *I'd forgotten that.* I'm laughing, clearly drunk, falling over myself. My eyes reflect the flames, making me look demonic, and my skirt's hiked up almost to crotch level, exposing thick thighs. Luckily, even zoomed in, the photo quality is bad because of how dark it was, but that hardly makes me feel better.

I know sabotage when I see it. Tina Marcus took these photos and just tagged me in them. I always knew she hated seeing me with Thomas, but this much?

In the photos, Thomas looks . . . Well, the me from yesterday would've said incredible. One hand holds a red cup and the other reaches for his hat. He's mid-laugh. Gorgeous.

But so much has changed. I stare at him, feeling confused, and repulsed, and sad beyond words as I click to make the photo go away:

Untag.

Heart thundering, I scroll to the next photo.

I'm sitting on Thomas's lap, my head on his shoulder. Not a good angle. Plus, I look passed out. Maybe I was. My thighs look even more gargantuan in this picture, with Thomas resting his hand on one. His face is turned to the side, talking to someone outside the photo, hat on backward, eyes half-closed.

Untag.

Next photo.

Oh god.

It's a direct shot of my ass. I'm on all fours in the grass, jean skirt hiked. Thomas is bending over me, arms hooked around my middle, trying to help me up. I'm sure my breasts are spilling out the front.

Untag.

Tina, you bitch.

Next.

My breath catches. This one's even worse. It's from the same angle except Thomas has finally helped me stand upright, arms still around me, though I'm bent over at the middle like a rag doll. Once again, my butt's hanging out of my skirt, though luckily the photo's too blurry to see details.

Untag.

But you definitely can see details in the next one.

Thomas is giving me a piggyback ride through the sliding

glass door. My skirt is hiked up so far, the top of my thong is clearly visible, wedged between bare butt cheeks.

Total humiliation.

Untag.

I try to scroll to the next photo, but it returns to the first. That's all of them. That's more than enough. I don't even check to see if anyone has commented yet. Anyone who would comment on something like this . . . no part of me wants to know what they'd say.

I refresh my profile till the photos disappear, then scroll through the rest of my page, looking for further posts. The only other new photos are the ones Caylee tagged of us in the bleachers at yesterday's lacrosse match.

I search for Amber's profile before I remember she doesn't do social media. That's a small blessing, at least. Then I look for Tina's. Tina tagged both Thomas and me in the photos so they're on his page too, though his profile doesn't even use his real name or link to his family. His last post dates back two days prior. It was about Saturday's game so there's a chance he hasn't been online and seen the photos yet. With any luck, he never will.

Caylee's page has the same photos of us in the stands, then a few photos at the party with her and Zac, his smile looking like a leer. He's wearing his letterman jacket, the arm without the cast draped around Caylee's thin shoulders while the casted one pulls at the varsity lacrosse patch on his jacket, holding it out for the camera like a badge of honor.

And Caylee, beautiful Caylee. Gorgeous smile, smooth skin. Her naturally sun-bleached hair falls around her face in perfect beachy waves. Suddenly, I hurt so badly, wishing everything could go back to normal, to yesterday.

I allow myself several deep breaths, then a sliver of relief. Devastating as the Tina photos are, I know it could've been so much worse. Thank god Mom's too busy (and internet illiterate) to maintain her account. I can only pray I got to them fast enough, not to mention hope the privacy settings I put on family members and family friends hold up, especially Dad's fiancée, who seems dangerously stalker-ish. Because she'd show it to my dad for sure. He'd be horrified, so disappointed in me. I feel the crushing weight of it on my chest. Not to mention what my nana and papa, Aunt Loren, distant cousins and relations, and friends of the family would think. Or maybe they will still see it. Does the tag get removed immediately? I have to make it go away. Now.

Through Tina's profile, I click on the first photo of me stealing Thomas's hat and try to find a delete button, but of course you can't delete something someone else posted. I search to find meaning or answers in the words, but they distort into a pixilated blur.

Forcing myself to focus, I flag each photo for removal one by one, hoping like hell all links to me will get severed before anyone in my family sees. Setting down my phone and leaning my head against my desk, I wonder what to do next. But there's nothing else I can do. Nothing.

I should've known Tina hated me this much. She'd laughed the hardest that day at Pizzaz when Zac and his shitty crew put a slice of pizza on my seat while I was in the back room flirting with Thomas.

All I'd done was go to use the bathroom, then I decided to stop at the vending machines to buy a temporary tattoo. But Thomas had startled me, coming over just as I was pulling the tattoo free. Together, we'd watched it sail straight under the PAC-MAN arcade game. But right then and there, on that gross-ass floor, Thomas'd gotten on his hands and knees and reached under, trying to retrieve it, even though all he'd gained for his efforts was a handful of grimy garbage. He'd wiped his hands on the back of his jeans, telling me the Gremlins must've eaten it, and I'd laughed. Then we'd stood there staring at each other, smiling stupidly, and it had all felt like an ellipsis—a *To be continued* I couldn't wait for.

When we'd gotten back to our seats, I'd been so focused on Thomas that I hadn't seen the pizza slice and had slid right into it. Of course it was the day I wore white pants. Of course Thomas had seen me do it and been embarrassed for me. Of course I hadn't said anything, just melted in humiliation as Amber told them all off in true Erica Strange fashion. But what his friends had done . . . it'd felt personal.

Head on my desk, I search my bulletin board for the note Thomas had left on my car alongside a rose:

Beautiful stranger dressed in
rainbows, Tell me where and I will
follow. The beach? The movies?
What is your vote?
(TBD in class over football-shaped
notes)
-Thomas the Rhymer

He'd written it the day after Pizzaz to make me feel better,
and it had, even if he hadn't said anything to his stupid friends
about what they'd done.

I've let my eyelids drift closed when my phone pings with a
notification. Lifting my head, I see a new message.

From Zac Boyd.

I scramble for my phone, ripping the charger free in the
process.

Zac's message reads: hey mouth been seeing ALOT of
your ass on here.

I read his message again and again. "Mouth"? It's the same
thing Ricky called me this morning as I came down the stairs.
But why is Zac messaging me? He never has before.

Another message appears: get it? literally your ass?

The muscles around my heart constrict, but I force myself to
stay calm. I need to find out what happened, and maybe Zac
is my best bet.

Hilarious, I type back, though it's anything but. Just

thinking about him on the other end, messaging me, makes me want to chuck my phone through the window. I can picture him in his room, sprawled against the pillows in the bed I passed out in only last night. Did he even bother changing the sheets? Surrounding him are those gray walls, piles of clothes, red cups, playing cards.

I swallow hard and type another sentence. **But seriously, what all happened last night? In your room?**

His response is agonizingly slow. So very *Zac* to draw it out: **its a shame you don't remember. we had alot of fun.**

My insides writhe as I read. I force myself to type words that can be calm for me. **I know you took my clothes off. Wrote your name on me. Why?**

I NEED TO KNOW.

It's a funny thing, the rift between needing and wanting, something my dad always tried to drill into my head growing up. Anytime I'd clutch some sparkly toy or bag of candy to my chest and tell him how much I *needed* it, he'd always respond, "No, hon, you *want* that. You don't *need* it. There's a difference." I think I've finally learned the difference because there's hardly a molecule in me that wants to know what happened. But at the same time, every thrumming vein and sparking nerve of my body *needs* to know. And everything that's standing between me and knowing is Zac, a fact he seems to be enjoying to no end.

His response pings through. **why not?**

I grit my teeth and type, **Who all was there?** thinking of all the people Caylee'd named.

It takes Zac ages to respond: **you and me and some of the guys. ricky and Forest and stallion. tina. your boyfriend thomas. he enjoyed it the most.**

So, Tina really was in the room. Thomas, too. I'd suspected it but seeing his name on the screen hurts so badly. Or is Zac just toying with me?

My hands curl into fists. Thumbs jab at letters. **ANDDD?!?**

and nothing, he replies. A beat and then he adds:

you liked being the center of attention.

especially after you passed out.

its how you got your new nickname you know.

I type the question I need to know. The one that's been haunting me. **What else did you guys do to me? Besides the writing.**

wow don't get your hopes up mouth. i'm not a fucking rapist. none of us are.

My fist comes down hard on the phone screen, and for a second I think I've broken it, but no. And yet, if they didn't rape me, then why do I feel so violated?

I suck in a deep breath and force it out through gritted teeth, typing: **Are there any photos?**

No. Please say no.

of... He's playing dumb, of course. Zac knows *exactly* what I'm talking about. He's drawing this out to humiliate me, only this time it's so much worse than a pizza stain on my ass.

A flurry of keys. **Photos. Of me. Your room.**

ahh... let me think... he replies.

I can't believe he's pulling this shit. But I can.

Are there any or not? I demand.

no need to go bezerka bitch, let a man think.

I hate you so much.

oh photos. you mean like this?

And there it is, up close, on my screen. A photo that proves my life really is over.

In it, I'm propped against a dresser, hair stuck to my sweaty face. I'm clearly passed out, though slivers of my eyes peek through mostly closed lids. But it's not my eyes I'm worried about. In the center of the photo are my breasts—pre-marker— large with pink nipples, laid bare for all to see. They fill the shot, so much so that I barely notice my lacy thong, which is still right-side out. At least, for now.

Delete it! I type. **Delete it right now!**

His reply is swift: **can't.**

What the hell do you mean you can't?

not my photo sweet tits.

Why not? Who took it??

ricky.

Who all has seen it?

knowing ricky... every body.

I stare at the word Zac has misspelled. It should be only one word. Though it's obviously another grammar error, his ripping the word in two is so much worse for what it highlights.

Every. Body.

Those two words bring up images of our school, crowds of rushing bodies. I imagine the mass of students that fill the bleachers at school assemblies. I picture everybody and *every single body* having seen *my* body, my breasts.

I sway in my chair, light-headed, nauseous.

Even though I want nothing more than to lie down and never get up again, I force myself back to the screen and its too-bright light. Who ever knew such a tiny device could cause so much pain?

A new message from Zac waits: you should be proud of those tits. their ace.

This time my thumbs move slowly, deliberately: Are there more pictures?

His reply is the swift slice of the guillotine: you'll have to ask ricky.

and i'm kidding mouth, he hasn't sent them to anyone outside our intimate little group. i made sure of it. itll be our little secret.

Despite his "reassurance," I go numb. There's no way to know if he's telling the truth or not. Hesitating for only a second, I do the only thing I can control. I click out of our chat, go to my account settings, and delete my account with the total and utter certainty that it's not enough. Maybe Tina will repost those pictures of me. Maybe they won't even get taken down to begin with. But I can't take the risk of Mom or any other family member finding those photos, and at least now they aren't linked to me. No one can tag me in anything.

For good measure, I close down every single social media account I've ever had. I only feel a momentary twinge of regret at losing every picture and comment I've ever posted, or even some of my earliest sketches and paintings that I don't have saved elsewhere, because what could it possibly matter now? My life is truly over. There's no coming back from this. No way to stop it.

Dread surges through me. Whoever said anxiety was a dark cloud hovering above someone like Eeyore and his rainclouds didn't know what they were talking about. Because fear is far more sinister, a black mold that lives deep inside you, waiting for the perfect opportunity to engulf your body. One minute, fine. The next, infected, and you're suffocating in it, watching your organs, brain, heart all rot from the inside out. Making you wish you'd never existed, that you don't exist now. That it would all just end already.

I can't do this. It's too much.

My old therapist used to say taking action was "the anecdote to panic," like it was a choice. But right now, there is no choice. I have to talk to Caylee. I have to tell her *now*.

My hands shake as I open my phone messages to her.

Changed my mind, I type, knowing Caylee will be at Juiced. **Be there in twenty.**

THOMAS

"THOMAS, MY MAN!"

As soon as practice let out, I tried to bail quickly, but I guess I wasn't fast enough. I sling my gear bag into my truck's backseat and turn. A blast of wind throws leaves in my face. Blinking hard, I spot Forest jogging my way, beanie pulled low over his eyes.

"How'd the audition go?" he huffs.

"Not so great," I tell him. "I fucked up the interview *and* the guitar."

"Shit, man. That sucks," Forest says, swiping a hand over his beanie, then glancing back toward the locker room. "Well, wanna catch a movie tonight or something? Get your mind off things?"

I get the feeling he means more than the audition, but before I can respond, Forest blurts out, "Wait, is that the great

Eleanor?" His gaze is on Eleanor's case, resting against the wheel hub. I'd set her there for only a sec to make room for my gear.

"Can I see it?" Forest asks as another gust of wind hits.

I slump, completely zapped of energy.

After today's practice, even standing upright is taking all my effort. Coach Mac had worked us extra hard till the end, knowing our hearts weren't in it. He and the other coaches had all seemed resigned when they'd left.

Then, to top it all off, in the locker rooms Zac had stood next to Ricky, holding his phone out, wearing a weird smirk. When I'd asked what they were doing, Ricky's "Talking to your mom" response had put me over the edge. I'd left my own phone in my truck, but even though I still needed to check it to see if Uncle Kurt had called, suddenly I'd wanted nothing to do with my phone, or the guys for that matter, or whatever stupid shit they were looking at that would drum up that brand of smirk from Zac. I'd changed quickly and left without showering.

Now Forest looks at me for a response about Eleanor. I hide my sigh. As a bassist, he's the only one who gets what a big deal she is to me, even if he's been too stoned to practice much lately.

"Yeah, sure, man," I manage. Pushing sweaty hair from my face, I summon the last of my energy and lift Eleanor's case onto the open tailgate. Some of the guys filter into the parking lot, but I'm too tired to even glance their way as I flip open the latches. With both hands, I ease Eleanor out and pass her to

Forest, feeling nervous about the wind buffeting the guitar too much. He's careful as he takes her, but still, I try not to look at where his fingers smudge her gloss.

It's because I have my back to them that I don't see them coming.

"Sweet ride, my man" is all Forest has time to say before Eleanor is snatched from his hands. "Duuude!" he exclaims, but too late.

I wheel around to face Zac, who's appeared out of nowhere. Not only him—Ricky, Steve, Stallion, and Mario stand watching too, all within a ten-car span. But my eyes stay glued to Zac standing a few feet away, gripping Eleanor by the neck with his good hand.

"Boyd. Be careful, man." I feel the empty guitar case beside me and everyone's attention on my face. I try to straighten up from where I've pitched forward, ready to spring. Because Zac wouldn't actually drop her, would he?

"Well, what do we have here?" Zac asks, eyeing her up and down.

Beside me, Forest's hair blows in the wind, his mouth slack. Two cars down, Ricky burrows into his red hoodie, grinning like an idiot. Stallion's paused next to his Mustang, keys suspended in midair, face unreadable behind dark glasses. Steve and Mario stand at his side.

Zac's in the middle of them all in his orange Syracuse lacrosse tee, Eleanor in his fist and me at his mercy. His thick fingers curl around her neck, squeezing her fretboard, base resting inches from the pavement. Zac runs his fingers over the silver autographs, leaving more smudges. "Nice toy, Music Man."

He wouldn't mess her up. He couldn't.

So, why's my heart pounding?

I try to stuff down the rising panic. "Thanks. But, uh, be careful with her."

"Her?" A smirk spreads across his face.

"Sounds like VanBrackel's got himself a new girlfriend," Ricky calls from his car, and everyone laughs.

I huff, uneasy, and reach out my hand. "Just give her back to me, okay? So I can put her away."

"If you want it so bad"—Zac laughs, swinging her by the neck like a gym bag—"then come get it."

"Boyd, come on." I clear my throat, trying to make my voice light. "She's . . . one of a kind." She's more than that. A reminder of the world beyond Bay City. A promise for the future. And it would take only one hit to do her in.

"Ah, man," Mario calls out, face caught between a smile and frown. "Give the kid back his guitar."

"No need to get your panties in a twist, Lorenzo," Zac fires back. With each swing, Eleanor's base barely misses the asphalt. "I'm just getting a *feel* for it."

"Give her back, man. Seriously." My voice pitches, and Zac laughs out loud.

"Don't worry. I'll give her back. After this cool trick. You ready?" Zac raises Eleanor high into the air again, fist gripping the base of her neck. "Watch this."

He drops her.

"No!" I lurch forward, throwing out my hands.

A startled huff—Forest.

"Oh shit!"—Ricky.

But Zac catches her by the top of her neck, centimeters before she slams pavement.

Hot adrenaline blasts through me. My heart slams against my ribcage.

"Whoa, man! Thought it was a goner for sure!" Forest says, delayed and too loud.

Zac's smirk falls at the look of what must be horror on my face. "Aw, come on, Music Man. You didn't really think I'd drop it, did you?" He swings Eleanor at me, her base hitting me in the gut and sending a hollow *clang* through the parking lot.

I fumble to catch her, deflating once I've got a solid hold.

Zac throws his good arm around my shoulders, squeezing hard. "Lighten up, VanB. So serious today! What's with you?" He slaps me hard on the back, then shoves me away.

Like he doesn't know the fucking answer. Like he's not always messing with people and pushing things too far just to watch the fallout. "Dumbass," I mutter, too bitterly, gripping Eleanor to my chest. I fixate on a water bottle, trapped by my tire.

"So, we're gonna meet up with the ladies at that smoothie place." Zac tries to catch my eye. "Interested?"

"Naw," I manage, even as I wonder if Erica'll be there. Probably not.

Ricky's "Later, Music Man" is supposed to sound like Zac's, only it lacks half the ego.

"Movie later?" Forest asks. When I nod, he drifts away.

"By the way." Zac walks backward, his shout almost inaudible over the sound of the wind. "Just had a friendly chat with your girlfriend. Till she signed off, anyway. We told her hi for you!" Then he turns and walks away.

Fucking *dick*.

I kick at the empty water bottle as I watch them leave, not daring to move till they get in their cars. Only then do I latch Eleanor in her case and settle her against the passenger's seat. Scrambling into the driver's side, I curse myself. Because I should've known better than to bring her around them. Why didn't I just tell Forest no?

But it's not just Eleanor. Zac said he talked to Erica. What did he say to her?

My phone buzzes, and I drag my gaze to where it sits in the center console. Speak of the devil: Zac just texted our group chat. He and Ricky have been blowing it up all morning, but I've completely ignored them. And right now, I really couldn't care less what they have to say. Still, I'm about to look anyway when I see the other alerts.

A jolt of panic hits as I scroll to the top. Tina's tagged me in some photos. Of course she has. But what photos? Pictures pop up when I click. They're of Erica and me, in Zac's backyard last night. Flipping through them makes me sick to my stomach. Worse, it opens up my brain.

"Hop on, little croc." Erica's tripping, landing on all fours, laughing. *"I fell!"* My arms wrap around her waist, trying to help her up. We both laugh as we fall . . .

The photos just went up, though I'm surprised it took Tina this long. Still, who else has seen them? There are already some comments and everything. It's shit like this that makes me not use my real name online. Not that it makes much difference.

Anger surges through me as I untag myself—Erica already must've—and type out a message to Tina: Enough with the photos already. You made your point, now delete them. Slamming my phone down, I crank up my stereo. The Hands's "Get Out" thrums in my ears, drowning out all other noise as I throw my truck in reverse. Today couldn't possibly get any shittier.

ERICA

PALM TREES AND SHOPPING PLAZAS WHIZ BY AS I NEAR
Juiced, replaying in my head what I'm going to tell Caylee.
Everything, my brain says. *You have to tell her everything.* I'll
start with the party and beg her forgiveness for not telling her
first thing when she came over. But how do I think I'll get the
courage to say it now if I couldn't before? Because I have to,
somehow. For a second, I wish I'd thought to save the photo
Zac sent before deleting my profile so I could show Caylee, but
it's the last thing I want floating around for someone to find.
It's bad enough she's probably seen the photos Tina posted.
Still, I cringe, thinking about Caylee finding evidence of my
naked body being inside Zac's room. Telling Caylee about that
part is going to be so hard already; I don't want her seeing the
gruesome proof, too.

I can do this, I tell myself. I can tell Caylee. Erica Strange would.

The parking lot is jam-packed, but I squeeze in between an SUV and a sports car, then hurry to the building, the wind tugging at my hair and sweatshirt. Though the Sharpie has mostly faded, I still need to wear max coverage.

Caylee and I have been to this place plenty of times, and I've always loved how clean it looks—so fresh and modern—even with its ridiculously priced ten-dollar juices. Rough wood planks and giant windows make up the outside, the metal edging catching the sunlight. Inside, air-conditioning blasts me in the face. It smells crisp and frothy even—a combination of wheat grass and lemon zest and something rooty, like beets. Small tables perch on tall metal stems that spring up from the floor like daisies. Bar stools filled with smoothie drinkers crowd each one. There's a long line leading up to the register that I avoid as I glance around.

Caylee and Amber sit against the far wall facing the window, their backs to me, Amber's frame a much wider silhouette than Caylee's. Caylee's crop top and skinny jeans look like they're ripped from a Lucky Brand ad, and Amber's in her customary dark colors, this time a belted navy lace dress. They would make a beautiful comic spread, Mermaid and Medusa, but I'm not here for art inspiration.

Neither has heard me approach. I hover awkwardly behind them, noting there's not another seat in sight even though I told Caylee I was coming. Come to think of it, she never texted me back.

"The musical's about some dumb beauty pageant," Amber's saying, "but that's the point. It's kind of this big commentary on the whole 'sexy beauty queen' thing, and it's got this incredible cast, largely female. Anyway, the director said she could probably get me the assistant stage manager gig if I wanted it."

Amber must be talking about the regional theater where she volunteers.

"What do your parents say?" Caylee asks, sounding a little uncomfortable, and I know what she's thinking—"Just more of Amber's 'psycho-feminist ideals,'" or so Caylee's always saying behind Amber's back. Plus, if the rumors are true, Caylee's mom was a beauty queen back in the day, and therefore part of whatever culture Amber's play is critiquing, which Amber must remember based on how long they've known each other.

Amber shrugs, seeming indifferent to Caylee's discomfort. "Mom One and Two are both totally for it."

"Hey," I say. Feelings of shyness and awkwardness swirl together in my stomach, surprising me. These are my friends. I shouldn't be nervous. But that was before.

Now they both turn in their seats.

"Hey," Caylee replies, but her voice is all wrong, her smile too tight. Is she still upset I wasn't thrilled by Zac declaring his love to her, or is this more than that?

"I texted you I was coming," I tell her. "Did you not get it?"

She shrugs. "Sorry. I just . . . forgot to reply."

Amber watches us, the space between her brows furrowing.

I fake a smile, wishing I were alone with Caylee. For half a breath, I almost consider just blurting everything out in front of them both. I picture pulling up a too-tall, too-metal chair that scrapes across the floor as it drags and laying everything out there. Amber would listen in, eyes fixed intently on mine, and Caylee would cry softly at her side, realizing she's dating a total prick. Amber may be a little distant and hard to read, but maybe she'd know what to do.

But, of course, I already know what Amber would do. When she smells injustice, she pounces, which is the last thing I need. This situation needs to be kept tightly under wraps.

Stalling, I reach into my bag. "I almost forgot. I brought you something." A B-Thin cookbook appears in my hand, which Amber rolls her eyes at, probably because of the name. "I was going to save this for your birthday, but . . ." Shrugging, I hand it to Caylee, hoping Normal Caylee will appear through the cracks.

"Thanks," she says, flopping the book on the counter, paging through it half-heartedly.

Why won't Amber just ignore me, glue herself to her phone like usual? This is awkward enough without an audience.

In the lingering silence, I gesture to the cookbook. "I thought maybe we could try to figure out how to make those bars you love so much."

Another shrug from Caylee. "Yeah, sounds good." And there it is again. The Something Different in her shrug. Agreeing to plans but like she doesn't really mean it. The way she won't quite look at me, hasn't called me "E" even once.

"Riiight," Amber says slowly, staring between Caylee and me.

Dread spreads its mold through my stomach. I came here to tell her my side. *Maybe someone beat you to it,* says a voice in my mind. I can't . . . I can't do this right now.

"I gotta pee," I say, turning and rushing away.

"What was that all about?" I hear Amber ask behind me.

I push open the bathroom door. *Do it already. Just ask Caylee if you can talk in private.* But somehow, it's so much harder to work up the guts now that Caylee seems to have already heard something, already formed an opinion. It's easier for me to stare at signs reminding employees to wash their hands than to talk to my best friend. I hover awkwardly until two girls ask if I'm in line for the bathroom. Then I stare at myself in the mirror. *Erica, DO IT NOW.* And the me in the mirror nods, cape and mask more or less back in place. I replay the line in my head as I return to the table: *"Caylee, can I talk to you for a second, alone?"* They'll both stare. Maybe Amber will ask me what's up again, or Caylee will, and I'll say, *"It's private."* And then Caylee and I will walk away to a different spot, and I'll tell her everything: *"Your boyfriend took off my clothes. He wrote on me. I didn't want to tell you because I was afraid you'd hate me."* Then at least my best friend will know what really happened. She'll hear it from me.

Momentum fueling me, I push open the door and round the corner.

I stop short.

Zac. And Ricky. And another teammate, Matt. Even horrid picture-posting Tina is here, sitting quietly on a stool she'd commandeered from somewhere. A wave of dizziness hits as I take in the scene. They're all here. Caylee's all smiles, looking tiny next to hulking Zac, while Amber watches in supreme annoyance, arms folded over her large chest.

Staring at Zac's powerful arm wrapped so tightly around Caylee, his muscled legs braced against the bottom rung of the stool, I feel ill. I imagine the Sharpie in his hand, leaning in as he writes his name, his breath hot on my thigh.

I whip out my phone and shoot Caylee a quick text: Meet me by the entrance.

Across the room, she reaches into her back pocket and pulls out her phone, then glances around, eyes searching until she finds me.

Tina follows Caylee's gaze, and with a shock, I swear she spots me too, but she glances away so quickly I think I must've imagined it.

I watch, confused, as Tina refuses to look up from the ground, as Caylee wriggles free from Zac's arm. It's very unlike Tina to sit so still, so quietly, but I whip around before anyone else has time to spot me. Maybe Tina really didn't see me, I decide, because if she had, she'd make it well known.

I hurry all the way to the entrance before turning back around, putting as much distance as I can between that table of monsters and me. Who knows what they'll say or do?

As Caylee approaches, I hiss, "I thought you said this was a girls' date."

Even though she seems upset with me, guilt ripples through Caylee's expression. We've had this conversation before, about how much time she spends with Zac. How she's always flaking out on plans we've made so she can be with him or inviting him along to every single thing we do. I usually try to turn my criticism into a joke to soften it a bit, so I don't make Caylee mad. But, especially lately, Amber has had no problem calling Caylee out on it, which has led to some serious friction between the two of them.

Caylee doesn't meet my eyes. "Well," she begins, voice defensive, "Zac got out of practice and asked where I was, and what was I supposed to tell him? 'Don't come'?"

"I just . . ."—*needed to work up the courage to tell you*—"wanted it to be you, me, and Amber. And now Tina's here. Did you see those pictures she posted of me?"

"Julie told me about them."

Caylee talked to Julie, from English class, who was also at the party. Who else has Caylee talked to?

"I hate her for you," Caylee says about Tina, but it feels automatic.

"I hate her for me too."

"What did Thomas say about the pics?" she asks, voice flat.

"I haven't talked to him yet."

"But weren't you guys, like, obsessed with each other five minutes ago? What happened?" She still won't look at me.

"Caylee, are you mad at me?"

Her frown deepens as she crosses her forearms. I'd draw her forehead in squiggles, deep vertical lines between her eyes, her mouth a sideways squish. "Why would I be mad at you?"

"You seem mad, is all."

Silence.

She casts a glance over her shoulder. Finally, she looks at me. "Well, Julie called me after I left your house."

Pause.

"What'd she say?" I ask.

"Well, there's been some kind of crazy rumors going around about you."

A few lines of Dad's Shakespeare hit me:

> *Rumour is a pipe*
> *Blown by surmises, jealousies, conjectures . . .*

I feel like I've swallowed rocks. "What do you mean? What kind of rumors?"

Pause.

"Well, you know, just some crazy stuff."

Pause. A thousand pounds of silence.

"Like what 'crazy stuff,' Cay?"

"Um, stuff like . . . about you. Like, getting naked in Zac's room and stuff." She rushes on. "But I know it's not true or anything. I mean, that's what I told her—that it's not true. I was there. And besides, Zac told me nothing happened. I mean, it's not like you're some slut, trying to steal my boyfriend." She lets out a nervous laugh.

Slut.

"No, of course not. Caylee, you know me."

Pause.

"Sure," she says.

"So, you know I'm not like that." *But Zac?* Caylee has no idea what he's really like.

"Yeah. I mean, that's what I told Julie. That you just passed out in his room. And Zac said—"

Caylee needs to know. Tell her now.

Erica Strange would.

"But that's not all that happened," I rush on.

It's out there now, hanging in the air between us.

On cue, I look past Caylee's shoulder to see Zac watching us. He winks at me and rises to his feet. I nearly choke. Is he coming over here? "I . . . I have to go," I blurt, tearing my eyes from Zac. "But I'm going to call you soon. Just . . . make sure you're alone. You're right, Caylee. Something happened. Something bad. But I need you to answer your phone, 'kay?"

As my eyes well up, Caylee's face goes completely blank. Behind her, Zac's closed half the distance separating us.

Go, go, go! my brain commands. *Leave!*

"I'll call you in an hour, 'kay? Pick up, all right?"

After a pause as big as a mountain, she nods. Zac nears as I wheel for the door.

"Talk soon!" I yell over my shoulder, then dart outside. Only after the door's slammed behind me do I realize Caylee hadn't asked what happened or if I was okay, like she already knew the answers. Or didn't want to know. But still, I'm going to tell her everything when I call.

I reach the parking lot right as someone ducks from a separate exit. For a bone-freezing moment, I think it's Zac racing out to corner me, or even Thomas, appearing from thin air. But it's Ricky, heading for his car.

Suddenly, I want to ask him about the photos. Though my guard's still sky-high, out of all the guys, Ricky seems the least physically threatening, maybe because we're the same height or because he's not built huge like Zac. He also acts differently when he's not around his buddies—less aggressive. And this could be the only chance I get to catch him alone. Just not too alone.

Channeling Erica Strange once more, my flip-flops slapping the pavement, I call out, "Ricky!"

He turns only long enough to see that it's me. Suddenly, Ricky does not want to be caught up with.

"Ricky, stop!" Halfway to his car, I grab his hood and pull, forcing him back. I cringe and drop my hand, knowing I had to stop him but hating I had to touch him.

He whirls, snarling. "What?" Ricky's a lot of things—unmotivated, immature, laughs at his own jokes—but he's never been hostile. Then again, there's apparently a lot about Ricky I don't know that's only now rising to the surface, now that it's too late for red flags.

Through my shock, I find my voice. "I need to know everyone you sent those pictures to. From . . . from Zac's room. I need to know if there are more." I'm shaking uncontrollably, my voice much quieter than Erica Strange's would be. "Please, it's important," I add, sensing his hesitation.

"I don't know what you're talking about." His eyes don't meet mine, but the malice remains.

Since fleeing Zac's room, I've played out a similar scene in my head a million times, one where I'd confront each of the guys for stripping me and writing on me. That was before I knew about the photos, of course, but even still. In all of my mental imaginings, I'd never prepared myself for one of the guys denying any of it. And, as I look at him, I realize Ricky's not just feigning ignorance of the photos. He's trying to deny everything they did to me, erase it all with his words as if none of it ever happened.

Could I have envisioned Tina sabotaging me with cruel photos to look cool to the guys? Yes. Zac turning it all into a sick game? Absolutely. But this? Pretending like the whole horrific nightmare never occurred? It hurts in a way I couldn't have predicted.

"Ricky, you know exactly what I'm talking about." He won't even look at me, hands jammed in his jean pockets. "Zac showed me," I add.

We stand there, facing off. Ricky glances around like someone will blow into the parking lot on the wind and save him from having to spend another agonizing second with me.

And then Ricky seals his own guilt. "I didn't do anything."

Something starts to ripple through me. Something with teeth and horns and claws. He won't even look at me. He was sure looking at me last night, and now he can't even meet my eyes? Can't even bother to tell me the truth? I yank the sleeve of my sweatshirt up to my elbow, exposing the faintest memory of his name across my forearm. Still he won't look. "If you don't remember, perhaps this will refresh your memory? Your name? Zac's and Stallion's and Forest's, all over me? The pictures you guys took of me?"

He cuts me off. "There aren't any pictures. They got deleted." *They. More than one.* Who is this guy, hunching his shoulders in the parking lot, trying to hide in his hoodie? How well do I even know him? How well do I know anybody at this stupid school?

A couple walks by holding cups of neon green juice. They glance at us, then away.

Suddenly ashamed, I clear all desperation from my face and yank down my sleeve. Fighting tears, I say, "Don't lie to me. I saw one of the pictures. Your handiwork."

I don't think Ricky will respond so it throws me off when he does. His voice comes out so low that I barely catch what he says over the noise of passing cars. "It was just a joke."

"What?" I ask because it's all I can think to say.

"A joke, Erica. Just a joke." At last, his eyes meet mine. "And any pictures got deleted. So, get over it already."

"Get *over* it? You and Zac and Stallion and Forest, you all wrote your names . . ."

"Yeah, you said that already. But I also notice how you conveniently keep leaving out Thomas."

"Thomas didn't write on me. I looked. His name isn't on me."

Ricky's face turns back into a snarl. "Sure, Erica. Keep telling yourself that." He hurries to his car, moving away from me in the darkening light like I'm disgusting, diseased.

Somewhere in my sketchbook, there's a drawing of Thomas and me at the beach, lying so close to each other on his blanket as I pointed out constellation after constellation in the night sky. I'd felt so proud that night, rattling on about Perseus on his winged Pegasus swooping in to save Andromeda, chained to the rocks, from the sea monster Cetus. And that night, Thomas had played me songs on his guitar, and even a song he'd written just for me, beautiful and haunting. And in that moment, swept up in his soft voice and the sweet melody, I knew I liked him so much it hurt. He'd made me feel like I mattered, like I meant something to him. Like I was special.

Nearby, a police siren blares, but it barely registers above the growing scream in my head.

Thomas?

THOMAS

IT'S DUSK, AND I'M NEARLY HOME WHEN MY PHONE RINGS.
Heart thundering, I stare at my uncle Kurt's name blazing
across my truck's caller ID. I take a deep breath and answer,
trying to prepare myself.

"Hey, Uncle Kurt."

"Hey, kid, how are ya?" Uncle Kurt sounds far too chipper,
and I know he's trying not to make me feel bad.

I flip my headlights on and switch lanes, getting ready to
exit. "I'm . . . I'm okay."

"Well, I wanted to let you know I had lunch with Ingrid
and Jorge."

Professor Kovich and Turtleneck Guy, I'm pretty sure.

"And I've got news for you," he continues.

My uncle can be tough to read, but there's no need to guess
what he's going to say this time. "You don't have to be nice,"

I interrupt. "I know I botched the interview. And the guitar. Badly."

"Yeah, you did, kid."

My heart sinks to my shoes. "I'm so sorry, Uncle Kurt," I blurt out. "I was late, and didn't sleep much, and I just . . . I just messed everything up. And after all your help, I couldn't do any of it right. The questions, our songs . . ."

"You had a rough start up there, no question, and your answers were far from what we'd practiced." His disappointment hurts the worst, though I'm surprised when he actually laughs. "Ingrid was not impressed, to say the least. She told me as much over lunch. *Several* times, in fact."

I'm about to tell him I'll pay him back for the sound engineer he hired to fix my audition tape when he continues. "Jorge on the other hand . . . he was truly blown away by your talent, kid. Not only as a songwriter, but as a performer, too. Honestly, it's the best I've ever heard you play. Not counting your rough start, of course. But Jorge understands, says he really wants to work with you. Said it took him a while to overcome his own stage fright, but that he believes in your passion. Could see it a mile away."

Work with me . . . I nearly miss my exit, swerving last minute. A horn blares behind me. "You mean I got in?"

This time his laugh is huge. "Well, not officially, but let's just say a little elf friend told me that, so long as you keep your grades up and your nose out of trouble, you may just find yourself at Thornton next fall semester!"

I can't speak.

Uncle Kurt rushes on, "But seriously, kid. You played your guts out up there, once you got out of your own way. It was incredible to behold. Coming back from the brink of failure like that. You did me real proud."

I got in. I got into music school. I don't know how, but I did.

Play something true.

Uncle Kurt's thinking the same thing because he says, "What was that song you sang up there?"

Erica's green eyes stare back at me through the hallway glass that first day. I clear my throat. "'Window.' Wrote it a few weeks ago."

"Yeah, that one. Great stuff, kid. Solid melody. The guys'll be so proud when I tell them. They're all dying to hear how it went."

Benji, Chad, Kobe, and Arjun. They'll know I made it.

I made it. I'm in.

"Uncle Kurt?"

"Yeah, kid?"

"Thanks for everything. Really."

I hang up the phone, staring at the spare tire of the Jeep idling in front of me. I made it. I'm going to music school. At Thornton.

When I pull into our drive, Dad's car isn't even in the garage. Perfect. I burst through the front door, breathing hard, and catch a whiff of garlic. Mom stands at the kitchen counter, seasoning raw steaks.

"Uncle Kurt just called."

She pauses, face hopeful. "What did he say?"

"That I made it. I'm in." I hear the daze in my own voice. "Not officially yet, but I'm in."

Mom holds up her dirty hands, like she wants to hug me. "Oh, Tommy, that's wonderful news!"

"Thanks. It's still hard to believe." And part of me doesn't yet. I've wanted this for so long, it doesn't seem real.

"I'm so proud of you, son. You've worked so very hard."

"Can I go to the movies with Forest to celebrate?"

She hesitates. "Of course, hon. Just . . . don't tell your father." Her smile falls as she glances away. "And listen, I'm sorry he was so tough on you this morning. I didn't mean to get you into trouble. I was worried, is all, when you didn't come home. But I'm sorry. I know I worry too much."

Irritation flares. How could someone be sorry so many times in one breath? "Mom, it's fine. It was my fault. I should've called or texted."

"I know, but I feel bad. I'm sorry that—"

"Mom, stop apologizing. It's fine. I deserved it."

She stays quiet a moment before reaching for the pepper. "Well, okay. So long as you're not upset."

"I'm not upset, Mom. Especially not with you." I turn to go before she can find something else to apologize for, agonizing over everything she's ever said or done. I hate it.

She calls after me, "We're having steaks for dinner. I hope that's okay!"

"Sounds great, Mom. Be back soon." I sprint up the stairs to change.

I got in, I remind myself. But in my head, green eyes stare back at me. Any elation I'd started to feel drops like a rock. I change quickly, chucking my phone on the bed as I leave. Usually I feel naked without it, but now it burns a hole in my pocket. It can stay here forever for all I care.

IT'S DARK OUTSIDE AS I PULL BACK INTO OUR PARKING LOT
and rush up the stairs to my room, thankful beyond words
that Mom's working late. Crossing over to my bulletin board,
I stare at the grainy photo of Thomas and me from the beach,
then glance at the note he'd left on my car. I'd kept the rose he'd
given me too, in a glass of water in my car, even after it had
shed aphids all over my cup holder. But it had started to mold
when I'd attempted to preserve it, so I'd had to throw it away.
Now I stare at the bottom of his note.

Thomas the Rhymer

His name. Ricky said . . . But I didn't see. . . .
Below the note is the ticket stub to the Los Angeles
County Museum of Art. Thomas and I had gone to see the

Edward Gorey exhibit, not because he'd known who the hell Edward Gorey was, but just because he knew I wanted to go. That day, I'd felt so *alive*, moved by the art of a man who wasn't afraid to be anything but his weird self. I'd told Thomas about my portfolio for CalArts and even confessed that I wanted to work for Disney like Tim Burton so Mom and I wouldn't have to worry about money ever again. Just when I'd started to get embarrassed, having thrown my hands wildly into the air in emphasis, Thomas had told me that that's what music was to him: freedom. In the middle of the exhibit, surrounded by all the strange museumgoers, Thomas and I had searched each other's eyes, smiling all the while. "I understand you," he'd said, grabbing my hand. "I understand you."

And I'd believed him.

Suddenly I'm choking on panic. I need to talk to Thomas. He'd tell me the truth, right? Maybe he could explain everything. I could call him. No, a text would be better.

Desperate butterflies dive in my stomach as I find his name in my contacts. My heart sinks as I stare at the picture accompanying it, Thomas in full lacrosse gear. I open a new text.

In the text history, it displays the last two texts we'd exchanged:

Here :)

:D

What I wouldn't give for a time machine so I could do

everything differently. But of course, that's impossible. All I can do now is type a new message. Because I need to hear it from him:

Hey, it's me.

SEND.

Crap! I didn't mean to send it yet! I wanted time to think about what to say, but now I have to rush.

Just wanted to say hi. Sorry I got so wasted last night.

SEND.

"Sorry I got so wasted"? Really?

Anyway, I really need to talk to you when you're available.

"Available"? This isn't a dentist appointment! But I punch send and wait, not breathing.

For a moment nothing happens. For a moment I think he's not near his phone or that maybe he won't respond at all. And then Delivered turns to Read 7:50 p.m. Then three dancing dots appear beneath my message, indicating he's typing a response.

I realize I'm clenching my phone. I pry my fingers loose, shaking my hand to relax it.

But then the dancing dots disappear.

Before my frown can form into a thought, the dots reappear.

What's he typing? Air refuses to push past my chest. The shallow breathing makes my head spin.

The dots disappear again.

Is it a long message? Him telling me off? Or something else? An explanation for everything? I need that explanation. I need it so badly.

I wait, telling myself not to hope for too much. But no new message appears. I glance at the time: 7:54 p.m.

Still no message.

I stare at the phone, trying to will a message to appear. I check the signal. Full bars. Several tense minutes tick by as I prepare for the worst. Nothing. No text from Thomas.

I gaze at the time again—8:02 p.m.—and let the cold truth sink in. No one takes more than twelve minutes to type a message, not even a long one.

He's not writing me back.

And yet, I can still hear him: *"I understand you."* Was that all a lie?

I stare at my phone, cursor blinking in the empty text box, looking like anything but an ellipsis. Because this time, maybe there is no *To be continued.*

Without giving myself a chance to think, I dial Caylee's number, then listen as her phone rings five times. But just like this morning, it goes to voicemail. I try again, but this time it doesn't even ring before her recorded voice tells me to leave a message. Is she intentionally ignoring me, after everything I told her at Juiced? I type out a text, asking her to call me back ASAP. Just as I hit send, my phone buzzes with an incoming call. I nearly leap out of my skin, but it's not Caylee.

Amber's never called me before. This can't be good.

"Hello?" My voice sounds wobbly.

"Erica? Hi, it's Amber. Tell me, what's going on?"

"What do you mean?"

"I mean, why were you and Caylee being total weirdos at Juiced? And why were the guys all laughing when they saw you? Did something happen . . . like, at the party after I left?"

Her questions send a spark of panic through me. Amber— she left the party early, she doesn't do social media, and even she's caught wind that something's wrong. "No. Nothing." The lie tastes like burned coffee.

"Then did you and Caylee fight?"

I know I have to choose my words carefully. "I just . . . got really drunk. Caylee was . . . annoyed she had to take care of me, is all. It wasn't my finest moment."

"Are you sure that's all?"

"Definitely. But, um, hey, I've gotta run. My mom's calling me for dinner, so . . . I'll see you tomorrow, 'kay? But thanks for calling. Seriously."

"Okay . . . ," she drawls out, not entirely convinced. "Well, catch you before school, then?"

Shit. "Sure." My shoulders collapse as I end the call, then I scan for any texts from Thomas. Still nothing.

My conversation with Ricky comes flooding back:

"His name isn't on me."

"Sure, Erica. Keep telling yourself that."

Ricky's words won't leave me alone. I've already looked for Thomas's name, though. I know I did. Did I not look hard enough? I head for the bathroom, deciding I need to be sure. If Caylee said she saw him coming down the stairs with everyone else, then I have to check again.

I drop my pants in front of the mirror, eyes scanning the dark smudges that used to be pictures and names, searching every inch for the name that's not there. Relief warms me. He couldn't have been in the room with the guys. Caylee must've been wrong about seeing him on the stairs with them. And there's another reason he was in the kitchen this morning, another reason he's not texting me back. . . .

It's as I stand in my underwear and turn sideways with my shirt lifted, convincing myself of the impossibility, that I see it, scrawled on my upper back right below my bra line, faded but still visible. All alone, it's in a place I'd never even thought to look—only a single word, a single name. And because of the mirror, I'm reading it backward. But I'd recognize that slanted writing anywhere.

THOMAS

THE SMELL OF BUTTERED POPCORN OVERWHELMS ME AS I wait for Forest in the entrance to the theater. I rock on my heels as a group of girls passes by. One giggles while the other two try to catch my eye. Big green eyes flash at me before I look away, my heart sinking, and shove both fists in my pockets. My hand hits something.

Frowning, I pull out a folded square of notebook paper. Before I even open it, I remember what it's from—a note Erica had slipped me in Spanish the last time I'd worn these jeans. I unfold the note, and Erica's drawing stares up at me. It's of us in the museum gift shop when I'd bought her that weird Edward Gorey poster. I'm holding it out to her like a baton, head bowed, saying, "One creepy scroll for Erica Strange." And she's reaching for it, responding, "Thomas the Rhymer, you shouldn't have!" Clearly that day had meant something to her, too, to record it on paper.

I flinch as someone calls my name, shoving the note in my pocket. Forest's heading toward me. We half-hug, half-clap each other's shoulders, and I smell the weed on him. Sure enough, his eyes are glazed as he hands me a ticket.

"Cool. Thanks, man," I say.

"No problem, my good man. No problem. Especially since snacks are on you."

I huff a laugh and follow him to the concession stand, where we load up on food. Forest and I each get a giant popcorn, then licorice for me and Milk Duds for him, plus two Dr Peppers. I even tell him about music school, and he pounds my shoulder. "Stellar news, my man!"

As the usher tears our tickets, I glance over at Forest. He's been my best friend since freshman year when a couple of us snuck out one night and rolled some old tires we'd stolen down a hill, hitting the house of this junior girl we thought was hot. We'd run like hell when it'd set off the house alarm. Forest can be a weird dude, and he's completely oblivious to the fact that he repeats himself when he's stoned, but he's as chill as they come, probably owing to him being half-baked all the time once Coach's drug testing is over for the season. And he's a solid friend.

We settle into the first row above the main aisle and recline our seats, footrests rising. I stuff my face full of licorice, realizing it's been a while since we've hung out, just the two of us. Between music school applications and practicing guitar, falling into the first-string goalie position, and keeping up on homework, things've been nuts. Plus, lately I've spent most of my free time with Erica. I brush against my pocket, feeling the note crinkle inside.

Forest turns to me, colors from a dental commercial flashing across his face. "You good, my man?"

I stop mid-chew, trying to rearrange my face. "Fine. Why?"

"Because you don't seem like yourself. Didn't at practice today either."

I swallow, feeling whole chunks of licorice scrape my throat, and chance a look at Forest. His face is so serious as he stares at our feet. I clear my throat, then wait for some moviegoers to pass by. "I'm . . . fine."

He shakes his shaggy head. "I've known you a while, my man, so I know when you're fine and when you're not. You avoided everyone all practice for sure." For the first time I see how tired he looks, maybe even more than a hangover's worth. "It was a shitty party, am I right?" he adds.

I cough on a piece of licorice and thump at my chest. Winded, I say, "To be honest, I don't really remember it."

He stares hard at me, looking as miserable as I feel. "If you don't remember, then why haven't you asked what happened?"

I push away the licorice. "I just . . ." But that's all that comes out.

He watches me as he sips his soda. "You see the photos, man?"

"Yeah, that Tina posted? She's so stupid somet—"

"Naw, man, those came down, like, an hour ago. I mean the ones from the group chat. From Zac's room."

I freeze. There are photos? From *inside*? But when . . . ?

Forest continues, "I'd show you myself, but I deleted that shit, you know?"

I'm still trying to wrap my head around it when Forest adds, "You talk to her since, man? Erica?"

"No, uh, not yet," I choke out.

He shrugs. "Maybe you should, dude. Seems like it's crushing you."

I blink hard, my throat going hot. I've never thought of Forest as observant, but today he's picked up on a lot more than I would've given him credit for.

The lights dim overhead, followed by a swell of music from the first preview.

Forest is still staring at me so I say, "We should probably . . . ," and glance down into the bright yellow of my popcorn, oil pooling over the kernels. Gross. I set it in the empty seat next to me.

Finally he nods and leans back in his chair. "That we should, my man."

I will my brain to turn off every thought of Erica. Thinking about her hurts too much.

But as we settle into our seats, tiny green aliens invade the screen. My brain says, *I think the gremlins ate it*, and throws me back to Pizzaz Pizza Parlor, reaching under that dirty arcade game to find Erica's stick-on tattoo. There's no escaping her. Erica is everywhere, and I realize I'd give anything to return to that afternoon, to be in that back room that smelled like fresh baked dough and floor cleaner, talking to Erica without a care in the world. Before the party. Before everything got so fucked-up.

I'm grateful for the dark theater as I wipe my eyes.

ERICA

JUST YESTERDAY, CAYLEE AND I HAD RUSHED ONTO THE
field after Thomas's lacrosse game to say hi. While Caylee went
to find Zac, I'd found Thomas by the benches, reenacting his
final winning save for Forest. And, just yesterday, when he'd
spotted me—red marks from his face mask running across his
forehead, hair glistening with sweat—his eyes had locked on
mine like I was the only person in the swirling chaos of that field.

"Erica Strange, you came!" he'd said, unable to hide his
excitement even though he knew I was there all along. I'd
watched him scan the bleachers earlier till he found me.

Thomas seemed completely oblivious to Forest watching us,
but I felt a little shy, one cheek full of the Altoids I'd jammed
in my mouth up in the bleachers. Still, I managed, "I'm hardly
one to break a deal, Thomas the Rhymer. That was quite a save
you made at the end."

Forest cleared his throat, and with a "Catch you in the locker room, my man," Thomas and I were alone. Bodies pressed around us, but—just yesterday—we were in our own little bubble together.

"Hi," he said.

"Hi," I said.

Then Coach Mac appeared suddenly, slapping Thomas's shoulder and startling us both. Thomas nearly dropped his lacrosse stick. "Hell of a save, Thomas! Hell of a save!"

I watched Thomas swell with pride, betraying how much his coach's words meant to him even as his coach disappeared back into the swirl.

Thomas cleared his throat then, eyes on his cleats. "Can I . . . walk you to your car or something?"

"Caylee drove," I said, "but I can walk you to your truck to put your gear away?"

His face lit up. "Deal!"

Nervously, I took his free hand, but when Thomas looked down at it, I thought I'd made a mistake or that my hands were clammy or something. But instead he said, "Your hands are so cold," then squeezed his helmet between his knees and held both my hands to his mouth, exhaling warm air onto them. I breathed in the moment, the smell of fresh sweat and spongy turf. The feeling of him so near me, consumed by his attention.

He handed me his gear, saying, "Better yet, mind holding this for a sec? I'll go grab you my sweatshirt."

"Sure thing," I replied, biting my lip and swooning as I watched him retreat. And—just yesterday—I remember looking around, wondering who would see me holding Thomas's stuff. I loved the weight of his gear in my hands, of being granted such close access to the small nicks covering his goalie stick, the scratch running through his helmet's BCP decal. In my arms, it somehow felt like the weight of belonging, even more so when he returned, handing me his sweatshirt to wear, then leaning me against his truck in the parking lot. Pressed against his driver's-side door, I noticed the splatter of freckles across his nose, the way he looked away shyly, scrubbing a hand through his hair when he said, "Erica, will you go out with me? Like, be my girlfriend?" And—just yesterday—all I could manage was a giddy "Yes!" as he tugged at my loose curls and our faces inched closer.

"Erica Strange?" he said.

"Thomas the Rhymer?" I said.

Then he cupped my jaw in his hand, eyes on my lips as he leaned in. *It's happening!* I thought, and it did. Our lips connected as he wrapped his arms around me and we fell into each other. He stopped only long enough to whisper, "You taste like candy canes."

Then Ricky yelled, "Yeah, get some!" and we reluctantly pulled apart, me telling Thomas I needed to go find Caylee. But Thomas squeezed my hand, stopping me. "I'll see you tonight, then?" he asked, voice hopeful.

I pulled myself back into him, nose close to his. "Definitely. To be continued?"

"To be continued," he echoed.

As I walked away, I heard Ricky slap Thomas on the back and say, "You are so gonna get laid tonight, VanB," and Thomas's "Shut up, Ricky" in return. But—just yesterday—Ricky's comment couldn't touch my elation, or overshadow Thomas's lips on mine, or the promise we'd made to each other: "To be continued." Instead, I'd rushed home to capture our first kiss on paper with my colored pens—so oblivious, so naive.

Because just yesterday, I was a girl head over heels, going to a party that night with my kind and captivating new boyfriend, whom I'd just kissed for the very first time.

Him, my Thomas the Rhymer. Me, his Erica Strange.

How wrong I'd been to place every hope in some guy I didn't know. Thinking he cared. Thinking I mattered. Because there it is, reflected back in the mirror. The name that changes everything.

Like the rest of the Sharpie on my body, the ink is partially faded, no longer the angry black scrawl it must've started out as. But because I didn't know it was there, didn't scrub it away like all the writing on my front, it wasn't washed near invisible like the rest.

As I stare at his name, the tiny spark that was hope—that I'd somehow kept alive since waking up at Zac's—splutters and goes out. A short-circuit behind my heart.

Thomas.

No.

But it is Thomas.

I can only stare, transfixed, at his name, scribbled in the same toppled letters, like those in the right-hand corner of his Spanish worksheets.

Not him, too.

I'm scrambling, scooting myself up and onto the vanity. It wobbles as I press my back to the mirror. I twist around, trying in vain to compare the two images—one mirrored, one inscribed that I can't quite see.

Thomas ƨɒmoʜT

No.

A feral noise escapes my throat, a sound so inhuman it terrifies me.

No.

But he did this. He did.

"How could you?" I don't realize I've said it aloud until I see my lips move in the mirror, feel the weight of the words hanging over me.

I slide off the vanity; it tips forward then crashes as it hits the wall, vibrating fury through my bones.

I turn and fling open drawers, grabbing fistfuls of stuff—a hairbrush, toothpaste, foundation—and hurl them at the mirror.

New mirrors cost money. But the thought drowns in a violent rattle of glass that refuses to break. The sound fuels the rage burning all traces of hope from my heart. More handfuls. Cracks split the mirror into several jagged pieces, but it remains standing.

More.

I tear and rip and throw.

Walking with him to class.

Claw and shriek.

Climbing into his truck.

Pummel and kick.

Cheering him on from the bleachers.

Thrash and break.

Feeling his gaze on me during Spanish.

Feeling his name on my bra line where he scribbled it with his friends. After they stripped me. Drew on me. Left me to wake to the looping nightmare of what they did—what *he* did—to me.

My palms hurt. My chest hurts. I'm panting hard.

In flickering stops and starts, my outline comes into focus in what is left of the mirror, sections of me reflected between the cracks. The mirror still stands, but barely, looking ready to cave at any moment like an important piece has fractured, fallen away. Below that is a massacre: crushed makeup compact with clumps of loose powder; hairbrush covered in creamy foundation; jumble of sticky pink lip gloss, tube of mascara, bottle of face wash, bobby pins, cotton balls, hair bands. A can of hairspray rolls free from the mess and off the counter. It hits the floor with a clang before coming to rest by the rug.

How could he?

In a single motion, I sweep everything from the counter. Stuff bounces off the toilet, wall, shower curtain. Something explodes against an exposed shower tile—a mirror shard.

And this time when I scream—"NOOOOOOOO!!!!"—I follow it up with slamming fists that unsettle the rest of the mirror.

But it still won't fall. I scream again. Fists pound. Again. Pound. Again. Pound. Until the mirror finally collapses in an ear-shattering deluge of glass shards.

The sight of blood stops me. It's splattered across the right side of the vanity and melting into the chalky face powder, turning sections a violent crimson.

I lift my right hand. Blood seeps from a deep cut on the side of my palm. For a long time, I watch the scarlet pool around the wound and run down my arm. It soaks into the sleeve of my shirt and drips onto the floor.

At first, I don't feel a thing. Like the girl from the mirror, the one they covered in Sharpie, this skin and blood belong to someone else.

Then the pain starts. First a throbbing, then something deeper, sharper.

And out of nowhere, the strangest thought enters my mind: *My pain smells like iron and salt.* But it's not this thought that scares the living shit out of me; it's the feeling that settles over me like a dark veil as I watch the blood collect then release, collect then release on my sleeve—a feeling like grim pleasure, a hollowed-out happiness. Relief.

I try to make myself puncture the feeling, to drive it away, but with each steady *plink* of blood hitting the bathroom floor, my breathing slows and steadies. My brain calms.

I will myself not to think of Thomas or his name written across my spine, but "How could he?" slips from my lips anyway, in a voice that's dead flat. Still, the crying girl trapped inside the glass shards doesn't bother answering. Or maybe I broke her along with the mirror.

THOMAS

AFTER THE MOVIES, I HEAD UP TO MY ROOM TO HIDE BEFORE
my father gets home.

Sitting on the edge of my bed, I lift Eleanor from her stand
and tilt her into the light to look her over. With the corner of my
comforter, I wipe a smudge from her glossy base and stare at the
shiny autographs. Eleanor means everything to me. She'd been
the only silver lining about coming back from winter break.

Till I met Erica.

I balance Eleanor's weight in my hands. My phone has slid
next to me, vibrating with a text as my conversation with Forest crashes back:

"I don't really remember it."

"Then why haven't you asked what happened?"

Because Erica's everywhere—*everywhere*—in my head. In
Spanish class, passing me her notebook when Señora Roberts's

back is turned so we can write each other messages. At the museum, glancing over her shoulder at me, giddy with excitement over that weird Gorey exhibit. In the parking lot at school, resting against my truck as I lean in to kiss her. Suddenly, I wonder what would've happened if I'd never transferred into her class. Would everything be different now?

"You see the photos?" Forest's words replay as my phone buzzes again. *"From inside Zac's room."*

The knot in my stomach grows as I set Eleanor down and grab for my phone. Ricky's texted, but he's hardly the only one. There are thirty-four unread messages in the group chat, which I know I've been avoiding all day.

Jumping to my feet, I pace the room. Last night had started out so amazing. Where'd it all go wrong? Everything had been perfect at first. . . .

"Hop on, little croc."

I squeeze my eyes shut. Tina's pictures crowd my mind, but I don't need her photos to remember. As I flop onto my bed, I can't hold back the memory any longer:

Erica stands next to the bonfire, staring up at me with her huge eyes. She holds my hat over the flames, pupils reflecting the light. Her smile alone is enough to raise my pulse.

My head buzzes with the three beers I'd chugged while waiting for her to get here. I ask if she wants to go inside, find someplace private to hang out.

She levels her gaze on me, but her focus slips. Whatever she's been sipping on from her purse all night has started to make her wobbly. She bites her lip. "Trying to get me alone, Thomas the Rhymer?"

"What if I am?" I ask, because I'm so ready, so full of adrenaline for whatever's coming.

Her smile tells me she's game to play. "I'd tell you you're not trying hard enough." She surprises me, grabbing my hand and dragging me toward the door. Only then do I realize just how drunk she is, how unsteady I am when I try to catch her. She stumbles, hand slipping from mine as she lands on all fours. I dart forward and can't help but see up her skirt. But she's laughing. "I fell!" This makes her laugh even harder, putting both hands over her mouth. I try to help her up and nearly fall too.

"Sorry, I'm not being very sexy right now," she says, but I can't agree. Erica knows exactly what she's doing with those eyes.

Inspiration strikes as I kneel beside her. "Piggyback?" I ask, already imagining her body pressed against my back, my hands on her thighs.

"You crocodile!" she giggles from the grass.

I'm only a foot away so I know I've heard her right. "Crocodile?"

"Crocodile!" she exclaims—so happy, so lively, my Erica. "Very playful little guys. Give each other piggyback rides all the time. Blow bubbles. But they get a bad rap. Chomping down on people."

"Like this?" I use both arms to mimic jaws and snap my curved fingers together like teeth. People can probably see us, but I'm past caring. "So how about that crocodile ride?" I ask, extending my hands for her to grab.

She blinks slowly up at me then takes my hands. I pull her to her feet. She wraps her arms around my waist and leans her head against my chest, and I feel so full of everything—the night, the possibility, her.

She nods her approval. "Yes. That'll do."

I pull away, keeping one arm out to steady her so she doesn't fall over again. Then I lean forward and tap the back of my thigh. "Hop on, little croc."

She does, and my hands grab the backs of her legs. Heat floods me when I feel naked skin. Her arms encircle my neck, and she rests her head against my shoulder. I can only hope she can't feel the pounding of my heart as I carry her inside.

Remembering everything feels like swallowing glass. All day long, I've tried so hard to push the memory away, but it hasn't left me alone. Because I'd brought her up to that room.

My hand's pulsing, and when I look over, I see my fist squeezing Eleanor's neck, practically crushing her fretboard. Horrified, I release her and jump away, picturing Zac's smirk from earlier, Eleanor's base stopping inches above the pavement.

Why do I screw up everything I touch?

A new text dings through, and I blink to clear my vision.

Shaking my head, I look again, but it doesn't go away, doesn't change. Not Zac or Ricky. Not even Stallion or Forest.

It's from her. She texted me. Erica just texted me:

Hey, it's me.

Two more texts follow in quick succession, their previews hovering at the top of my screen.

Just wanted to say hi. Sorry I got so wasted last night.

Anyway, I really need to talk to you when you're available.

Thoughts gladiator battle in my head: *Sorry?* is quickly taken down by *She wants to talk to me.*

My thumb clicks into messages, touching two keys before I even realize it. I stare down at the single word I've typed: ok.

But then *She wants to talk to me* is dragged off by *What would I even say to her?* And that opens a whole can of ugly. What *can* I say? I delete the text.

The next thought that fights through is that she can tell I was typing and that I still haven't replied. Shit. I have to say something. Anything. But what?

For the second time today, the cursor blinks at me, awaiting input. Maybe there's nothing left to say. Or maybe there's everything, and a text could never cut it.

I remember. I *remember.*

And Erica's texting me now, saying she's sorry? She's *sorry?*

Before I can talk myself out of it, I click into the group chat.

It takes only two seconds of scrolling to find a photo. The bottom drops out of my stomach.

No. Fuck. No. This can't be happening.

My phone flies across the room, punching a large dent in the *M* of my Ramones poster. I hear glass crack before the phone crashes to the ground. But then the poster replaces itself in my head with the weird Gorey one I'd bought her at that museum. *"I understand you,"* we'd told each other that day.

No matter where I turn, there she is. Everywhere. She's *everywhere*. I can't get away from her. And I'm going to have to see her tomorrow, which, after that photo, after everything . . . I can't do it.

I rip the poster off the wall and hurl it. Chest heaving, I glare down at my phone lying on top of a dirty practice jersey and dread having to pick it up again. Because then I'll have to see the last few screens open—a text from her asking to talk to me, saying she's sorry. She's *sorry*. And next to that, group chat messages I can't read and a half-naked picture of Erica with her boobs scribbled on, probably just one of many from Zac's room that I can't make myself look at.

I stomp down on my phone, putting all my weight into it till it crunches under my Chucks. Ruined. I broke this, too. What else am I going to break? But even as I think it, the air gushes from my lungs and a sick relief washes over me. Now I won't have to keep looking.

ERICA

I PACE AROUND MY ROOM, THINKING ABOUT SCHOOL TOMOR-
row and roasting in my pajama pants and long-sleeved shirt.
The whir of the box fan only blasts me with warm air, doing
nothing to unclench the knot in my chest.

I've since wrapped my palm in a white hand towel, even
though I know better. The fibers will stick to the wound, and
the color white makes everything look more gruesome. I know
how to clean a cut, but I didn't have the strength after scrubbing down the bathroom. And there was no resurrecting the
mirror, though luckily, it's the only visible casualty aside from
some duct tape on the shower curtain. I don't even know what
I'm going to tell Mom. It's not like you can accidentally tip
over a mirror mounted to a wall. But judging from the light
growing through the window, Mom should be getting here any
time now.

After the mirror incident and scrubbing Thomas's name off as best I could, I'd tried to draw. It's been several days since I've posted any new material to my webcomic—not that anyone but me has access to my uploaded cartoons, even though I keep vowing I'll make it public soon. Still, earlier I'd fetched my notebook and markers out of my car, arranging the pens by color on the coffee table. It's my rainbow ritual, and normally it soothes me. *Start with the last panel*, Erica Strange always urges me. *Figure out where you want to end, then how to get there will follow.* But then I'd made the fatal mistake of paging through the notebook. It was all there: the original Thomas doodles and cartoons, the notes we'd written back and forth in between, the teasing in his slanted handwriting about me liking "creepbucket" Edward Gorey, and, of course, the quick sketches of Thomas's lacrosse game, of our first kiss. I'd slammed the sketchbook shut then and flung it across the room. It was all too much. Everything is a reminder, a portal back to freezeframes of Last Night, to finding his name on me. I told myself my hand hurt too badly to draw anyway.

And now, thinking about tomorrow, I can't shake the sick feeling I get thinking about seeing my classmates again. Every single one of them is a ticking time bomb—lean one person who knows against the wrong someone else, and they explode my whole world. I would give anything in the world not to go tomorrow. But I need to get it over with.

Caylee must know most of what happened by this point. At

least she thinks she does. It's why she won't return any of my calls or texts, even after what I told her. She probably called everyone she knew after leaving Juiced and has decided she knows all there is about the party. So, now I really have to make sure she hears my side of things tomorrow. Maybe she's even seen the naked picture of me, but she can't blame me for being passed out. She can't.

Amber, on the other hand, texted me immediately after our phone call, trying to solidify her plan to meet up before class. I didn't text back. But if Amber's even wondering what happened still, then that must mean she hasn't seen any photos. At least, not the ones of my bare breasts.

As for Thomas . . . I need to look him in the eye tomorrow and see what he has to say for himself. Erica Strange would. I just hope I have the nerve. I think of the five names on me—Thomas's name—and my chest feels ready to implode.

Stop. You have to stop. But my mind keeps yo-yoing back. How the hell can I go to school? There's no pretending this didn't happen.

But what did happen? What do I know to be true about last night? I know I was in the backyard with Thomas, that we went upstairs together. And that's where everything gets hazy. I remember Thomas giving me a piggyback ride inside, probably upstairs to Zac's room. Wait, do I remember that? Or is that just because Caylee told me it happened? Regardless, I know I was in Zac's room with everyone Zac mentioned—Zac, Ricky,

Forest, Stallion, Tina, and Thomas, too. So, six people were in the room with me. And Caylee confirmed that those same six people later came down the stairs together.

But between going upstairs with Thomas and them all coming down later, someone took my clothes off, or maybe they all did, and everyone wrote their names on me, plus other horrible stuff. Everyone but Tina. At least, I never found her name. But she did take photos of Thomas and me in the backyard, and Zac said Ricky took photos in the room—topless photos of me passed out. Zac said they didn't rape me, and when I checked this morning, I didn't feel raped. Not in the way I normally think of it, anyway. But I . . . I still feel so *violated*.

Tears spring to my eyes. So, what am I missing? I more or less know what happened, just not who did what or why they would even do it. Ricky called everything a "joke." Was that all it was to them?

I press hard into the memory, eyes clenched shut, trying to root around in my mind's dark corners. In Zac's room there's . . . not a memory. Just a feeling. Anger, maybe? But is someone angry at me, or am I angry at someone, or is my mind just throwing up faulty support beams under a collapsed memory, trying to make sense out of nothing?

My head starts to throb, and I drop my focus.

Plopping down on my bed, I snatch up the pile of anatomy books I'd borrowed from the library in the hopes they'd help my form drawing.

In a particularly dusty anatomical guide, instead of human figures like I'd envisioned, the pages contain morbid illustration after illustration of disfigured skeletal creatures interspersed with text. Not exactly uplifting. I toss the book—it hits my hamper and bounces to the floor—and shove aside the remaining volumes.

Staring up at my bulletin board, then over at the folder of all the drawings I'd done of Thomas and me, I feel stupid beyond words. I texted him tonight—*texted him*—and the whole time his name had been on me. What's worse, he hadn't even texted me back. Erica Strange would be so proud.

Maybe he was with them right now—the guys—laughing over my texts. Laughing at the stupid girl who thought she'd mattered, who thought she could be a part of it all. With Thomas, with Bay City. Maybe Ricky was right and it all was a stupid joke to Thomas. Because why else would he do it? I haven't taken his picture down all day because, somewhere in me, I truly thought there could be a different explanation. And I've been waiting for him to offer it up. To tell me that his name on me wasn't or couldn't mean what I thought it did.

I've been so foolish.

My room is full of Thomas, but it won't be for long.

I take down half the cards and mementos tacked to my bulletin board and scattered around my desk: the Lead Paint album cover; the LACMA ticket stub; Thomas's failed Spanish homework; the photo of us from the beach; the note he wrote me. Next comes the folder of drawings.

I grab the old printer-paper box from my closet that's filled with knickknacks from my childhood that I haven't looked at since we moved months ago. The towel wrapping my hand snags on a corner of the box, but I tug it free. Then, folding over the tape of each Thomas memento so they won't all stick together, I stack each reminder, each memory inside, tucking them away on the highest shelf in my closet, in my mind. Next, I cast around the room for his sweatshirt and shove that in my backpack, trying not to smell him on it. What would he say if I tried giving it back to him tomorrow? Maybe I should just leave it on his truck.

Having closed down every visible reminder of Thomas, no tears come. Only the realization that the world is not the place I thought it was.

Something presses—has been pressing for a while now—at the back of my mind, tugging like an impatient toddler I only now noticed. It's been with me since this morning when I woke up in Zac's room, since the walls were gray instead of purple.

It's a simple thought. A statement, really. Only a subject, verb, and modifier dancing on the wind like rustling leaves.

I want to die.

Maybe this was the only way the thought could fully reach me—in this new state of numb, like all the tubes of paint colors have been bled from the world and mixed together into a murky grayish brown. The no-name, throwaway color that your paintbrush rinse water turns to after one too many dunks.

I crawl into bed, eyes staring beyond the neon green stars of my ceiling. I can't do this anymore. I don't want to. It's an obsidian thought, a black shiny sphere, cold and smooth, as I roll it around my mind.

I'm up and out of my bed, yanking open my closet door and dragging the sagging box of childhood memories back out, now topped with reminders of Thomas. Tossing everything Thomas aside, I find the ratty stuffed bear Mom and Dad had bought me at a toy store in Milwaukee; stacks of birthday cards from years past; journals covered in stickers and filled with earnest hopes; a lone surviving tiny teacup and saucer from a Peter Rabbit tea set; picture after picture of Isabela and me from grade school, reminding me I was once so young and impressionable, that I had a best friend I had to leave behind, one I forgot to call or text after I met Caylee.

Below that is my ballerina jewelry box, filled to the brim with the shiny, candy-colored necklaces I used to wear by the dozen; a bracelet that changed color with body heat, the coolest thing to my fifth-grade self; a ring with a pink stone I'd gotten from my great-aunt for my eighth-grade graduation.

I dig my hand in until my fingers find the familiar soft worn leather. I pull the pouch free, its bulge and weight telling me it's still filled with the marbles Grandpa Joe gave me the Christmas before he died. Before he shot himself in his basement. That

Christmas trip had been the last time Dad had gone to Seattle with us, and he and Mom had fought a lot. Dad had never wanted to go in the first place since he hadn't been a big fan of Mom's dad, calling him "moody" and "antisocial," but that was before Grandpa Joe's death, after which Dad stopped mentioning him at all. Not that Dad could've known, but I don't think Mom ever forgave him for it.

During that Christmas trip, in Grandpa Joe's living room that always smelled like fresh oranges, Grandpa had handed me this pouch, unwrapped, his craggy face holding no expression. I'd been around eleven at the time, not sure what to make of it. He'd taken the pouch from me and dumped them into his palm, as worn and leathery as the pouch itself. Holding each marble up in turn, he'd explained each one's meaning based on its color. Though I can't remember them all, a few stuck in my mind:

The red one: love

The yellow one: friendship

And then he'd gotten to black. Holding it up, he'd said, "And this one . . . death."

Maybe it was because he'd died shortly after that, or maybe it was because I'd been so young at the time, but that moment left a strong impression on me, one I've never forgotten. I'd sort of been afraid of the black one after that, and it had always stayed in the bag while I played with the others until some point when I forgot all about the marbles.

But then, a few years ago, around the time Mom and Dad

started fighting for real and my anxiety got super bad again, I rediscovered the pouch. I don't remember how it began, but I started squeezing a marble in my hand depending on what emotion I was trying to conjure in that moment. Yellow for hope. Green for safety. Blue for calm. After Dad left, I practically wore the shiny finish off the blue one with all my squeezing, rolling, fretting, and especially trying to ward off panic attacks, something my old therapist called a "healthy coping mechanism." In truth, each color got a lot of use back then to help calm me—all except that black one, probably because it still reminded me so much of Grandpa Joe and the devastation on Mom's face when she and Dad had sat me down and told me what'd happened to him. It also felt . . . dangerous somehow.

Then, when we moved, I'd put the marbles back in their pouch so they wouldn't get lost and sorta forgot about them again. I told myself I didn't need the marbles anymore, that they were stupid and childish.

But now, they don't seem stupid *or* childish. And now, it's the black marble I want.

I dump them all into my palm and roll them around, feeling their cool surfaces, hearing the soft *clink* as they bump together: orange, green, red, yellow, white, purple, even the slightly dulled blue.

For half a second, I don't see it, think it's disappeared, or wonder if Past Me threw it away. But then the blue one shifts and exposes a sliver of obsidian. I pull it free, a dark orb with shimmering silver flecks, and stare at it in wonder. *Like a caged constellation.*

It's the black one I rest in my palm as I dump the others back in their pouch and shut them away in the box. I roll it between my fingers as I curl up in bed, then squeeze it tight. It calms me somehow.

Lying alone in the dark, I hope tomorrow will be better. The dark marble brings me comfort—the hard sphere pressed into my palm like the heavy thoughts clinking around my mind.

Through the living room, I hear the click of the front door unlocking, then the sound of creaking hinges and jingling keys. Mom's old-lady shoes squeak across the entryway and onto kitchen linoleum, followed by the fridge door breaking suction.

Squeezing the marble in my hand, I swing my legs off the bed, left hand holding the towel to my right, and check that my long-sleeved shirt covers any trace of writing.

In the kitchen, the yellow light of the fridge casts a greenish tinge across Mom's scrubs. She must sense my presence because she glances around the side of the fridge, then leaps into the air. "Dear God, Erica! You scared me!" Her hand flies to her heart. "What are you doing up so late? It's nearly two in the morning. You should be in bed resting."

"Sorry, Mom." I'm already tearing up.

Concern twists her face. "What is it, Bug? Are you feeling . . . Wait, what's wrong with your hand?" The fridge door slams, and then she's next to me, cradling my fist and slowly unwrapping the towel.

"I cut it." Tears stream down.

"How?"

"The bathroom mirror . . ." My voice breaks, falling away.

She pulls at the towel, but the blood has stuck it to the wound. "I need better light." She flicks the overhead switch, the sudden brightness blinding me momentarily and pulling at the ache behind my eyes.

"Have you washed it yet?"

I shake my head.

She throws on the cold tap. "Well, this isn't going to feel great, but it needs to be done." After checking the water's temperature, she leads my hand under the stream, soaking the towel. Carefully, she pulls it free, exposing the wound. Slowly, the dark red falls away, revealing an angry pink slit.

"Oof, Bug, it's deep. Does it hurt much?"

Though it hurts far less than I'd expected, I nod through my runny nose.

"Keep the water on it, okay?" She disappears into the bathroom, where I can hear her pull open the cupboard and rifle through the contents.

I catch a glimpse of my reflection in the mirrored heart-shaped ornament that hangs above the sink. What's reflected back isn't pretty. Bloodshot eyes stare out from a halo of frizzy hair. Without a blot of makeup, my features seem blurry, like watercolors gone wrong. My mouth is a taut line, emphasizing how puffy my face is.

Mom comes back with a plastic bin containing an armada of medical supplies, which she dumps onto the counter. Gauze, medical tape, and old prescription bottles spill out. On reflex, I flinch as Mom raises my hand for closer examination.

"Sorry, Bug."

Without all the blood, it doesn't look nearly so bad.

"Well, you're borderline in need of stitches, but it's nothing a few butterflies won't fix."

She rips a box of adhesive strips from her first-aid stash and pats the wound dry with a pile of gauze, following it up with a thin line of ointment then butterfly Band-Aids that squeeze the skin back together.

The tightness on my cheeks tells me my tears have nearly dried.

"So, you did this on the bathroom mirror?" She applies another line of ointment. "What happened?"

"It fell and broke." My voice does the same. "And it cut me."

She pauses. I know she must be wondering how I managed to break a bathroom mirror bolted to the wall, or maybe she's thinking about the cost of replacing it since we're only renting this place.

"I'm sorry about the mirror," I blurt out. "I'll buy a new one. With my birthday money."

She lays several cottony squares of gauze over the wound.

"Don't be silly. These things happen. I'm only glad this isn't worse. You could've really hurt yourself. I'll call the landlord and tell him he should've properly mounted that thing." Thank god she doesn't ask *how* these things happen as she reaches for her tape, or maybe she's too tired for the truth today. "What'd you do with the broken mirror?" she asks.

"Dumpster."

Her brows squish together. "Bug, I don't want you going to the dumpster at night by yourself. Next time you leave it by the door for me to take down, okay? Alleys are no place for young women after dark."

Her words spring an image to mind, one of Mom in the early hours of dawn, walking down the apartment stairs in her scrubs after a long shift to toss away my trash. The scene is so depressing, though I don't know why, exactly. It pulls at something in me, threatening to bring more tears.

Out of her line of sight, I roll the marble between the fingers of my free hand and manage a nod.

"Good." She finishes the last of the tape before looking up at me. Only then can I see the exhaustion lining her forehead—from working overtime to support us, to pay the portion of my school's tuition not covered by my father or scholarships.

"Thanks, Mom. It feels better now."

She gives me a tight squeeze. "I'm glad. And remember not to get that wet, okay? Wear a bag when you shower so that wound will close properly."

"I know, Mom. Thanks."

"Of course." In one motion, she scoops all the supplies back into the bin.

"How was work?" I ask, trailing her to the bathroom. She pauses in the doorway but doesn't say anything about the missing mirror before sliding the armada into a cupboard.

"Oh, you know, the usual aches and pains of the elderly. It's hard for them to sleep much." She turns to me. "I'd give you something for that, but given the condition of your belly earlier, I'm not so sure it's a good idea. Did you eat some dinner?"

"A little something," I lie. After finding his name, I couldn't stomach any food.

Mom makes for her room, slipping out of her scrubs and into a nightgown before heading to the bathroom to brush her teeth.

As I watch her wash her face, I know I should leave her to sleep, but instead I keep hovering behind her like a ghost.

She pads down the hall and climbs into bed, about to turn off her bedside lamp when she sees me lingering. "What is it, Bug? Your hand still bothering you?"

"Mom," I begin in a voice from my childhood, "can I sleep with you?"

She sits up straight and stares at me, puzzling over my words. Then she pulls the comforter down next to her, patting the bed. "Of course you can."

When I crawl in beside her, she adds, "You've had a rough last few days, haven't you? Cutting your hand on top of being so sick."

I nod, then add a wet "Yes." The tears have returned full force, silent but shaking my core and tugging at my lingering headache.

Mom curls her body to fit mine, then wraps her arms around me. "But that's not everything, is it, sweetheart? Do you want to talk about it?"

I shake my head no.

"Is it something serious?"

It takes everything I have not to nod yes. The shake of my head lies for me.

"Well, if it's not serious, then I won't push, but you know I'm here for you, right? For anything?"

I nod, wishing I could somehow tell her but knowing it's impossible, hardly breathing for fear I'll start shaking with silent sobs.

"Dream with the angels," she murmurs. Minutes later her breathing deepens, and I know she's found sleep. Only then do I let myself go, if silently, until the crying stops, until the hiccups and shaking smooth. Lying awake in the dark, I feel Mom's warmth press against me, her puffs of breath blowing my hair.

Even before this weekend, nights have always been the hardest for me, right as my mind tries to settle into sleep. Especially at my most stressed, it's always been the point when I've felt too tired to use the coping tools my old therapist gave me, like deep breathing or combatting "distorted thoughts" by writing down the truths and lies of them on paper. And at night, every mistake I've ever made, or every single stupid thing I've ever said or done has haunted me, stuck on a loop to pound against my brain again and again until I've felt truly worthless, insignificant, unlovable. And that was before my whole world turned to hell.

As if on cue, my thoughts drift to Thomas.

Stupid. You're so stupid to have trusted him.

He'll be waking up soon, getting ready for school. I wonder again how his audition went today, or what he'll do if we run into each other tomorrow. Will he even care?

Why do you care about him? Clearly, he doesn't care about you.

I want to die, my mind repeats.

I roll this last thought around my head like the marble in my hand until at last I fall into restless dreams of razor-sharp words and cloth soaked in blood. I shudder awake, but the heaviness of my eyelids wins.

Before sleep can come for me again, a strange thought takes hold—one involving expired pills, going to sleep, and never waking up. Then I wouldn't have to face anybody about anything. My grandpa chose to leave, didn't he?

I start, eyes wide in the darkness. No, no, no. I can't think like that.

And yet, as I search for the marble that's rolled away and press its smoothness against my palm, a part of me knows that yesterday was only the beginning. Today is going to be a living hell. Everyone will know. They'll talk about me behind my back, about the pictures Tina posted and how drunk I got. Maybe they'll know everything. They'll judge.

Bitter tears burn my eyes as my mind churns. *What can I do? What would Erica Strange do?* But I already know the answer. She wouldn't hide from the world, the truth. She'd face it head-on *and* every single guy whose name marred her skin. She would confront Caylee with the truth, and Thomas, too, once and for all.

Face them. You have to face them. Promise me.

"I promise," I whisper into the dark while Mom snores softly beside me.

Only after I've made my oath to Erica Strange, to myself, does sleep come for me at last.

PART TWO

MONDAY

ERICA

BEFORE I LEAVE FOR SCHOOL THIS MORNING, MOM ASKS
why I'm so quiet.

"Just thinking," I reply, which is like mentioning the monster's shadow but not the monster. Truth is, I'm rehearsing what
I'll say. To Thomas when I return his sweatshirt. To Caylee
when I finally tell her my side of what happened. To the Tinas
and Zacs of Bay City, who everyone knows live for moments
like this. Because they're coming for me. They all are. I'd be
stupid to think otherwise.

Concern twists Mom's face as she leans toward me over the
kitchen nook. "Bug, I know something's up. Can't you please
tell me?" My cat hoodie and black leggings have already earned
me a "You're dressed a little dark today" when I first entered
the kitchen, not to mention my overly caked-on makeup that
clearly pinged her Mom Radar. For years, Mom's been saying I

"catastrophize," always playing out the worst-case scenarios in my head. It's probably what she thinks I'm doing right now—blowing up something small and obsessively worrying about it. Little does she know there's a legit reason right now, a legit catastrophe.

Mom speaks again, confirming my suspicions. "Is it your anxiety, Bug? Maybe time you started up with a therapist again?"

Her words fill me with fury. Like "anxiety" covers it. Like we could even afford a therapist anyway. But I shove down my anger with everything I've got. I have to backtrack, put her mind at ease, or she'll never let this go.

"Everything's fine, Mom. Really. I'm just . . . stressed about school and don't feel super great."

"Are you sure it's nothing more? You seemed so upset last night."

"I was tired is all, and this new school's really demanding. Been trying to keep my grades up."

She hesitates, and I know she's thinking about the GPA I have to maintain to keep my scholarship. "Well, can I at least help you rewrap your hand before you go?" she asks.

I breathe in relief. "I did already." I'd replaced the bandages right before I texted Caylee for the eighth time. That'd happened somewhere between me sending her the first text right when I got up and the last one while picking dehydrated apples from my oatmeal. And yet, to all of the above, there's been no response. Nothing. Cell silence. I need to find her alone and get her to hear me out.

Breaking her hard stare, Mom kisses my forehead. "Well, I've got one more night shift today, then it's off for four days! I'll need to catch up on sleep, but then maybe we can go see a movie tomorrow night? Caylee can come too, if she wants."

Mom hates going to movie theaters—she says they're over-priced and too loud for her "old lady ears"—so I know she's only trying to be nice, which wrings my stomach. That, and her saying Caylee's name. I manage a grateful smile for Mom and a "That would be fun" before scooting out of my chair and reaching for my backpack.

Mom stands as well, gathering up the bowls of oatmeal. "Why don't you stay home today, sweetheart? You could get some more rest, take care of that hand."

I huff in a way that lets her know she's being ridiculous. "Mom, I'm fine. I wouldn't go to school if I wasn't."

Weren't, Dad's Grammar Police voice says in my head. *It's subjunctive.*

"Now please drop it. I gotta go." I try to load as much finality into my voice as possible, because the truth is I'd love nothing more than to stay home—bolt to my room, throw myself under eighty layers of blankets, and smother myself in my too-hot breath and sweat until they find me, a shrunken mummy, years after the Sharpie's long since faded. My brain shrieks

RUN! Go anywhere that's away from school and everyone who must know by now.

Shutting down my social media was the only option I had yesterday, but it also means I have no idea what fresh-grown horrors the day could bring. And even though only a select few have my phone number—Thomas, Caylee, Amber—I still thought I'd somehow wake to dozens of cruel texts. Texts from unknown numbers saying things like Nice tits and Get sum!!!! and Everyone knows you're a whore and Slut and I'd hit that. But there was nothing like that. Not a single text, which was almost worse. The quiet felt so unnerving. I tell myself that, aside from Caylee and Thomas never texting back, it's maybe a good sign, that nobody cares. That this really was only a stupid prank, and it will all blow over soon.

From inside my hoodie pocket, my marble reminds me that this doesn't feel like a stupid prank—any of it—and I'd be fooling myself to think this level of gossip isn't on everyone's lips. I roll the smooth glass between my fingers as I head for the front door. It helps for some reason, though it still takes everything I have to imagine Erica Strange's cape rustling behind me, feel its hem graze the backs of my legging-clad thighs, imagine peering at the world through the eyeholes of a violet mask. I think to myself: *Erica Strange would go* and *Just get through today. It's only one day.*

And the part I hate myself for the most: *Thomas will be there.*

Maybe he'll explain. Because what could he possibly say that could change anything? I was so stupid to text him last night, but I won't be again. I'll confront him and that will be that.

"Have a great day at school, Bug!" Mom calls after me. She has no way of knowing how impossible her words are. That today, "great day" and "school" go together like "poison" and "small children." Not that I blame her for being clueless. She couldn't possibly know what's going on inside my head, which is a tiny gift from the universe.

As I walk to my car, the words keep playing over and over in my mind, pounding with each footstep: *Erica Strange would go. Erica Strange would go.* Even though Caylee hasn't texted me back and Caylee *always* texts me back, *Erica Strange would go.* I need to get this over with.

THOMAS

EVERY TIME I CLOSED MY EYES LAST NIGHT, MY BRAIN flooded with the picture of shirtless, passed-out Erica, merging with flashes from the audition stage. When I'd finally fallen asleep, I'd jerked myself out of one shitty dream and into the next, feeling like I was gonna puke.

Though none of my actual dreams were about Erica, they were all disturbing. Heavy. Full of giant lizards with sharp teeth. Lacrosse balls that turned to dust mid-flight. Dark auditoriums with no lights or doors. Microphones that screamed like they were being murdered. And Eleanor. In nearly every single dream, there was my guitar—splintering, cracking, breaking. And I could never stop it from happening.

In one dream I was sprinting through the woods, trees whizzing by. Then suddenly there was a break in the trees, and I nearly fell off a cliff, catching myself just in time. A few feet away, Zac materialized, gripping Eleanor by her neck, holding her over the cliff's edge.

"VanB," he calls out. "Tell me not to."

But I'm rooted to the spot, can't move or speak.

A grin splits his face. I watch in horror as he removes one finger at a time from Eleanor's neck like a sick countdown.

I jolted awake, and by the time I managed to fall asleep again, the sky outside had already started to lighten.

It's a new day, the first time I'll see Erica since the party. And midway through brushing my teeth, I've made my decision. I'm going to talk to her, try to catch her before class and say hi. I should've just texted her back last night instead of smashing my phone like an idiot. Those pictures Tina posted sucked, but they weren't as awful as the ones Zac sent. But at least those didn't get posted online so it could've been a lot worse. And Erica hadn't seemed too upset in her text messages so maybe we can move past this. *Everything will be fine,* I tell myself as I open my truck's backseat and slip her boots into my bag. *It wasn't that big of a deal.* We can meet before the bell, talk in Spanish class like we always do. I'll say I had nothing to do with those Tina pictures, and Erica probably doesn't even know about the others. I'll tell her I'm sorry I didn't text her back, that my phone's broken, tell her the good news about my audition. Maybe she'll even be happy for me.

When I get to the school parking lot, her car's not here

yet, so I drop her boots in her spot. I know she'll be worried about them.

But then I don't make it thirty feet past the front doors before Steven, our lead defenseman, bumps fists with me in the hallway. "VanB, heard you like adult coloring books."

I stare at him blankly.

"With Sharpies," he adds.

I feel my panic rising. "Where'd you hear that?" I ask.

Steven's smile falters. Clearly, this wasn't the reaction he'd been expecting. "Just something Ricky shared with us."

"Shared what with you?" But I already know.

"The pictures, man. The video."

The video?

"You were there, right?" he continues. "Don't tell me you haven't seen them. If so, you're definitely the only one who hasn't. . . ."

I stare around me in horror. I knew there were pictures, but a *video*? From *Zac's room*?

Why the fuck did I smash my phone? Why'd I try so hard to keep myself out of the goddamn loop? I just didn't want to see . . . But ignoring everything didn't make it go away either. Not by a long shot. Deep down, I knew it wouldn't. Shit like this doesn't just go away. *Coward. You fucking coward.* And now there's a video? What the hell is on it? Am I on it?

"Weren't you, like, into her, man?" Steven adds, a little hesitant. "Probably not anymore, am I right?"

Where the hell is Zac? I'll *kill* him. Or more important, where's Erica?

But if today's anything like last week or the week before, I know exactly where to find her when she gets here. With any luck, I can still catch her before anyone else does.

ERICA

MOST OF THE SCHOOL IS ALREADY HERE BY THE TIME I PULL in. I'd wanted to get here early, well before first bell, but I stalled too long. Seeing all these people—*every body*—makes me physically ill, but I can't skip school. Not after pushing so hard to come. Plus, the office would notify my mother, which would be yet another red flag she could stick in her cloud of "What's wrong, Bug?" suspicion.

But there's something in my parking spot. A black cat, or a trash bag, or a pile of . . . boots. My boots. I stop, halfway pulled in, and hop out. The car behind me honks and whips into the spot across from me.

There they are. My boots. Did Zac put them here? I didn't realize how much I've missed them until I scoop them up and, hopping on one foot, replace my ballet flats with them. Even without socks, the boots feel so comfortable, like a long-lost friend, which is exactly what I need today. I fight the memory of when I last saw these boots, that insists on asking if the white scrape on the left toe is new and how it got there. Hoisting my backpack over my shoulder, I try to summon Erica Strange—I need her more than ever today—and head for our usual mermaid meeting spot.

Caylee's car is here, but there's no sign of Caylee even though it's where we always meet. Still, I knew today would be different. She's ignored me since Juiced.

Turning in a full circle, I still don't see her anywhere. What I do see is a senior girl staring at me and laughing as she closes her car trunk. I recognize her from the day Mom and I came to enroll me here. The girl had been in the principal's office cursing up a storm then, and I hadn't talked to her. But now she's gawking at me, sticking her tongue in her cheek and moving her hand in the universal sign of a blowjob.

My skin crawls. Clearly I'm missing more puzzle pieces, and here's one of them.

Worse, Amber spots me two minutes later, hair as red as her lipstick. She's sitting on a bench right outside the main doors, dressed in her usual dark lace, and for once she's not on her phone. My chest tightens. I didn't expect her to let me go all day without talking, but I also didn't expect her to seek me out so intently.

I'd decided on the way to school that the best way to deal with today was to pretend like none of it mattered, to slap a plastic grin on my face, but that's a hell of a lot harder in front of no-bullshit Amber. Still, all I want to do is find Caylee and force her to listen.

As I walk up to Amber, I hide my bandaged hand in my sweatshirt pocket and manage some warped version of a smile, plastered on top of my face full of makeup—my real-life version of Erica Strange's mask, a shield of indifference against the world. Amber rises from the bench when I near.

"Hey," I say, testing the waters.

I expect her to comment on how much makeup I've caked on, or my godawful fake smile, or a snarky something else. Instead, she launches straight into what I really don't want to talk about. "Erica, what happened after I left the party? Really? Did someone hurt you?"

Moldy panic spreads through my chest as I stretch the plastic smile to breaking. "What do you mean? It was nothing like that."

"Then what? Because Caylee's furious, and everyone else seems to think something's so hilarious, which makes me think that whatever it is isn't funny at all."

"Well, what does Caylee say?" I ask, buying time.

"To ask you. But she's pissed. Royally."

She found out more, then, and she's furious. I knew she would be, but it still hurts deeply to hear.

"You can tell me, you know. Anything," Amber insists.

Yeah, and have every adult in the land find out. Still, Amber's guessing too close to the truth. It's probably only a matter of time till she figures it all out too, but I can't let that be right now. I need time. Thinking fast, I say, "You're right. I wasn't entirely honest with you. Something did happen."

Amber's lips form a perfect *O*.

I shrug, faking a calmness I don't feel. "You know Caylee. Always so jealous when it comes to Zac." I don't realize it's what I planned to say till it's fallen out of my mouth. Still, the sliver of truth seems to work because Amber's nodding, absorbing my every word.

I rush on. "Well, Zac wasn't paying enough attention to her at the party, so she got mad and accused me of flirting with him. And I was so drunk I didn't really know what was happening . . ." My mouth goes dry, sickened by my words—lies and truths smushed together like modeling clay. I'm teetering on an edge I don't want to fall over. "But nothing happened. No one . . ." I can't finish the sentence, so I cover it with another shrug and avoid her gaze. "I'm just"—my voice breaks—"so embarrassed, you know?" The truth of it strangles my throat and stings my eyes. "Being so drunk and stupid."

For a second, I think she believes me, that she'll make some biting remark and drop it. Then she says, "Erica, there's something you're not telling me. I can feel it. And I'm sorry, but I'm going to find out what it is. Zac . . . he did something to you, didn't he? And Thomas?"

The plastic smile shatters. "Amber, please," I choke out. "There's nothing."

Amber's expression is the softest I've ever seen it. "There's something, Erica. And it's not okay, whatever it is. But I can help you."

"I gotta go."

"Erica . . ."

"There's nothing to help!" Whirling, I rush toward the entrance, ignoring Amber's loud protests. I yank the door open, forgetting for a second about my cut till it burns hot. Fumbling for the marble in my pocket, I clench it, telling myself that, even if Caylee's mad, she can't blame me for what happened. Not really. Or, at any rate, she won't after I get the chance to talk to her. She'll hear me out. She has to.

At least, that's what I'm telling myself. And, as one of Dad's most-quoted lines from Shakespeare's *Measure for Measure* reads, "The miserable have no other medicine. But only hope."

ERICA

RUSHING THROUGH THE HALLWAYS, I OBSERVE EVERYONE from behind my eye mask and clutch the marble in my pocket. Running my thumb across its smooth surface helps me stand up straight, put on my best face of indifference, all the while telling myself that these people don't matter. I couldn't care less what they think. But I've never been so acutely aware of everyone around me. Every laugh, every glance, every whisper behind a closed palm feels like a poison-tipped arrow aimed at me. I strain to feel out the air around me, press my finger to the pulse of the passing bodies. *They know*, my senses tell me. Because of course they do.

Stay strong, Erica Strange says in my head, so I tell myself I'm invisible, that they aren't talking about me, can't see me under my cape, behind my mask. And even though I hate myself for it, my eyes dart around, searching the throng for Thomas, to see if he's looking for me.

I wonder what would've happened if I'd been able to confide in Caylee at my house when I'd had the chance, if I'd told her everything then. Or even at Juiced before the guys got there. Would today be so much easier or exponentially worse? Would she have barred me from her life or helped me figure out what to do about Thomas, about everything? But if there had ever been a "right" time to tell her, it had slipped out my bedroom door with her yesterday. So, I need to find her and tell her everything right now. Then she can choose to hate me or not.

I search the hallways, but she's nowhere, then I shoot her another text and get no reply. I know she's here because of her car, but where? I don't want to have to wait till English.

By the time I make it to my locker, my hypervigilance is exhausted. Busying myself while I try to figure out what to do, where to go, I slip my binder from my backpack and open it to the homework folder. I didn't do any of it this weekend, and I have a freaking history quiz. Mr. Jenkins will want my head on a spike for missing my lab write-up, and Ms. Adams will be so disappointed when I don't turn in my vocab sheet. And of course, these are the least of my concerns.

Then there's Spanish.

Staring down at my Spanish folder, I see my unfinished subjunctive worksheet, translating and completing it in my mind.

Please fill in the blanks and select your answer below:

Sofía **hopes** the rain will **stop**.

Fernándo **wishes** that his boss would **give** him a raise.

Erica **hopes** Thomas will/will not **attend** class today.

How do you say "false hope" in Spanish? Because what could Thomas possibly have to say that could explain his name on me?

Stalling for time, I fling open my locker, then recoil. Sticky red consumes my field of vision.

Oozing through the locker vents and running the length of the door are half-dried rivers of scarlet. The goo seeps down the front of my Edward Gorey poster, over the giant block letters spelling "AMPHIGOREY." It's the poster, my favorite poster, that Thomas bought for me on our second date.

As he'd pulled out each wrinkled bill and smoothed it on the counter to pay, I'd felt a strange urge to cry. No guy I liked had ever bought me anything before simply because he knew I'd love it.

Now, fighting tears of frustration, I touch the poster, bringing a blob of red to my nose and sniffing.

Ketchup. Someone squeezed ketchup in my locker. It's splattered across my textbooks and coffee thermos, my mirror and pack of colored pencils.

"Ew, gross!"

I turn slowly to face some girl I don't know, with bushy hair and braces.

The girl studies my face. "Is everything all right?"

"It's fine," I say, even though it isn't.

"God, who would do something like that? What's wrong with people?"

"I don't know." I shrug.

The girl studies my face. "You should report this."

I snort. Another Amber. "Yeah," I say without conviction.

"Do you . . ." She searches for words. "Do you want me to?" Clearly, she doesn't know who I am, or I doubt she'd be caught dead helping the school leper.

I shake my head. "Naw. I'm just going to . . ." I set my binder on the floor and slowly peel the poster out of my locker. Ketchup drips onto the bandage on my hand, and I know I'll have to stare at it all day and remember this moment. Careful not to drip on anything else, I walk to the nearest trash can. People leap out of my path as I throw away the poster and tell myself it's not a big deal. Because why the hell should I care anymore?

The girl with braces has disappeared by the time I stoop to pick up my binder. Holding it, I stare into the mess in my locker, feeling strangely numb.

I'm reaching for the marble in my pocket when my locker door bangs shut. The binder I'm holding hits the floor and paper explodes from it like confetti. I wheel around to see Zac wearing his letterman over his cast and a shark's grin, flanked by Kevin and Cole.

Zac stands a foot from me, unpredictable as a live wire. The urge to reach down and pick up my scattered papers is shot dead by his proximity. He's standing so close, towering over me, that the idea of giving him any more of a physical advantage makes me ill. Fear rises in my stomach as I look away from his bulging chest muscles and the lewd Sharpie drawings on his cast that remind me of my skin.

"I was looking for you, Mouth." He places the palm of his good arm across my locker door and leans in, smacking his gum. I've never realized how much I hate spearmint until this moment. "You slipped out the other morning without saying good-bye," he continues. "Didn't say good-bye online, either."

All my senses feel heightened, on overload. I try to hide how much he's caught me off-guard. "That was so messed up, what you guys did."

His smile is a deadly weapon. "You seemed to like it."

"I was drunk, Zac. Blackout drunk." Panic tinges my words.

"Whatever you say, Mouth."

"Why do you keep calling me that?"

"Well, if you don't remember, then it's for me to know and you to find out."

Breath isn't reaching my lungs. I need to get the hell away, but I know I need answers more. So, I do the very last thing I want to do. Glancing behind Zac at the others, I ask in a shaky voice, "Can I talk to you? In private?"

His smirk splits into a wide grin. "We can do anything you want in private."

Kevin snorts. Cole looks uncomfortable, but neither leave.

Because I can't get any smaller, I try pleading. "Zac, please. Just tell me what I don't know." Bodies swirl around us. Lockers slam. People yell to one another. It registers as a hum to my ears, my skin.

"Don't worry, sweet tits. Your secrets are safe with me." He stares purposefully down at my chest, having ignored my request.

I cross my arms over my sweatshirt.

"Come on, man," Cole says. "Bell's gonna ring."

Zac eyes him, says, "In a minute," then turns back to me. "Oh, I almost forgot. You left something behind in my room."

He left my boots in the parking lot, I think.

But no. Zac pulls a smashed pink object from his back pocket. My bra. The one I couldn't find before leaving his room. It's like I've stepped into a furnace. I grab for it, but he holds it above his head with his casted arm, just out of reach. I don't want to get any closer, and the humiliation of having to jump for it would kill me.

People are starting to stare. Everyone can *see.*

"Give it to me," I demand.

"What are you gonna give me?" he asks, amused.

"You're revolting."

"Incoming," Kevin warns. "Your woman just rounded the corner."

Caylee.

Zac drops his hand. I snatch my bra, brushing against his gross cast as I do, and shove the bra deep in my backpack. I turn in time to see Caylee approach, hands gripping her bag strap, a terrible look on her face.

"What was that?" she asks, glaring from Zac to me.

Shame drops my gaze to her ballet flats—the two-hundred-and-fifty-dollar Tory Burch shoes from Nordstrom's I'd gone with her to buy last week. I force my eyes up. "Caylee, listen . . ."

Zac cuts me off, all pearly whites and veiny arms pulling her in. "Hey, babe. Just catching up with Erica here."

Her mouth squishes into a frown. "That's not what I asked you. What was that thing? In your hand?" Her eyes flash to mine. "Erica, what did he hand you?"

"Caylee, I tried calling and texting you multiple times. You never responded. I told you I needed to talk to you!"

But her eyes are only for Zac now. "You told me nothing happened in your room. You *told* me that everyone else—"

"Babe, chill," Zac interrupts, gaze darting around the hallway. "Why are you always freaking out on me?"

It's impossibly hard to do in this hallway, in front of these guys. It's impossibly hard to ask Caylee for what I need most.

But I have to, audience or not. "Caylee, please talk to me. I need to talk to you." I reach out, touching her arm, but she rips away from me like I've stung her.

"I don't want to hear anything you have to say." Though she says it quietly, addressing the air pocket to the left of my head, it's a deadly sort of quiet. I reel back from the truth of it, from the sudden certainty that as hard as I've tried to avoid telling her, tried to avoid the moment we'd have to have this conversation, all along she's been trying just as hard not to hear it.

Zac pulls her away by the arm, hard enough it looks like it hurts, as if suddenly Caylee's a lit match and I'm a bomb fuse and keeping us apart is the only way to avert disaster. But she lets him lead her away from me, from my plea for her to hear the truth—again—until Zac and a sullen-looking Caylee are swallowed up in the throng of moving bodies. Cole gives me an apologetic glance and takes off with Kevin, both looking awkward as the warning bell rings.

Every part of me imagined that telling Caylee would be unbelievably difficult, that she'd try to avoid hearing the truth, but no part of me thought she wouldn't even listen when the time came. At least, no part of me that I'd let fully surface.

I stand frozen, numb, as somewhere behind me I hear paper ripping. The contents of my binder have launched across the entire hallway, people stepping all over everything. I vaguely notice the shoe print on my empty Spanish worksheet as I stoop to pick up the pages.

As I flip over an old Spanish homework, my gaze snags on the upper right corner where Thomas had written his name as a joke. I'd had to cross it out and write my own name above it before turning in the sheet. He'd told me he was going to pretend the homework was his so he could finally get a perfect score on an assignment.

I linger over the name—the way the letters slant, the way the top and base of the *T* don't quite meet—as the final bell rings overhead. Without trying to, I'd given Thomas plenty of opportunity to meet me before class like he had all last week and the week before that. Maybe he isn't even at school today but, more likely, he just doesn't want to see me. What does it say about me that I wish he had come? What does it say about me that I thought Caylee would at least hear me out? And what does it say about her that she wouldn't even do that?

Shoving the paper mess into my backpack, I duck into the science classroom I know will be empty before a hallway monitor can get to me. I'm not about to go to first period and sit near Tina for a whole class, even if they will call Mom about it. I just can't.

As I slide into a desk in the back, my eyes catch on the life-size skeleton hanging in the front corner of the room, the one I used to practice my figure drawing on during lunch before I met Caylee. Its jaw hangs loose on its hinges, revealing a gaping mouth lined with less than half its teeth. The skull looks like someone punched it in the mouth, something I wouldn't put past certain male classmates strutting the halls. I used to think the skeleton looked like it was smiling, and I'd always drawn it that way—like something Edward Gorey would draw inspiration from or like one of artist José Guadalupe Posada's famous dancing, grinning calaveras. But today it reminds me of a poster covered in dripping ketchup and just looks sad.

I glance out the window, spotting the tops of the stadium lights. For a fleeting moment, I feel a tinge of the excitement I'd felt on that lacrosse field after Thomas's game, before the feeling plummets, turning bitter in my stomach. And I wish again with my whole being that I could magically teleport myself back in time and do Saturday all over again—to walk off that field and never return, never go to that fucked-up party.

Overwhelming grief washes through me. I press the marble in my bandaged hand till it hurts, to stop the tears from leaking out as a plan starts to form in my mind. If Caylee thinks she can ignore me and that I'll simply go away, she's wrong. I just need to wait it out till fourth period. I'll see her in English, without Zac, where she won't be able to flee. Or if not then, at lunch. I'll corner her and tell her everything—about the party, about her gross boyfriend. Then she'll be forced to listen to every single thing she's been trying so hard not to hear.

THOMAS

I'M TOO LATE. SHE'S STANDING BY HER LOCKER, BUT SHE'S not alone.

It's my first time seeing her since the party, and it knocks the wind out of me. Zac's standing there with Kevin and Cole, though I'm too far away to hear what he's saying. But anger flares in me at the way he's leaning in, practically crushing her as she shrinks against her locker. Why doesn't she say anything to stop him? She's in all black—a hoodie with a white cat, tights, and her boots. She'd found the boots, then. It's the least colorful outfit I've seen her wear.

They all turn in my direction, and I duck reflexively behind the guy in front of me. But their gazes fall short, landing on Caylee, who walks ahead of me. Still, I see what Erica is trying to stuff into her backpack so that no one else'll see—a pink bra, the one she wore to the party that I couldn't find the next morning. It wasn't anywhere, but I couldn't wake her. . . .

Erica looks like she's about to cry, blinking hard, shaking her head.

I can't do it, can't talk to her. How could I explain? Those pictures. And a *video*?

Stomach churning, I hurry past Erica's locker right as Caylee joins them, looking upset. With any luck, none of them saw me, especially Erica.

I'm such a coward.

My body feels like a sack of dumbbells as I make for the gym, thinking about how I found her, curled up into herself. There can't be evidence of that going around. There can't be. But I know there is. Maybe I could ask any one of these people, and they'd show me everything. What did Zac start?

As I burst into PE, I curse under my breath, remembering the sport-of-the-week is Ultimate Frisbee. There's too much shit bouncing around my head to care about flinging Frisbees. I hang back, not helping out my team. Besides, everyone seems to be whispering, and I don't want to hear any of it. Then a girl sprints past me, dark hair loose around her face. I turn, holding my breath, but no, she's only a sophomore. She doesn't even look like . . .

Some freshman pounds into me, but I manage not to fall. The Frisbee clatters to the floor, and I pick it up, flinging it as hard as I can, surprised by how good it feels. I don't even care when it goes out of bounds. Then it's like I can see the gym around me for the first time today—bright overhead lights, Panther-blue basketball hoops with stiff nets, three dozen students staring after the Frisbee as Coach Lee nods his approval.

For the rest of class, I'm unstoppable, everyone leaping out of the way as the Frisbee whizzes by them to crash into the bleachers, the wall, the basketball hoop. My team doesn't score many points since everyone seems afraid of being guillotined, but I don't care.

And today's far from over. We're not even halfway to lunch and then comes Spanish, meaning I have only a few hours to figure out what the hell I'm going to say to Erica when I have no choice but to face her.

ERICA

I SOMEHOW MANAGE TO MAKE IT TO FOURTH PERIOD, though I lose my Erica Strange mask on the way to English. All morning, the whispers, the smirks have pulled at it, slowly loosening the knot. Then Stallion saunters down the hall, his name a faint memory on my inner thigh. He points his index finger at me like a loaded gun and calls out, "Mouth! Take it off! Yeah, girl!"

As half the hallway dissolves into laughter, I duck away, feeling the mask slip from my face entirely and float to the floor. Who was I kidding? There's no hiding behind stupid masks. Everyone knows, probably even Stallion's girlfriend. What awful things would she say if we ran into each other?

I squeeze my marble, feeling the hard press of it as I round the final corner. But Amber's outside the classroom door talking to our English teacher, Ms. Adams. People filter past into class, staring after them. From how seriously Amber talks and how intently Ms. Adams listens, I know Amber's made good on her promise to find out what happened. And now she's telling a teacher.

Oh, Amber, how could you?

I turn and pace the hall even as the bell blasts overhead. I'm trapped. I can't go to class now.

Instead, I slip around the corner and slide against my backpack down the length of the wall. The tile feels cool through my leggings.

"Excuse me."

I look around.

"Yes, you." The hallway is entirely empty except for a woman approaching me. The hanging badge overtop her wraparound sweater tells me she's a hallway monitor.

"Why aren't you in class?"

"I just . . ." I take a deep breath. "I just needed a break."

Her eyes go soft, and she pats my knee. "I know high school can be rough, but it's not forever. So, power through, okay? I don't want to have to write you up."

I nod and slowly rise, knowing it doesn't matter if I "power through" today. All this mess will still be here tomorrow and the next day and the day after that. I'm damned no matter what I do, though I'm not about to explain it to this woman.

The hallway monitor watches as I once again round the corner to English. Only this time, Ms. Adams stands alone beside the classroom door. She closes it when she sees me, then crosses her arms and stares at me over rhinestone-studded glasses. "Erica?"

Shit.

"Yes?" I shove my bandaged hand in my sweatshirt pocket and approach her, trying to conceal my growing dread.

Ms. Adams beckons me closer. "Come over here a minute, please."

Please don't let her know! Please don't let her know!

But of course she does. I see it in the concern wrinkling her eyes. Amber found out and told her.

"Is everything okay?" Ms. Adams asks, voice lowered.

I swallow hard and run my thumbs over my backpack straps, realizing too late I've exposed my bandaged hand. "Everything's fine, Ms. Adams."

Her gaze roves over my hand as she leans forward, shimmery nails pressing into opposite arms. "Are you sure?" She wants me to look at her, but I can't. I don't trust what would come out of my mouth.

I nod, eyes locked on a pencil with a foam apple topper that someone dropped near the door. I wish I could be any-where else because then I wouldn't have to be here, lying to my teacher about the fact that I'm not okay, that I'm Saturday's party removed from okay, that I need to talk to my friend to find out if she could ever be my friend again or if she's gone forever.

"I'm fine, Ms. Adams," I repeat, but I've lost my mask and she can read my face. I press my palm against my pocket, feeling for the marble. "Really, everything's fine."

"Erica, let me be blunt. Some rumors have been brought to my attention"—my heart stops, no beats—"rumors that have frankly disturbed me." Her voice stays low.

"What sort of rumors?" The pencil topper gleams in the light, unnaturally shiny.

"People talking about a party. And you. People writing on you." She shifts. "Did anything happen at a party?"

I imagine squeezing the foam apple in my fist, feeling it pop as the hard shell gives. "No," I say, and when she doesn't respond, doesn't believe me, I add, "Just, you know, some people messing around. It's no big deal. Really."

She hesitates, and I glance up, catching an expression of deep concern. No amount of outlining in pen could duplicate on paper how heavy her eyes look.

"Listen, Erica." Her mouth is tight, words barely audible. "If you are getting harassed, or if, god forbid, you were assaulted, then I can't ignore it. I'll have to take this to the principal, the police."

Assaulted. Police. A strangled sound chokes from my throat as tears wet my cheeks. I think about my mom finding out I lied. That I got drunk. That all those guys saw me naked, wrote on me. My mom who still thinks I'm a virgin. She'll see the photos of me, naked and stupid drunk and written all over.

"Please, don't do that," I sob into the echoey hallway. "There's nothing to report."

"Erica. Honey. It's my job to make sure that—"

I turn and run, ignoring Ms. Adams as she calls after me. Sprinting down the hallway, I'm blinded by my tears, backpack slapping my spine as I turn one corner, then another, then another.

It's as I push through the main doors, thinking I've finally found freedom, that I smack right into him.

THOMAS

I'M BRINGING AN ATTENDANCE SHEET TO THE OFFICE, HAVING just taken a shortcut outside through the quad. And I'm about to push open the doors to enter the main building when Erica comes bursting out of them. She slams into me, startling us both, but she recovers first.

"Thomas, hey . . ."

Her eyes are wet, and I've never seen her so on edge. She tries to smile through her nervousness, but it only makes her look desperate.

I don't even know what part sets me off. Maybe it's everything from the last few days. Maybe it's because she's caught me off-guard. Maybe it's her smile—the nervous part that says she's scared to be around me now, that I've somehow earned her fear, or the fact that she's trying to smile at all. Because it's this last part that I pounce on.

"Why are you smiling?" I spit, disgust pooling in my words.

It's enough to make the forced grin disappear—flicker then die altogether.

My rage dulls for a moment, then returns in a flood with her reply.

"What?" she asks, even though I know she's heard me. She just needs context to pin my question to. But I repeat the question anyway.

"Why are you smiling?" The hostility in my voice surprises me, but I want to know. What the hell's she even doing here, out of class? Standing just outside the main entrance, having plowed into me and trying to smile like everything between us is okay. Like anything between us could ever be okay again. "I mean, why are you even talking to me right now?"

It's a question with teeth. Why does she make everything so hard, appearing out of nowhere, not only right now but always? Couldn't she have just stayed out of my way and I would've stay out of hers, and we could all pretend like nothing ever happened, pretend like no one even knows?

"Why?" I ask, louder than before because she still hasn't answered. She's still just standing there looking stunned, somehow surprised that this is where things are now. Her genuine shock makes me even angrier. Hasn't she heard what people are saying about her, about us? Even before, they were always looking at us. From the beginning, staring at me, at her, at us together. The new girl, the crazy dresser, the artist, hanging out with that guitar kid. *"Isn't he that big-shot lawyer's son?"* they'd ask behind my back. *"That goalie filling in till Zac's arm heals?"* Or *"Doesn't she live in, like, an apartment or something?"* they'd ask me, like I knew exactly, or make some crack about her boots like she had no other shoes. And now here she is again, making everything harder. *"Weren't you, like, into her? But not anymore, am I right?"*

Erica still hasn't moved. I stare down at her stupid boots and her stupid cat sweatshirt like I hate her, because right now I do. What did she expect, trying to talk to me? Smiling? Acting like nothing ever happened? She doesn't even look mad.

"I'm sorry . . . ," she starts, and I lose it. Sorry. She's sorry.

Like my mom. Sorry dinner took five minutes longer than planned to get on the table, even though she'd spent five hours preparing it. Sorry it was cold outside and she'd forgotten to remind me to bring a coat. Sorry my father's a complete dick and she puts up with it. She's always sorry.

And now Erica's sorry. She's *sorry*. For what, getting wasted? For my friends seeing her naked or talking about her body in front of me like I wouldn't mind? For sharing photos of her? Because why would I care? They did me a favor—showing me that the girl I liked doesn't matter, that none of it matters, right?

"Don't," I spit with a voice so full of rage that it startles even me. "Just . . . don't. Don't talk to me. In Spanish either. I don't want anything to do with you."

New tears spring to her eyes, but she doesn't answer. She's stunned. Motionless. Crying silently while I watch.

I just made her cry. I did this.

"I thought you were different," she whispers. Blinking furiously, she jams a hand in her backpack and tosses something at me. Instinctively I grab it, dropping my gaze to the light gray fabric. It's my sweatshirt, looking like the world's heaviest olive branch I just snapped in two, the one I gave her after my game before kissing her. Before the party. Before everything got so fucked.

"Erica Strange . . . ," I whisper. But she's already blasted back inside, her black-and-white checkered backpack a blur.

I watch her go, horrified, the angry words I spat at her replaying in my head. I sounded just like my father, everything I always feared I'd become, and I hate myself for it.

ERICA

MY CAPE STRINGS RIP FROM MY NECK AS I RUSH BACK INSIDE
the empty hall. My nerves zap like sparklers. Or maybe the
sound is coming from my brain.

What freaking delusion made me think I could ever be Erica
Strange?

After turning for the bathrooms, I hurry inside and into a
stall, throw my binder over the toilet, and sit on it. Suddenly,
I'm overheating in my long sleeves and boots. I cross my arms
over my breasts, breasts Thomas and all his asshole buddies
have seen. I'd wanted to ask Thomas so many questions. Why
he didn't text me back last night. Why he didn't meet me at
my locker this morning like before. But those weren't the questions I really needed to ask: *Why did you do it?* Why would
he write on me, humiliate me like that? Did I mean nothing
to him? Did our dates, our kiss, mean nothing? Did he just

ask me to be his girlfriend as some cruel joke, knowing all the while what he and his sicko friends had planned for me? Was Thomas the one who blacked out my nipples? Scribbled on the rest of my body? Had he liked it? Derived some sick pleasure from dragging the Sharpie over my bare skin while the other boys snickered? Or did they all pass the marker around like a torch, each one taking his own turn as I lay there, passed out, Thomas writing on my back so he wouldn't have to look at my face while he did it? But I didn't ask him, didn't say much like always. Erica Strange would be so proud.

I think about standing on that field after his game in a sea of people, feeling girlfriend-like pride for getting to hold his almighty helmet while he went to fetch his stupid sweatshirt for me, telling myself all the while that the weight of it in my hands *meant* something.

I press both hands to my face. Thomas hates me. Caylee must too. And everyone thinks I'm a whore. I need to get out of here, but I can't leave yet. I'll never make it to the parking lot between classes without being seen, especially since Ms. Adams probably sounded the alarm. And if I wait till lunchtime, I know where Caylee will be. It's Monday, which means Zac and the guys go to Junie Bee's, and Caylee's not invited. She'll be by the picnic tables. And she needs to know what really happened—who her boyfriend really is—whether she wants to or not.

I pull out my notebook and touch pen to paper, to write or

draw, I don't know, but the pen takes over and before long the entire page becomes a mess of blue scribbles. As I circle the pen again and again, the pen tip threatens to punch through. I keep at it until it does, till navy ink bleeds onto the next page and the page under that, until I've dug a soggy crater that's layers deep. It hurts the cut in my hand, but I don't stop, only push harder.

After ages and no time at all, the bell rings for lunch, the outside hallways humming to life. The outer door to the bathroom bursts open three, four times as girls filter in, bringing with them the roar of lunchtime chaos.

I'm throwing my notebook into my backpack when I hear Tina's voice.

Through the gap in the stall, I see her at the mirror, talking to Kelly. Tina turns, then stops, eyeing the bottom of my stall. I shrink back, and for a split second I think she somehow knows I'm here, but then she and Kelly pull open neighboring stall doors.

Over the sound of tinkling pee, Kelly's voice asks, "Where do you want to go for lunch?"

"Junie Bee's, of course," Tina calls back.

"You only want to go there because the guys will all be there," Kelly responds.

"And?" Tina asks, a challenge.

Two toilets flush, zippers zip, and doors squeak open. They reappear in my line of sight at the sinks.

"Well, what about Erica?" Kelly asks, pulling up her sleeves.

"What about her?" Tina's reply carries over the sound of the tap. "It's not like she'll dare show her face after Saturday night." Tina's raised voice hooks attention, faces turning toward her to listen, clearly as she intended. "God, you should've seen her. Fat-ass couldn't even stand up straight. I've never seen anything more disgusting in all my life. Making out with everyone. She probably gave them all mouth herpes or something."

What is Tina talking about? I only kissed Thomas that night. At least, I think so?

And even though Tina's made it very clear she doesn't like me ever since I started hanging out with Thomas, I've never heard her be this cruel. The quiet Tina from yesterday sitting awkwardly on a stool at Juiced suddenly enters my mind, almost like she'd regretted posting those pictures. Guess that moment roared by fast.

"I know you don't like her," Kelly says. "But did you have to send that video to Caylee this morning? Or anyone else for that matter? It's pretty foul."

My chest sears with heat. She sent a video? To Caylee, to everyone else? Of me in that backyard or worse?

"Yeah, but so is she," Tina responds.

Bitch!

I fly to my feet, bursting with all the unspent anger from my encounter with Thomas, and shove open the stall door with a bang. "What'd you send Caylee?"

Kelly's eyes and mouth fall wide at the sight of me, though Tina doesn't look at all surprised, like she expected this. And then I get it. My boots. Tina saw them under the stall door, knew I was in there the whole time. Talked about me *because* she knew.

Tina stands there, looking like a stupid yoga ad in her tight leggings. "Well, look who it is," she sneers. "What'd you do to your hand, Erica? Too many hand jobs?"

I advance on her, fury and fear pulsing through me. "Tina, what the hell did you send Caylee?"

"Just some documentation about what a shitty friend you are. But looks like you haven't seen it yet, have you?"

I have to fight the urge to recoil at the look she's giving me— the sick grin of a sadistic executioner right as he swings his ax.

"Well, I'd be happy to show you, if you really wanna see," Tina adds.

"Come on, Tina." Kelly pulls at her arm. "Let's just go to lunch."

Tina brushes her off. She takes her time scrolling through her phone to find what she's looking for: the video I don't want to see; the video I need to see. Another missing puzzle piece. Tina holds her phone up for me, and my heart plummets. I'm not sure what's scarier—her evil smile or Kelly's cringe.

A video starts playing. And then I stop breathing.

The video is poor quality with very little light. But it's enough. I'm passed out, naked, curled up on the edge of Zac's bed, sheets tangled at my feet. Standing beside me is Zac, a sloppy grin on his face. On the floor below sits Ricky, blacking out a nipple on one breast, his face scrunched in drunk concentration. From this angle, you can see my bare ass, but not quite between my legs. Laughter ripples through the bedroom, then someone says, "Do it again, Zac. I'm recording now." Tina's voice, behind the camera.

She zooms in on Zac, a lazy smirk on his face. His pants are unzipped, half-hard penis hanging out. He moves closer, penis right next to my face. Then he starts thrusting.

Laughter roars. I hear a "Get some!" from Stallion, and even Ricky stops his scribbling to watch as Zac's penis slaps against my half-open mouth, my cheek, my chin, again and again. One thrust hits my nose, rocking my head back.

A small part of myself—the detached, logical side—says, *Well, that explains "blow job girl" earlier*, while the rest of me screams and Screams and SCREAMS.

Tears gush from my eyes and down my face as the video cuts out, freezing at the start like the world's cruelest sketch: a girl, passed out. A boy groping her breast. Another boy, pants unzipped, ready to humiliate, assault.

Assault *me*. *My* body.

Mouth.

This is what everyone's seen. My entire naked body. Zac's penis in my face. On my face. Ricky's hand on my breasts. While I just lie there, passed out.

Was *that* rape?

Nausea balloons in my stomach as the bathroom rings with silence. No one moves. Then the door swings open. In my periphery I see Amber enter and know I've been discovered, but I don't look away from the freeze-frame of my humiliation, ready to play again at the touch of a finger.

Tina lowers her phone, turning to Kelly. "So yeah, I almost didn't share this with anyone, but then I woke up this morning and thought, 'What the hell? Caylee deserves to see what kind of friend Erica really is.'" She shrugs. "And now she has."

I whirl, fist flying, hitting Tina right in the mouth. The contact makes the wet popping sound of a soda can opening. I gasp as my butterfly bandages give and my cut rips wide.

Tina staggers, dropping her phone and covering her lip. The phone hits the tile with a crack, protective case and all. She stares down at the webbed glass, stunned. "What are you, psycho?"

Kelly wheels on me, alarm coloring her face as she stoops to pick up the broken phone.

"Screw you, Tina," I spit.

Amber pushes her way to me, getting right in Tina's face. "You disgust me, you disgrace to womankind. I'd punch you myself, if Erica hadn't already."

Tina snarls at Amber, but Kelly tugs her away. "Come on, Tina, let's go!"

"Yeah, and tell Principal Renall she's got psychopaths on the loose!" Tina yells before shoving past Amber.

As the door swings shut, Amber calls after them, "Hope it hurt, Tina!" Then she takes in my tears, the hand I'm clutching, and grabs my upper arm. "Come with me."

She leads me out, parting the sea of girls with her anger.

I realize I'm shaking. Holding my hand to my chest, I feel the reopened cut spreading liquid heat across the gauze. I've never been sure if Amber likes me. She's always snorting when I say anything, or she's been too interested in her phone and texting her college boyfriend to pay me much attention. And when she told Ms. Adams earlier, I thought maybe she did it for a sense of "right." And yet, here she is, the only one who's stood up for me today, looking as fierce as I wish I felt, but I'm as small as the marble in my pocket, like I could drop and roll into a grimy corner, never to be found again.

In the busy hallway, Amber drops my arm and whirls to face me. But for once, I get in the first word. "Amber, you told."

She shakes her head to clear it. "Erica, I had to. What those guys did, what Tina did . . ."

"It wasn't your story to tell," I say. She hesitates, and I turn for the exit, swinging my backpack over my shoulder. "I'm going to talk to Caylee."

She grabs my arm. "Erica, you need to talk to an adult. Everyone's looking for you."

I slip from her grasp, not caring who in the hallway hears me. "Amber, please! Listen to me. I need to find Caylee first. She blames me, I know she does, but I have to tell her it's not my fault, that I didn't ask for this, for any of it, okay? Then I'll . . . I'll do whatever you want." I promise her this, not knowing if it's true or not but feeling my world close in even as I say it. I watch Amber waver, so I repeat, "I have to tell her my side. She wouldn't listen to me earlier, so please let me do this first. Please."

Amber stares at me for a long time, then she nods once and says the one thing I need to hear right now: "Fine. Maybe she needs to hear the truth coming from you." She points at me. "But then you're coming with me after that, got it?" Amber turns, not waiting for a reply, and blazes the trail ahead.

THOMAS

MUSIC BLARES THROUGH MY TRUCK'S SPEAKERS AS I RACE TO Junie Bee's. It's where the guys and I always meet on Mondays, but today, everything's changed. The gray sweatshirt Erica returned to me slides off the front seat along with my backpack, but I don't slow, blasting the playlist I made this summer that feels like a lifeline. Vocalists scream. Guitars wail. The truck cab vibrates with the noise of it all. I want to drown out the voice that keeps asking me what the hell happened outside the main entrance with Erica, but my head won't clear.

There's a video, and everyone's seen it. Except for me.

Whose fault is that?

I'm fully wound up by the time I get to the restaurant.

Zac and the guys already sit around a table in the far corner. From the door, I can see Zac, Ricky, and Steve huddled around Ricky's phone, Forest across from them. The folder from Coach with practice plays we're supposed to be studying sits untouched in front of them. From the expressions on their faces, they're absorbed in whatever shit they're watching. And I'm pretty sure I know what that is.

As I near, my suspicions are confirmed when Ricky laughs. "God, Zac. You're such a perv."

I slap both hands on the table and ask, "What's up, guys?" My words are sharp. Still, no one across the table glances up, though Forest nods in my direction, flipping his red order number in his hands and looking uncomfortable.

"What's so funny?" I demand, voice deadly.

Finally, Zac's eyes meet mine. He shoves Ricky. "Show Van-Brackel. He must've not seen it yet."

"Show me what, exactly?" My voice pitches, dripping sarcasm. "Or maybe it's this video I've been hearing so much about?"

Zac rolls his eyes and yanks the phone out of Ricky's hand.

"Aw, c'mon!" Ricky protests, eyes tracking the phone.

Zac shoves the screen in my face. "Tina sent it this morning, but you'd know that if you ever checked your messages."

My insides go cold as I take in the visual. Here it finally is. The video.

It's . . . her. Of course it's her, but she's naked, covered in writing. Ricky, the Sharpie in his hand. Tina's voice.

Then Zac is . . .

I shove the phone away. "The fuck is that?" When no one answers, I demand, "The fuck did you do, Zac?" He's done some twisted shit before, but this? To her?

"Calm down, VanBrackel," Zac hisses, eyeing the nearby tables. "Don't get so worked up."

"Are you fucking kidding me right now?" They're all staring, like me raising my voice is the problem here and not them sitting there laughing, watching that messed-up shit on repeat while eating their goddamned french fries. Like it's all just another one of Zac's "Big Funny Jokes" and he hasn't gone way too far this time. "That video is all over school," I hiss. "Do you have any idea how much trouble we could get in?" Like that's the half of it.

Zac's face freezes into an icy calm. "That's a far cry from what you said Saturday night."

I explode back from the table, slamming into a waitress and upsetting her tray. Hot sandwiches and parmesan fries rain down around me, warm lunch meat sticking to my back.

"Oh! I'm so sorry!" the waitress exclaims, and I cringe at the apology. Another fucking apology. She holds her arms away from herself, her red-and-white striped shirt covered in melted cheese and barbecue sauce.

"It's . . . it's my fault." I back away, brushing cheesy roast beef to the floor.

"I'll be right back." The waitress turns and flees.

Forest's on his feet next to me, looking for a way to help, but there's nothing he can do. It'd take an industrial-sized broom to undo the mess I've made.

"Nice going, VanB," Zac says, but it's not him I'm looking at.

Ricky's phone sits on the table where it fell during the chaos. I snatch it up, dropping it in Forest's Dr Pepper. Bubbles erupt. The phone hits the bottom of the glass with a plunk. I can only hope it won't survive.

"What the hell, Thomas?" Ricky demands, but I hardly hear him. Fries and sandwich bread squish beneath my Chucks, food still falling from me as I leave. I don't care that I have no idea where I'm going. I just need to drive. Because I can't go back to school yet. Everything's so fucked-up, even worse than I thought. Zac and the pictures from his room, the pink bra, those were bad enough. Now there's Ricky and his phone full of videos and god knows what else, plus the waitress who smells like vanilla, which is to say like Erica, who apologizes for things that aren't even her fault.

I made her cry at school just now. I yelled at her. And they . . .

Panic squeezes the air from my lungs. *Everything's so fucked. I'm so fucked.*

Zac, laughing. Holding her up like a doll. His hands all over her. Like she belonged to him. Like everything fucking belongs to him.

As my truck roars to life, I crank up the music as far as it'll go till my ears ring with it and nothing else. I tear at the steering wheel, slamming against it as I try to rip it free. The music mirrors my yell as I shout into the dash. Tires spit gravel as I peel out of the parking lot and away from Ricky, from Zac, and any other prick I was stupid enough to call my friend.

ERICA

I FOLLOW AMBER OUT OF THE BUILDING, NEITHER OF US
speaking. As we near the quad, I see a group huddled around a
phone and know without asking what they're looking at, a fact
confirmed when I walk by and one guy glances up then hits
the arm of the other. Pretty soon they're all staring me down
with faces that span a whole spectrum of emotion: amusement,
confusion, disgust, horror. My face scalds, vivid images of
exactly what they're looking at playing in my mind. I squeeze
the marble: *I want to die.*

"You guys got a problem?" Amber asks. "Because if you
know what's best for you, you'll stop staring like a bunch of
creepbags."

All the while, I search for Caylee. And I find her, right
around the corner.

She sits with Julie at one of the picnic tables lining the

East Building hallway, which is two tables down from the one Thomas leaned against when I first saw him. Because of course it is.

I know before I even reach Caylee that there is no going back to the way things were with us. It's the way her jaw sets and posture tenses when she sees me coming. It tells me what I've already known all day.

She's not going to listen. She blames me for what happened, and she hates me for it.

As I approach, I try to brace myself, but there's no way to prepare. "Caylee, you need to hear me out."

"There's nothing you can say that I want to hear," she snaps.

Several years back, Mom had been cooking in the kitchen while I did my homework at the table. Dad had rolled through, giving her a kiss on top of her head and asking if she was cooking any more mushrooms, because if she was, then he would kindly excuse himself from whatever meal that entailed. Mom laughed, swatting him with a spoon.

He'd turned to me, winking, spouting yet more Shakespeare: "No legacy is so rich as honesty!"

Only now as I stand in front of Caylee, her face contorted with rage, do I realize something about that quote: It doesn't talk about what to do when someone doesn't want to hear your honesty.

Beside me, Amber says, "Hear her out. She's got something to tell you."

"Stay out of it, Amber," Julie cuts in.

"Caylee, please," I repeat. "All you need to do is listen, but I have to tell you what happened." I slap my chest. "My version."

Caylee throws up her hands, then stands, crossing her arms. "Oh, now you want to tell me what happened? Your *tragic* version of all this? Well, don't bother. Because at this point, I'm done listening. I've heard about all I can stand for a lifetime, Erica."

She's said my name like a curse, like I'm the monster in all this. She's yelling—at me. "Well, tell me what you've heard, then," I start, voice wobbling. "Because I have no idea what you could possibly have heard that would make me the villain here. And if you would've picked up your phone yesterday like I asked you to, then I would've told you—"

"Oh, I'll tell you what I heard," she interrupts. "It's the part where you stripped in front of my boyfriend. Does *that* ring a bell?" She fights to keep her voice low, but her aversion to creating a scene in public can't win out over her anger. Several people stop to stare.

I lower my voice. "Caylee, it wasn't like that. You know it wasn't."

"Oh yeah? Then please tell me because I'm dying to know. What was it 'like'?"

She doesn't understand. How can I make her understand? "I was passed out, Caylee. They took my clothes off when I was asleep, wrote on me while I was beyond drunk. And I can't even remember what—"

"How can you not remember, Erica? How the fuck can you not remember getting naked in front of my boyfriend?"

The hushed quad rings with her words.

Several things about this sentence are so un-Caylee that it shocks me into silence. My Caylee would never get angry, would never yell. My Caylee would never make a scene. My Caylee would never drop the F bomb. But she's doing all those things—at me—in the middle of the courtyard.

"Caylee, if Erica was unconscious and Zac, or anyone else—" Amber starts, but Caylee interrupts.

"Shut *up*, Amber! *He* didn't do anything! But this slut?"

Erica Walker is a sluuut.

Amber tries to interject, but I cut her off, my chest flushed with heat. "You think I'm a slut, Caylee? Because I passed out and a bunch of guys humiliated me, including your boyfriend? In case you haven't noticed, Zac's not a good guy. Have you seen the video, what he did?"

"Don't you dare!" Caylee's pure fury now, shaking and crying nearly as hard as I am. "Don't you *dare* blame it on him! I *defended* you, Erica. When everyone talked shit behind your back, laughed at you for being so drunk, I told them off. Told them they were wrong about you, that you were a good person. So, don't you *dare* blame it on Zac when you're the problem here."

My eyes burn with devastation. She really believes it. Everything she's saying. She actually believes it. "Caylee, please, you don't mean that. Please, just—"

Caylee scrubs at her eyes, smearing her perfect makeup. "Please what, huh? Calm down? Don't make a scene? Stay everyone's good girl who never does anything wrong? Or were you going to say that I should trust you? Because that's not going to happen. Not anymore. In fact, I should've believed everyone from the start when they all told me that my best friend screwed my boyfriend, something I know you've wanted to do for a long time. I've seen the way you look at him. Don't even try to deny it."

A splintered silence follows.

And then I can't help it. I laugh. It's a deranged laugh, and I know it. While I'm at it, I should shout to everyone staring: *"Welcome to the Erica Walker: Exposed exhibit! On display now! Come one, come all!"* But my eyes don't leave Caylee's as I ask, "Are you freaking serious right now? Because your boyfriend's a sick bastard, Caylee, and I'd never sleep with him. The truth is you're dating a monster. He doesn't love you, doesn't appreciate you. He never has, he never will, and everyone knows it but you." It's a truth I've held on to for so long, but saying it aloud tears at my heart, especially as I watch Caylee's face crumble.

She's a mermaid out of water, gaping mouth sputtering. "You liar!" she screams. Fat tears stream down her face, eyes hard as the marble clenched in my fist. She slams her chest with her open palm. "Zac loves me. He *loves* me. But you're just jealous because I have everything you want. And what do you have? A porn video and a shack of an apartment. So, screw you!"

Amber gets in Caylee's face, her entire body red with fury as she shouts at Caylee to wake the hell up. But Caylee only rips her purse from the table and storms away, Julie rushing after her. Watching Caylee race off, I feel a hurt so deep I can't see the bottom. A heaviness falls over me, heart choking with suffocating mold. Gawking faces surround me—faces that have witnessed the worst moments of my life and seen everything taken from me. Faces that have studied my naked body, watched Zac humiliate me in the halls and Tina humiliate me in the bathroom, and looked on as I lost my best friend, a best friend who believes her predator boyfriend over me.

There is no hope.

Red lips, ivory skin swim in my vision—Amber trying to get my attention, asking if I'm okay. But she can't understand that it's not okay, that nothing is, that it will never be okay again. Caylee was my last okay. She blames me for everything. There was never any going back. From the moment I woke in Zac's room, there was never any chance of going back. And now she's gone forever. I have nothing, no one.

Go.

I turn from Amber, pushing her hand from my arm, and start to run, rushing past all the judging looks, pointing fingers, humming whispers. My boots crush spongy grass as behind me Amber calls out, telling me to "Stop! Wait!" But for the second time today, I ignore her.

Go.

Grass gives way to concrete, concrete to asphalt, as I sprint. Even after reaching the parking lot, my body refuses to slow.

Go. The word pounds with my pace like a mantra until I spot my car. *Go. Don't stop.*

And I don't, even after I'm in my car, tearing out of the parking lot. To hell with them all. To hell with this place. Why did I ever come back? I fly away, leaving behind Bay City—and all the Thomases and Tinas, Zacs and Caylees—for good.

THERE'S A NEW ERICA RUMOR TO TOSS ONTO THE PILE.

I'm late to sixth-period precalc, after skipping Spanish. I know I'll catch shit for it, but once I saw that video, there was no way I could sit between Erica and Ricky for a whole class.

I'm sneaking into my desk when Nick Frasier hits my arm. "Dude, did you hear? Your girl Erica punched Tina Marcus in the face!"

I collapse into my seat. "Wait, what?"

Nick's leaning sideways in his desk, not exactly whispering, and everyone a desk-length away is in full hearing range. He takes in his audience. "Yeah, I just heard about it from Nadeeyah. I guess she was in the bathroom when it happened. Said Erica socked Tina right in the face. Seriously!"

"Tina 'never shuts up' Tina?" Jerod Kellor asks. "Sporty chick?"

Nick nods. "That's the one."

"Good," Farah adds. "That's the least Tina deserves for what she did. God, that poor girl, I can't even imagine. I only hope Tina gets what's coming to her, and then some. Her and anyone else involved."

"Oh, for sure," Jerod says. "Like, who even does that?"

My stomach bottoms out even before Farah turns to me. "But, oh my god. You two were dating. You must be livid. You don't know who else was in on it, do you?"

"Thomas?" Ms. Hollis calls from the whiteboard, and I nearly have a heart attack. "Nice try sneaking in here, but you know the rules. Go to the office and bring me that late pass."

I'm sweating bullets as I pull open the office door . . . and come face-to-face with Tina. What are the freaking chances today? She's holding an ice pack wrapped in a paper towel over her lip.

"So, I guess you heard," she says, lifting the pack and rolling her eyes. The hint of a smirk tells me she's enjoying the attention.

"I heard something," I say.

"Yeah, your little girlfriend? She attacked me at lunch, so there's that."

"I'm sure that's exactly how it went down, Tina. And it had nothing whatsoever to do with that video you made." I thumb toward the principal's office. "Did you tell Principal Renall about that video while you were ratting Erica out?"

Tina scoffs, lowering the ice to reveal a split lip. "Are you trying to make me feel bad? Because that video proves how disgusting Erica is. She was totally wasted and all over Zac. Or did you forget?"

Like I could forget.

"So, I did you a favor," she continues, "exposing her for what she is."

I lean in. "Do you have any idea how much trouble we could get in, or are you that much of an idiot?"

Her mouth opens then closes. "We're not going to get into trouble. If anyone is, it's her and Zac. They're the ones who—"

"Because you had nothing to do with it. Someone else must've taken the video. It's only your voice that's behind the camera."

For the first time, something like fear flashes across Tina's face. Is she only now realizing how bad this could get? "What do you want me to say?" she sputters. "Erica's disgusting. I merely gathered the evidence."

I huff out a laugh. "It must have made you so happy—so damn giddy—to be in on the action, huh? Always trying so hard to be a part of it all. Bet you couldn't wait to pull out that Sharpie and get started."

"So, this is my fault?"

"Yeah, it is."

She advances on me, ice pack hitting the floor. "Look in the mirror, you shit-stick. Because I sure as hell didn't sign your name on your stupid slut of a girlfriend. And who did that again? Oh yeah, that's right. You."

I close the gap between us.

Her eyes and mouth pop wide as my face comes within inches of hers.

"Tina," I say, voice poison, "if you ever talk to me again, I swear to god you'll regret it."

I slam the office door in my wake, leaving behind a stunned Tina, for once shocked into silence.

"Thomas, wait up!"

The school day's finally ended, and Amber's cornered me by my truck, hair blazing red in the sun. *Perfect. Just perfect.* She looks more intense than usual, out of breath. "Hey, have you heard from Erica? Do you know where she went?"

I'm supposed to be grabbing my gear bag from my truck. I'll be late to practice, should already be on the field by now, but I've been stalling since school got out. Which was clearly a mistake.

"What's that?" I ask, pretending like I didn't hear, like Amber didn't just catch me staring at Erica's empty parking space, the one next to the fence, away from the other cars.

"Erica," Amber repeats. "She took off at lunch, and I'm really worried about her. Do you know where she is?" Amber studies me, which makes me more uneasy than I want to admit.

I clear my throat and unlatch my tailgate. "I'm . . . sure she's fine."

Amber huffs. "She punched Tina in the freaking face, then got in a blowout fight with Caylee, then took off in her car. And now she won't answer her phone, so no, she's not fine, Thomas."

"Well, I don't know where she is, okay?"

Amber huffs again, disbelief on her face. "What, are you, like, done with her now?"

I pause, gear bag halfway to my shoulder. "What do you mean?"

"Don't get cute with me. You two had a thing, and then the party happened, and some fucked-up shit went down with Zac and Ricky that Tina filmed, and now you're acting all shady. So, I want to know what the hell happened and if you're done with her now."

I don't meet her eyes. "I don't know what you're talking about." I wish it were true. I wish so many things. "Erica and I never had a thing." I try so hard to believe it all, try to avoid glancing at her empty parking spot again.

Amber stares at me for so long, I start to wonder if she's even going to respond. Then she slowly shakes her head. It's a gesture I know far too well from my father. Bitter disappointment. "Well, don't you sound just like Zac," she says. "Though I was somehow under the impression you were better than that. A good guy, even. So, why are you protecting him?"

"Listen, Amber. I gotta—"

"Unless . . ." Realization dawns across her face. She backs

away, finger aimed at my chest. "Unless you were in on it too." She exhales, face incredulous at whatever expression's on my face. "You too, huh? Un-freaking-believable, Thomas. Un-freaking-believable." Her face hardens, and a chill rolls through me. "You listen to me, Thomas VanBrackel. You're going to be held accountable for what you did to that girl, you can bet your ass. You along with every other creep in that room."

Cold sweat washes over me as she climbs into her Del Sol and speeds away. Heart sinking, I have no choice but to shoulder my gear bag—and my impossibly heavy guilt—and head for the field.

ERICA

I DRIVE AROUND FOR HOURS, STEERING WHEEL CLENCHED IN one fist, marble in the other. I'm trying to stop the thoughts, trying to stop *crying*, but neither is working. My entire school has seen that video. And Thomas and Caylee—how could they both yell at me like this is my fault?

I think of Thomas, all we shared together. Exchanging notes in Spanish class and making up rumors about Señora Roberts's wild after-school parties. Walking together to my history class and agreeing to that stupid deal about going to his game so he'd come with me to the party. His hands raking through my hair when he pressed me against his truck and kissed me hard. It's gone. All gone. And Caylee? She's been my best friend since I moved here. I don't know how to do Bay City without her. She took me under her wing and gave me a place to belong—at lunchtime, and in her shimmery car, her shimmery house, her shimmery life.

Before I know it, I'm zipping through my old neighborhood, toward the house Mom and I lived in with Dad, one block over from a busy street. At first, I drive past it, unseeing, then have to back up and crawl past it again, parking just beyond the driveway. I don't know what I was expecting. That the lawn would've died of thirst. That the fuchsia roses Mom loved so much would look scraggly and diseased. Maybe I'd even hoped so, that something else had gone to shit. But it's not like that at all. The new owners have transformed it, repainting the house a crisp buttercup yellow. The lawn has fresh sod on it and looks as pristine as the lacrosse field. Even the curtains through the windows—brilliant white with large blue dots—look amazing, like someone happy lives here.

The stupidest part of me expected Dad's old Miata to still be parked in the driveway. But it's not, of course, since he sold it to a former student before moving to Boston. Still, I picture him in his cramped office at the college here, on the second floor of the Comp Lit building, reviewing his notes for an eighteenth-century British literature seminar. I've heard people say he was a good professor. Well, assistant professor, anyway.

I always did try so very hard to impress him. And sometimes I managed. I would know when I did because he'd call me his 'Rica Girl and invite me to come sit with him in his study and read the books on his shelves. Or he'd take me on an outing, just the two of us, to a museum or bookstore, and he'd let me pick anything I wanted to take home, so long as it wasn't too expensive. I'd follow him all around the house and recite Shakespeare quotes to him, or watch him practice his lectures with rapt attention, or even help him grade multiple-choice tests. Everything was great . . . till I grew up.

Then practically overnight, Dad was always too busy for me, impatient when I was around, scolding me for not knocking before I came into his office or not picking up the books I'd left on the floor. It wasn't till later that Mom and I found out he'd started getting close to another professor and was trying not to get caught. Still, even as I watched him drive away with all his stuff piled in a U-Haul, I didn't tell him how angry I was or how he'd ruined our family. How much he'd hurt me, hurt us. Because even then, I didn't want to disappoint him and not be his 'Rica Girl! anymore, even though it felt too late for that. But when the boots came in the mail for me, the ones he'd seen me eye for months, they felt like an apology he didn't know how to give.

I stare down at those same boots now, scuffed and faded next to the dirty floor mat. What would Dad think of his little 'Rica Girl now?

My phone rings. It's Mom again. I click it to silent. Word has surely reached Principal Renall by now of what a delinquent I am. Recalling my conversation with Ms. Adams, I hope that's all that's reached the principal, but I doubt it.

I roll the marble in my hand and think about today, of Thomas and Caylee, so full of hatred for me, of Amber spilling her guts to Ms. Adams, or Tina and the video, the sound of my fist hitting her mouth. As I hold it up, the silver flecks in the marble shimmer in the light, throwing strange shapes onto the ceiling of the car that, through my tears, seem to morph and dance.

I don't want to do this anymore. I can't.

I pull out my phone and type in my search. Turns out when you Google "How to commit suicide," the National Suicide Hotline pops up first. But that's the exact opposite of what I want.

The next entry is some creepy guy's website with an e-book you can purchase detailing all the ways you can "make it count" by doing it right the first time. It makes me wonder if he's followed his own advice, or if not, what he thinks when someone actually purchases his morbid book.

I start over with a simpler search—"Suicide"—and scroll down, getting to a link about warning signs. This intrigues me. I almost laugh out loud as I read the second one: *Searching online for more information on ways to kill oneself.* At least they know what they're talking about.

Other warning signs follow, eerie in their accuracy: Giving your stuff away (or at least giving Caylee her birthday cookbook early and Thomas his stupid sweatshirt back), displaying extreme mood swings (check), and using more alcohol or drugs (do drugs involving the actual suicide count?). Because that's how I'd do it. Pills.

Clicking out of the search engine, I realize I found what I was looking for. Not so much how I'd kill myself. That I knew. I sought reassurance. And I know I've found it since finally fully acknowledging the thought that's been tugging at me—*I want to die*—because a strange calm settles over me. Which brings me to "Additional Warning Signs," including feeling lighter, calmer, more energetic.

I don't know about "more energetic."

But I do have options.

Is this how Grandpa Joe felt before he shot himself? Did he do what I'm doing now? Feel what I feel—this unbearable heaviness?

Then I can't breathe. This car closes in, and I realize I don't want to die. Plus, how could I do that to Mom?

No, there must be another way. I'm going to send Caylee a message. Maybe she's had time to calm herself, and if I write everything down, tell her what happened in detail, or at least everything I can remember, then she'll get a notification and have to read my side of it. Then maybe she'll finally understand that I didn't want any of it, that all I wanted was to make out with Thomas, maybe even sleep with him. But I'd wanted to remember it, and I'd wanted it to matter—*I'd* wanted to matter—then everything had gone so horribly wrong.

Even as I think all this, I know that hoping for a positive outcome with Caylee probably isn't realistic, that sending a message might not help anything. But somehow, despite so many things not mattering anymore, the truth still does, at least to me. So I'm going to tell Caylee everything. Every gruesome detail that I've had to live through since those guys put their hands on me. She needs to hear it all, especially where it concerns Zac.

On my phone, I click into my website. The last post I'd scanned in is the illustrated spread I did of Thomas kissing me after his game. It's sloppy art at best, given the limited time I'd had to throw it together before the party. But it makes no difference now.

I've been adding to my website for the past few months, saving it as a space just for me, keeping it private while I tried to figure out what I wanted it to be. And as it stands now, the site contains every doodle or illustrated spread I've created since December. In one column are the sketches of Erica Strange and Sparky. The other holds my entire life at Bay City—Caylee and Amber (our little Mermaid Gang), Thomas the Rhymer, Gross Zac and the guys, Evil Tina. Even Ms. Adams and Mr. J's skeleton make a few appearances. I drew out whole panels about meeting Caylee, getting to know Thomas, and everything in between, all the while keeping the illustrations a secret, even from Caylee. But now I want Caylee to see it. Let her know my private world and all that I've lost.

I open a new post and start typing, my first-ever post that's not an illustrated panel:

Caylee, you don't want to hear from me.
You made that clear enough today, but if
you're going to hate me, hate me because
of the whole truth . . .

The words pour from me in a tangled mess, then I go back and push those words around until they're in some sort of order and begin to make sense: Getting ready and pre-partying. Driving myself to the party in case she stayed the night with Zac. Thomas kissing me in Zac's driveway. Flirting with Thomas by the fire. Zac and Stallion shooting off fireworks. Me, downing vodka to calm my nerves. Going inside with Thomas.

Then nothing. Charcoal black where a memory should be.

Tears stream down my face as I relive waking up in Zac's room, but I push through and put it all in there—every drawing, word, and name on my skin, my missing skirt and bra, even my inside-out panties. I describe the drunken photos Tina posted and having to discover what happened to my body alongside the entire student body, the photos from Zac's room that must've circulated. Then comes the video. I describe it so that maybe Caylee will finally see who the real monster is in all this.

Tears turn to sobs as I narrate surviving school today: wanting to tell her all along but fearing she'd blame me. Zac returning my bra in the middle of the hallway. Stallion and his "Take it off, Mouth!" Ms. Adams asking about the rumors, saying she had to report everything. Thomas telling me he never wanted to speak to me again. The senior girl and her blow job mime. Punching Tina over the video. The group huddled around a phone, staring at me like I'd chosen to get stripped and humiliated. My fight with Caylee when she wouldn't listen, wouldn't acknowledge any blame on Zac's part.

As I type, for the first time since the gray walls, I feel a little lighter, each word a tiny weight breaking free. All the while, my marble sits in my lap. I look at it, resting against my black leggings, unable to articulate even to myself exactly what it means to me—how comforting it is to hold. I nudge it with my finger, then roll it up the valley where my legs meet.

By the time I post, it's mid-afternoon. I copy the link and send it to Caylee in a text, along with my login email and password, knowing it's my only chance of being heard. I doubt it'll change anything, let alone save our friendship, but I hope she at least takes the time to read it.

Suddenly the car can't contain me anymore. I get out and, without even knowing what I'm doing, I approach my old house. I find myself in front of a rosebush, plucking a single flower like the one Thomas left on my windshield. As I touch the satiny petals, a line from Dad's incessant Shakespeare recitations snakes its way into my thoughts: The roses fearfully on thorns did stand, / One blushing shame, another white despair; / A third, nor red nor white, had stol'n of both . . . and something about "A vengeful canker eat him up to death," but

I can't remember the rest, and I don't even know what it means anyway.

The front door opens and an elderly woman steps out, her face a frenzy of wrinkles. She reminds me of Mrs. Pensacola, the retired oil painter from Mom's work. "Hello?" the woman calls. "Can I help you with something?"

I hold up the flower, like I'm Belle's dad from *Beauty and the Beast*, caught with a sacred bloom. "I'm sorry. I was just . . . these are so beautiful."

"My roses? They are nice, aren't they? Feel free to have one. Even two." She winks at me.

"I . . . the one is enough. Thank you so much." I turn away from her. "Sorry for trespassing."

"It's quite all right. Flowers can have a rather intoxicating effect!"

I hurry to my car and throw the rose on the dash, feeling the old woman's eyes on me as I pull past the house and down the street. It was a mistake to come. Dad doesn't live here anymore and neither do we. Any dream I'd had of going back in time is just that—a dream. I should've just left the house as a memory.

My phone rings. It's Mom again. I don't answer. I'm not sure who Tina said what to, but I'll assume it really did involve Principal Renall and the word "psycho," and that's if Ms. Adams didn't get to the office first. Mom's going to be . . . what? Livid that I lied to her about the party? Disappointed in me, which is somehow always worse? Or frantic with worry and about to go off the deep end racking up even more debt, trying to fix me when it's clear I can't be fixed? Whatever the case, I don't want to know.

I make a U-turn and head home, comforted by my marble and telling myself that Caylee's probably reading my message right now. And if she's going to chuck me out of her life, at least she'll know deep down that she's chucking the truth out right alongside me.

THOMAS

A WHISTLE BLOWS AGAIN. COACH GESTURES ME OFF THE field. Again.

"Thomas, sit this one out." He's staring at his clipboard, disappointment oozing from him. I've been playing like shit all afternoon. As I near, Coach gestures to the bench. "Cole, you're in."

Cole leaps up, ready to take my spot.

"What?" I demand from the goal, so he'll have to look up from his stupid clipboard when he repeats it.

Coach levels his eyes on me. "I said you need to sit this one out. You're up, Cole." To everyone, he yells, "Okay, guys, let's bring it in."

The guys all huddle up as I storm off the field and throw myself onto the bench, stick and gloves hitting the ground, as far from Coach as I can get.

I realize too late that Zac stands to my left, ignoring the huddle and staring me down. "The hell has gotten into you, VanB?" He looks amused, head tilted as he chomps his gum.

I spit out my mouthguard and hurl my helmet. "What the hell has gotten into me? Are you kidding?"

He laughs, and my hands fight fists. "What's your problem, man?" I shout.

Zac leans in. "My problem is you, VanBrackel, acting like a pretty pink princess, and pretty pink princesses don't belong on my team."

I scoff. "*Your* team? Don't kid yourself, man."

His face dares me to keep going so I do, rising to my feet. My thumbs squeeze around curled fingers. I want to punch the smirk right off his face. "You know what, Boyd? You think you own everything. That everything is yours for the taking. But guess what? We've won every single game without you. We don't need you."

Down the bench, Coach yells something, but I don't hear. Blood thrums in my ears as Zac's face gets inches from mine, gum popping. He drops his voice to a low growl. "Wanna know what I think, VanBrackel? I think you're butt hurt about that Erica chick because she got a taste of my cock before yours. But it's cool. You can have my sloppy seconds."

When my fist makes contact with Zac's face, it's bone against bone—a sickening crack of knuckles hitting jaw. He staggers backward, nearly falling, then regains his balance and runs at me like a bull, taking my feet out from under me and hurling me beside the bench. I slam the ground, ribs absorbing his full weight, back of my head smacking turf.

Someone yells out as our fists fly. Elbows, knees, shins collide. He's on top of me, forearm pressed to my windpipe. I buck him off, elbow crunching the bridge of his nose. Cartilage gives but he doesn't slow. While I've got height advantage, Zac's hours in the gym have paid off. But I'm wearing full padding and he's not. Several blows bounce off my chest protector. We scramble to our feet, crouched and ready. He charges, tearing at my head, ears, hair. I rip free then throw all my weight into him. No padding cushions his fall, but it's his injured elbow that does him in. He lands on his bad side, breath gushing from him. I jump him and land blow after blow on his face, a few connecting with the forearm and cast he throws up to block me. His muscles tense, a sure sign he's gearing up for an offensive. Then someone yanks me to my feet, arms looped through my armpits. I pull and kick, but whoever holds me doesn't budge. Stallion's dragged Zac to his feet too.

"Thomas, enough!" Coach yells.

"You're an animal," I spit at Zac, only now realizing how much I hurt all over.

Blood streams down his nose and chin. He's wheezing, though his voice is calm. "So, what does that make you?" He smiles, blood catching in his teeth.

I stare at Zac, shaking my head in disbelief. He looks

completely unhinged, grinning at me like everything's a fucking game and everyone's only here for his entertainment. Me, Erica, Caylee. The whole goddamned world. Like he can just put his hands or his big-man cock wherever he fucking wants to. Always strutting around with that smug smirk on his face doing messed-up shit like none of it matters.

But it matters. It fucking *matters*.

Jesus. I didn't see it—didn't *want* to see it—so I blamed it all on her.

But it was him. He did this. Went way too fucking far this time.

Zac's grin widens at whatever expression's on my face. He's the worst kind of person.

So, what does that make me?

I shake off whoever is holding me. Forest, I realize.

"You good, my man?" Forest asks, only a trace of his usual calm.

"What the hell is going on over here?" Coach demands, but I don't answer.

Abandoning my gear, I turn toward the parking lot. Home. I need to go home.

"Only a little friendly fire, Coach. Music Man's too sensitive," Zac yells after me.

Before, his words would've turned me around. Would've dragged me back onto that field, pushed a helmet over my head, and forced my arms into movement. His words would've looped through my mind for the rest of practice and into the night. I would've wondered if he was right, if I'd overreacted. If I'd been too weak.

Now, I don't bother responding to Zac, or Coach's yell to get my ass back there. I keep marching off the field and as far away from Zac Boyd and his bloodstained grin as I can get.

WHAT I'M SEEING DOESN'T MAKE ANY SENSE.

I've just pulled into the parking lot of our apartment, car idling. I stare at my phone, trying to puzzle it out, but the synapses in my brain are not connecting. How did everyone find out about my message, my website? I sent the link and login info to one person and one person only, so how did anyone else get it?

Caylee. She must've shared the link, going so horrifically far as to make my website live before blasting it to everyone. It's the only thing that makes sense. But why? She has to know I wrote to her in confidence even if I didn't explicitly state it. The post was addressed to her alone, full of mortifyingly personal details, and she still made it public? Showed it to everyone?

I feel blindsided but so stupid at the same time, like of course I should've seen this coming. We're not friends anymore. She'd made that clear enough. But to give away the last shred of my privacy? It's a level of cruelty I wouldn't have believed from her, even given everything.

No matter how many times I refresh the page, it stays the same: 1 post, 43 comments. I scroll to the previous entry, the rough sketch I did of Thomas kissing me after his game, and the one before that of us at the Gorey exhibit, and all the rest, dating back to the beginning. But no matter which post I click on, it's the same. Piles of comments on posts that weren't meant to be seen. At least, not now. Not like this.

Yet now they've seen everything. And not only my message to Caylee about what they did to me at the party, but everything I've ever written. All my comics since the beginning. All of it. Every confession of love for Thomas. Every time I missed my dad and wished he missed me, too. Every single insecurity or worry—about living in a shitty apartment, about what Erica Strange would do. Everything. It's all there because who was going to see it? No one.

Had I known . . .

I can't even begin to go back far enough with that sentence.

I didn't read the comments from the pictures Tina posted, but these—on my website, about my art, about me—I can't look away from.

> "Ahaha! LMFAO Mermaid Gang. What are we, five?"

"Thomas would never go for a fat whore
like you."
"You wanted everything you got. And then
some."
"Clearly she just wants attention. So here
it is. Erica got laaaaaaaaaaid!"

But the one that cuts the deepest:

"Who wrote this, a kid whose puppy
got run over? Get over yourself. Or do
the world a favor and KILL YOURSELF
ALREADY."

They're all the comments I'd been prepared for this morning, only to arrive when I had no idea they were coming. I can't
figure out which one it is: Do people really have no idea what
they're saying, or do they truly take pleasure in hearing bones
snap, heartstrings pop?

What will it feel like to kill myself?

I already regret all the art I won't get to make, all the things I
won't draw, characters I'll never create. Maybe CalArts could've
made me happy, given me a place where no one knew my name
or had seen my naked body. But none of that matters now. I
won't be finding out.

Mostly I feel sad leaving Erica Strange behind. Which seems

weird, considering she's me. Well, the best version, anyway. The better version. The version I couldn't ever be.

I wonder what my mom will do with my drawings. Keep them up for a while or clear everything away? What will Valerie say, or Father Christoph? Will he even remember me? It's been ages since I've gone to Mass. At least he and Valerie can comfort Mom.

I drag myself up the stairs to our apartment, knowing Mom's home and I'm going to have to face her. But for once since Saturday, I don't feel panicked. Only a settling calm.

As soon as I open the door, Mom flies at me. "Erica? Where have you been? I've been trying to reach you for hours!" She's dressed in clean scrubs, hands thrown up—the same agitated wasp from yesterday morning. Except now someone's gone and whacked her nest a couple dozen times, that someone being me, apparently.

I shrug. "Driving."

"Why didn't you answer your phone? I've been worried sick! And why the hell is your principal calling me, saying you assaulted a classmate? And what does she mean some boys drew on you at a party this weekend or 'possibly worse'? Did something happen to you, Erica, that you haven't told me? I thought you were at Caylee's!"

I shrug. "Sorry, guess I lied."

"You *guess you lied*? Erica, you don't answer any of my calls even though I've been trying you for hours, and that's all you have to say? I had to call in sick to work because I didn't know where you were or if you were dead on the side of the freeway. I've been worried to death about you, so you're going to have to do a whole lot better than you 'guess you lied.' Start talking, young lady. Now."

"I don't know what to tell you, Mom. Maybe your perfect daughter isn't the precious little angel you thought she was." There's only a trace of fire in my voice as I push past her. I'm tired. So very tired.

"Erica, come back here. Please." Mom follows close behind, desperation replacing any anger. "Talk to me about this party. About this girl you punched. About these boys. Tell me what happened."

I turn, arms up in defeat. "Why? So I can relive it all yet again? No thanks."

Mom's entire irises are visible. "Please, honey, just tell me what's wrong."

"Everything." I move into the bathroom, shove the door shut though it doesn't close all the way, pull open the medicine cabinet, and dump several random pill bottles into my backpack. If nothing else, at least I have options.

Mom rushes in, hands raised to halt me. "Erica, please stop. Explain it to me. I'll listen."

"There's nothing left to say. You can't fix this. No one can." I push past her. At the entrance to my bedroom, she grabs my arm, but I wrench free, slamming the door in her face and locking it.

The knob rattles. "Erica? Erica Rose! Unlock this door right now!"

I drop my backpack on the bed and hurl my marble across the room. It hits my bookshelf, toppling the POP! Rapunzel figurine Caylee had held just yesterday, before clattering to the floor and rolling under the bed. Ripping open my backpack, I scoop out the pill bottles, empty each one onto the bed, then scour the floor for the weird-ass anatomy book I'd tossed there last night.

"Erica, please! Open this door! Won't you just talk to me? Please?"

It takes me twenty seconds to find the page I want, the one I'd spotted earlier nestled between those morbid illustrations but hadn't let myself read. I read it now, scrolling over the title—"Dialogue Between Frederik Ruysch and His Mummies"—to the poem below, captioned "Chorus of the dead in Ruysch's laboratory":

> *O death, thou one eternal thing,*
> *That takest all within thine arms,*
> *In thee, our coarser nature rests*
> *In peace, set free from life's alarms:*
> *Joyless and painless is our state.*
> *Our spirits now no more are torn*
> *By racking thought, or earthly fears;*
> *Hope and desire are now unknown.*

I skim the passage, lines I crave to hear springing up from the page, about vanishing earthly troubles and souls no longer vexed. At the end of the poem, the final stanza shines like an omen:

> *Our portion now is peaceful rest,*
> *Joyless, painless. We are not blest*
> *With happiness; that is forbid*
> *Both to the living and the dead.*

As Mom continues to pound on my door, I realize that this time, nothing about the book scares me, and maybe that's the scariest part. Because "peaceful rest" sounds like utter bliss.

THOMAS

WHEN I'D COME HOME EARLY FROM PRACTICE, MOM HAD made a big fuss about all the blood on my jersey (mostly Zac's) and the blood dried to my knuckles (mostly mine). I'd been sent upstairs to clean up with an ice pack for my hand and the unspoken understanding that Mom would call my father as soon as my feet hit the stairs.

Now I sit on the edge of my bed holding Eleanor, flexing my bruised hand. So much has gone wrong these past few days, but I'm unable to shake the feeling that something else is about to happen. Something worse than my father finding out about Boyd's face.

Running my fingers down Eleanor's struts, I ignore the ache of my raw knuckles, but no words, no chords come to me. Before, even thinking about my fingers on Eleanor's strings, her soft weight in my hands, always made me push down on my truck's accelerator a little harder to get home. But today, holding her in my hands, I can't find the enthusiasm.

Heart sinking, I think back to yesterday's audition, how I'd completely lost myself in the music, and the text Uncle Kurt had sent later on: So proud of you, kid!

I got in. I'm going to Thornton, I remind myself for the millionth time. I should be ecstatic, but every time I think about it, the ray of light that is music school dims a little more. Still, I've waited so long for this. I *need* Thornton, maybe now more than ever.

There's a knock at my door, and Mom comes in, looking apologetic as she holds out her phone to me. This can only mean one thing: It's my father. Mom leaves as I lift the phone to my ear, dread growing. "Yeah?"

"Do you want to explain why I just got a call from Coach MacDonald and your mother, telling me you got in a fight at practice?" my father barks.

"Zac's a dick."

"I don't give a damn if Zac's a dick. I want to know why the hell you are fighting on school grounds and walking away from your coach. Are you trying to make me look bad?"

"Make you look bad? Not everything is about you, Dad."

The line goes deadly quiet. When he starts up again, his voice is scary calm. "Let me make something very clear to you because I'm only going to say this once. If you have any hope on earth of going to that fluffy music school of yours—and that is a *serious* maybe at this point—then you will call Coach MacDonald back and you will apologize to him, to Zac, to the team for whatever you've done because you're lucky as hell I was able to convince Coach MacDonald not to report the fight. So, you will fix this, and you will fix this now. And if you put so much as one more toe out of line, you will regret it for the rest of your miserable life. Do you understand me?"

"Yes."

"Yes, what?"

"Yes, sir."

"You're damn right, yes, sir. Now fix this."

The phone goes dead. I chuck it to the floor, teeth clenched.

But I can't fix this. I can't. Everything's so fucked-up. And I've lost her. . . .

Inspiration striking, I lift Eleanor, plugging her into the amp and dialing the volume low.

My fingers fly. It'd taken me weeks to write that one song for Erica, but now new words pull themselves from the air like magic. Now that everything's already gone.

It's a song about an electric green-eyed girl in a cape and mask, with lyrics about boots flung under a couch, spilled orange juice and broken glass, unsent texts and a snapped olive branch.

All at once, the final lines pull from my throat:

> *"I'm sorry" hangs heavy from closed lips*
> *A broken ellipsis after a kiss*

Choking, choking, on words unspoken
Just a man drowning in lies

I lay Eleanor, still vibrating, across my lap. She means everything to me.

Like Erica did.

Did. It's like she's dead.

And I'd just walked out of Zac's room and left her there.
And finding her Sunday morning, lying on her side . . . the
memory will haunt me forever:

Right before dawn, I wake, drenched in sweat. Flailing in the
dark, I sit up, staring at a broken coffee table. Forest snores on
the floor next to me, Stallion beside him. Ricky's on the couch
above us, half his body falling off. Blinking several times, I
realize I'm in Zac's living room, feeling like I drank rat poison.
I had no idea someone could feel this shitty.

Lying back down, I force my brain to think. Last night, we
were outside by the bonfire. Then Erica and I . . .

I bolt upright. The world spins, but I force myself to stand.
Was that . . . ? Did it actually . . . ? But I already know the
answer.

My feet are bricks as I trip over Forest. Mounting the stairs,
I stare ahead at Zac's closed door. It squeaks as I push it open.
I hold my breath, then peer in.

Oh god.

Erica's curled up on her side in the middle of the bed.

She's naked.

Black Sharpie covers every inch of her skin. And there it is—my name on her back—but that's not the half of it. Ricky's name, Forest's. Shitty words, drawings, all over her.

Where are her clothes?

Up close, she looks so small, like a little kid pulled into herself who'd played with markers and fallen asleep before her bath.

The night before I'd been so furious, but this?

What did they do?

What did I *do?*

I feel lost. About to cry, sink to my knees, punch a wall. I search around for something, anything, I can do to make it better.

There. A tiny gray pile on top of scattered cards. Pink hearts with lace. Her underwear.

I pick them up, move closer to her. But I'm frozen. I can't do anything but stare at her legs tucked underneath her, arms pulled into her chest, the words that cover her, the names—my name—on her back.

Erase it! my head screams.

But there's no way to wipe Sharpie off. There's nothing I can do. I can't take it back.

I blink hard, sliding the underwear up her legs. Even though she's on her side, I try to avert my eyes from the space between her legs. But Stallion's name, Zac's, catch my eye.

Fuck. Fuck fuck fuck!

Searching for her skirt, her bra, I find only her tank top. Pulling it over her head, I loop her arms through. It's slow going, she's so curled into herself. And I can't look at her—her body or scribbled-on boobs. *If she wakes up, finds me here . . .*

I pull the sheets to her chin. With the words covered, for half a second, I trick myself into believing that it didn't happen. That it couldn't have happened. But then Erica shifts, exposing her forearm and Ricky's name.

God, when she wakes up . . .

I trip over a backpack as I sneak out, closing the door softly behind me.

What the hell did you do, Thomas? my mind roars. *What were you thinking?*

But there are no answers.

There can never be answers for what happened that night.

My fingers squeeze Eleanor's neck as the memory crumbles. I knew even then that everything had changed. Because with some things, there's no coming back.

I can't fix this. There's nothing I can do. Everything's fucked-up. Everything. I've lost her. I *betrayed* her. And there's no coming back.

I swing with everything I have. Eleanor hits the edge of the bed with a bang. Her amp screeches in protest, nearly bursting my eardrums. She drives dent after dent into the wooden bedpost, but I don't stop swinging. Not until the strings have popped, one pinging loose and stinging my face. Not until the cord has ripped free and the amp goes quiet. Not until Eleanor is little more in my hand than a neck of snapped strings and bashed-in base.

No words. There are no words. There can never be words to fix this.

The stinging brings me back, first my cheek, then my fingers. I wipe at my face. Blood.

"Tommy?" Mom's voice, distant and worried.

Cuts zigzag the fingers gripping Eleanor. I peel the top string from where it's sliced into my middle finger—High E, the thinnest string. Eyes burning, my hand cups around the pooling blood.

No words.

What did I do? I see Erica's face, streaming with tears as she hurries away from me. Scared of me. Scared. Of *me*. Just like my father, like Zac. I'm no better than them. I'm worse.

She *trusted* me.

Eleanor drops to the floor. *What did I do, what did I do?*

The door swings open. Mom's hand flies to her mouth as she takes in Eleanor, the bed, my bloody cheek and hand. "Tommy! What happened?" She grips my forearm. "Are you all right?"

I'm fine, I want to tell her. Another lie. Everything I say is infected with lies. My hand drips, and I wrap it in the front of my shirt. I've made a big enough mess.

"It's fine," I manage. But my voice is wrong, high and stran-gled.

What have I done?

No words.

Brushing off Mom's hand, I make for the bathroom, step-ping over what's left of Eleanor as I go.

ERICA

I used to play thiss game with myself where I pretended I'd die tomorrow an today was my last day to live. It sounds a little morbid, given how things have turned out,but I didn't mean it like that. Not back then. The whole point was to inspire myself to live for the moment! Is't that what everyone says these days: You only live once?

But sometimes once is one ttoo many times.

Here's what I'd do, especially if I were nervous about something. I'd tell myself that it didn't matter,, that I would be dead tomorrow of [insert sudden, inexplicable tragedy here!], so whatever I did, I better make it fun DAMMIT because I only had one day left to live! And it worked. For a while anyway. I'd head out, confidence blazzing, until life got in the waay.

Sorry if I'm a little off right now. Blame it on the vodka, baby!!! There's nothing like it. Mix with Redbull and it's like drinking Skittles. Instant liquid confidence. Taste the freakin' rainbow. Only I've Never combined my liquid confidence with pills beforee.

Turns out when your mom's a nurse, pills aren't toohard to come by. Medicine cabinet's full of them. Aspirin, sleep aids, old prescriptions of vicoden from when I tore tendons in my ankle. I had my pick of the litter; 56 blue sleepers, a whole bottle of orangey-brown aspirin (149 to be exxact), and 20 white to kep the pain at bay— because WHY THE FUCK NOT?—guzzled away by clear fire liquid that burned the wholeway down. I ran out of Redbull by the end. Mom thinks sugar will kill you. Ha.

"FOr in that sleep of death what dreams maycome…. Shrugging offf this mortal coil."

Or somesuch bullshit shakespeere. I could never get those stupid quotes right.

Speakin of stupid, Erica Strange is in thhe trash now. like I couldve ever been her anyway. I tried but it Doesn't matter—she's gone. Know why I wrote her in the first place Erica Strange—the first time? Because s mean ol man followed me aroun a store once and scared me half to death, See? I thought thos where the guys to stay away from. Ones who scared little girls in stores. I thought she'd help me be tough, But shes gone now. Erica Strange.

Well, I guess I'll leaves you with that. Starting to get a lil sleepy. Mom if you see this post I'm sorry I lied, couldn't say goodbye. Wish I could ave been the dauughter you though I was. The good girl who allways did as she was told. Aorry for follwing Grmpa Joe. But it's better this way. WIthout me.

Sorry Dad. I'm sorry. The boots weere great

Goodbye said the slut on her way to lie down..

But here I am, still typing. Still tappin away at the keys only to here them clic. I could do it forevr. At least my screwed up version of forever limited as is now. But no I want t be lying on my bed in internal repose. Internal inside? Eternal yes. Eternal repose. Not slumped over like som drunkard. Like wheen it happen.

Call me dramatic, but here goes: You chisel me with your names laughter photos (Thanks for that Tina. HOpe your mouth feels better, yoou bitch) You all took something from me I can't never get back. And what's worse—you don't evn care. Right Cay mermaid? You were my best frien and still you choose Zac. Hope it was worth it. He's He's an animal but in your hearts of hearts you already know that.

Not even you Thomas the Rhymer.

God, I liked you so much. Thought you we different. A good person. even. How completely stupid of me. But there's no time to dwelll on such things. Not anmore.

I read in National Geographi once that some cultures don't let yo take photos of them. THey think a photo will captures their soul and steal it away.

They were right my soul was ripped form my body alongside my cloths. On little wings it flew away. But will this reunite us, my sooul an me, or will it mean were are forever seprated?

Unknown. Unknowable. Goobye.

Head swirling, I push back from the desk and lie on my bed. My thoughts are a torrent of rushing noise and wind. Prisms of color pop before my eyes. Burst, shimmer, swirl.

And then the roaring falls away. Ears mute. Silence. Heart slows. Calm.

Only a kaleidoscope: neon stars of morphing shapes and too-bright colors. A frantic carousel, spinning and spinning and spinning so fast, like my marble.

My marble. Cold, smooth. Obsidian. A galaxy of stars. I almost forgot. I *need* it. To hold. Its weight in my hand.

Too far away?

I stumble, flop. Hands, knees, crawl to backpack.

Zippers. Too many. Which?

Small.

Sliding. Fumbling. Grasping.

Nothing.

A realization.

Not there.

A realization.

Dropped it.

A realization.

Death.

Realization.

My death.

Now?

Scared.

Scared.

SCARED.

Not ready?

Black clouds gathering.

Smothering.

Not ready.

Choking.

Scared.

Rising.

Not ready.

Not Ready!

Hurting.

Can't breathe.

NOT READY!

"Mom!"

Aloud?

NotReady.NotReady.

Hurting.

Can't breathe.

Scared.

The door.

Try?

NotReady. NotReady.

Hurt.

Locked.

Breathe.

Can't!

Dark.

NotReady.NotReady.NotReady.

HURT.

BREATHE. CAN'T.

DARK.

NotReady.NotReady.NotReady.NotReady.NotReady.
NotReady.NotReady.NotReady.NotReady.NotReady.
NotReady.NotReady.NotReady.NotReady.NotReady.
NotReady.NotReady.NotReady.NotReady.NotReady.
NotReady.NotReady.NotReady.NotReady.Not
F
  a
    l
      l
        i
    n
  g
  .
    .
      .
F
  a
    l
      l
        i
    n
  g
  .
    .
      .
    .

PART THREE

TUESDAY

THOMAS

I'M IN SPANISH CLASS WHEN THEY COME FOR ME.

I've been staring at Erica's empty desk, feeling caught between disappointment and relief. Mostly relief. Everyone's saying she got suspended for punching Tina. But who could blame her for snapping? Everyone has been an absolute prick to her.

Me especially. God, the look on her face as I tore into her yesterday. The image won't stop haunting me.

At the front of the classroom, Señora Roberts discusses our homework, but even if I cared, I forgot something to write with. Last week I would've welcomed the excuse to talk to Erica and ask to borrow a pen. She would've said, "What'll you give me?" or "It'll cost you, Thomas the Rhymer." Because Spanish used to be so much fun, us tossing each other notes behind Señora's back. Erica'd fold them into these complicated origami creatures, and I'd have to guess what animal it was, plus unfold the note without ripping it. But I could never get the note back to its original shape so I'd either fold it at random or wad it up. Normally the latter. She'd raise her eyebrows at the paper wads and whisper, "Lemme guess. Another lacrosse ball?" To which I'd reply, "What are you trying to say? It's a baseball. Can't you tell?"

But today I can barely bring myself to look at her desk—it's never been empty before—or the crack in the plastic chair that always catches her hair, or the "ES" star logo she scribbled in the top corner. I press my feet against the metal legs trying to push Erica from my mind, but the whole desk slides forward, ramming into Victoria's back. She swivels around, a question on her face.

Sorry, I mouth, straightening as I do, wincing with how much my body hurts all over. I can only hope Zac's as sore as I am today.

It's fine, Victoria mouths back with a small smile as she turns around.

Sorry. What I couldn't say to Erica yesterday. Not that anything I could've said would've changed much. Or maybe it would have. I don't know.

Ricky shifts in his desk behind me, and I wonder if he's thinking about Erica too, or yesterday's practice, or maybe his phone that, with any luck, I wrecked. I haven't said a word to him since lunch yesterday, or anyone else for that matter, which is fine by me. I did hear rumors about Jasmine breaking up with Stallion last night, which is crazy because they've been together since eighth grade, and apparently it got pretty ugly. But that's all I've heard, and maybe that's a good thing.

What's going through her mind right now? Does she hate me?

God, my body hurts.

Red and blue strobes flash through the open windows from the direction of the parking lot, blazing across the walls and whiteboard. Señora Roberts's dry erase pen halts mid-word. Everyone who's ever seen a crime show knows what those lights mean. Someone's in trouble. But police at Bay City Prep? It's gotta be a first. We all crane our necks for a better look.

A radio crackles through the parking lot. Two doors slam in unison. I wipe my palms on my jeans as the strobes keep flashing. This couldn't be about my fight with Zac, could it? Or Erica's fight with Tina?

Who am I kidding? The cops wouldn't show up over a few punches thrown yesterday. This has to be . . . bigger than that.

I swallow hard and glance back at Ricky. He shrugs, though his whole body's tensed.

The class erupts into whispers, but for once Señora doesn't use her annoying trill to quiet the room. Even she's craning to see. And even though Señora has a cellphone jail where she locks up any phone used during class, I reach into my backpack to pull mine out. Chances are good someone's got an explanation. Then I remember it's on my bedroom floor, crushed.

Several people stand, and Señora moves over to the window just as I'm pulling my Band-Aid-covered fingers from the front pocket of my backpack.

The classroom door flies open. Principal Renall strides in and over to Señora. They hold a hushed conversation before Señora points in my direction. I freeze as a sea of faces turns on me. "Thomas VanBrackel. Richard Demoine." Principal Renall beckons Ricky and me forward. "Boys, accompany me to the office."

I stumble out of my desk. Ricky follows. He's always been good at following.

"Grab your things," Renall adds.

Heat sears the back of my neck as I scramble for my backpack. Every eye drills into us. The rumor mill's about to explode. I shouldn't care, but I do.

It's happening.

Renall leads us down the hall toward her office.

Panic hammers in my chest with every step. This definitely isn't about my fight with Zac. They called Ricky in too.

Ricky walks beside me, head bent. He whispers, "Is this because of her? 'Cause that was just a joke."

Her—Erica.

Renall throws a glance over her shoulder. "No talking, boys." She leaves Ricky in her office with a somber-faced secretary before marching me into a small conference room.

Two police officers sit at the table. Both rise as I enter.

Renall takes her seat at the head of the table, gesturing for me to sit across from the cops. She introduces them as Officer Rodriguez and Officer Shiva.

The female cop, Rodriguez, holds a file of papers—*Papers about me?*—and studies my face. The male cop, Shiva, is well built and knows it. He leans forward on massive forearms. Renall explains that the cops want to ask me questions once my father arrives.

We sit in awkward silence. Thoughts bombard me:

What do they want?

She's not at school. . . .

A coincidence. Has to be.

But why isn't she at school? Did she call them—the cops?

What do they want?

And the scariest question of all: *Where the hell is Erica?*

ERICA

i'm floating
cool waves lap at my skin threads of silk tendrils
    run through my veins
           muscles
           organs
i drift
    settling onto the
        surface of the water

                    how strange
it cushions me smooth and buoyant i will not drown peace
finally at peace the clouds
   above my head
   look spongy if i could only reach up but no something
            tugs at my elbow like an
      anchor

my arm feels so heavy so heavy pulled to the bottom
of the lake
> by an invisible rope hooked

into the
crook of my elbow
> but i want

> > to move

it's silent here
> just a tiny cicada screeching

eeeeeeeeeeee

> > through thick

> cotton in my ears i
want to hear the water the cool
lapping waves that ebb and flow through
me i reach my other hand not the anchor hand to my ears
but again the
> tug this time from the tip of my finger anchoring my
movement stuck what if i tip over pulled down cant
break free from my weights now the lake is marbles count-
less obsidians press around me sink suffocate drown me i try to
scream but marbles fill my mouth no a snake slithered down
my throat i choke
will die out here a prisoner in this lake of dead calm heavy
spheres and no one will hear me
die

i start to twist rolling left then right pull my arms from my side writhing and i feel the anchor on my finger slip slip away and then the tiny animals i didn't know were there chattering but then the one pinning my elbow cuts into my flesh with its beak tearing a hole i cry out but don't hear the sound the snake blocks my throat and then there is

movement on the lake surface creatures wading their ripples run through my veins and then the liquid splashing over me in me so cold hurts running running through me and i am

lost

    sinking into obsidian

    darkness

again

THOMAS

THE CONFERENCE ROOM DOOR BURSTS OPEN AND MY FATHER surges in, all crisp suit and legal briefcase. "You haven't answered any questions, have you?" he barks at me.

I shake my head no. For the first time in years, my father's presence brings relief. That is, until Principal Renall has made the introductions and my father's settled next to me. In a voice low enough that only I hear he hisses, "Jesus, son. What the hell have you gotten yourself into?" Then, all pretend casual, he asks the officers, "So what's this about?" But I know my father. Can practically see the snake coiled inside him, ready to strike.

Twirling her pencil, Officer Rodriguez answers, "That's what we're here to find out. With your permission, Mr. VanBrackel, we're going to ask Thomas a few questions."

My father throws out a hand, dismissive. "Be my guest." He'll play nice. For now.

Officer Rodriguez addresses me directly. "Thomas, do you know a young woman by the name of Erica Walker?"

This is about Erica. *You knew it was.*

My father looks at me, eyes betraying nothing, then nods his head once. *Answer.*

For the millionth time, I wish I could take it all back—my petty, drunk anger from Saturday, cram it into a jar, and hurl it off a cliff. I hadn't really been mad at her that night. Not really. But it's too late to take any of it back. And if I think about her, talk about her . . .

I'm sunk—we're all sunk—for what we did to her.

The clock on the wall ticks loudly, so loudly it echoes through the small room, through my brain. I can't think.

Get it together.

"Thomas?" Officer Rodriguez prompts. Officer Shiva's pen hovers over his notepad.

Focus, Thomas. Because I don't have a choice. Because I have to answer their questions or I'll look guilty, and guilt is what drags you under.

I clear my throat and lean forward, hoping to appear calm, not cocky. "Uh, sure. Erica. Yeah, I don't really know her that well . . ."

Lie.

". . . We hardly ever talked . . ."

Lie.

"Let's start small, then," Officer Rodriguez suggests. "How do you know Erica?"

A nod from my father.

"She, uh . . . We have Spanish class together."

"And have you ever spoken with Erica? Had any conversations in or outside of class?"

Another nod from my father.

"Yes."

"How often would you say you've had contact with Erica?"

Contact? "Uh, do you mean how often I talk to her?"

"Correct."

"Um, a handful of times. But not . . ." I trail off.

"But not what, Thomas?"

But not since yesterday, when I yelled at her outside. "Uh, nothing. I didn't mean to say that."

My father leans forward, ready to pounce on my next slipup.

"And how would you describe your relationship with Erica?"

"Um, friendly enough. Like I said, I don't really know her that well. She only moved here a few months back—"

My father cuts in. "Answer the questions directly. Nothing more."

Officer Rodriguez fixes him with a sharp look before turning back to me. "When was the last time you saw Erica?"

"Uh, yesterday?"

"And did you speak with her?"

"No. No, I didn't."

Lie.

"Did you see Erica the night of Saturday, March 11?"

Letters and numbers collide in my head.

My father's eyes tear into me.

"Um, when?"

"This past Saturday. What were you doing Saturday night?"

The party. They know about the party.

What did Erica tell them?

"I was, uh, at a party. At Boyd's . . . Zac Boyd's." *Erica, standing in the driveway. Short jean skirt. Lucky boots.* "Him and I are captains for the lacrosse team. We had a game, then went to his place afterward."

Keep it short, Thomas.

Officer Rodriguez looks me over. I wipe my sweaty forehead, unclench both fists. "And was Erica at this party?" she asks.

The bonfire. My hat on her head. Body pressed into my back as I carried her. "Maybe. Pretty sure. Yeah."

"Where is this leading?" my father snaps.

Outside, a raised voice carries into the conference room. "Is anyone going to tell me what the hell's going on?" It's Boyd. Which means someone must've dragged all the guys—Stallion and Forest, too—into the office to wait with Ricky.

"You were saying?" Officer Rodriguez presses.

I swallow. "It was a normal enough party. Broke up around one. Everyone went home."

Lies. All of it.

Officer Rodriguez's frown screams disbelief. *She knows.* "Thomas, are you aware Erica had a website?"

My oxygen shuts off.

"No more questions," my father barks.

"Are you aware your name showed up on that website a total of"—eyes scan notes—"sixty-seven times?"

My father throws back his chair, rising. "Son, don't answer that. He's not answering any more questions."

What did Erica say about me?

"Her mother found her last night, Thomas. She wasn't responsive."

Her words slam into my chest with the force of a linebacker, crushing all breath from my lungs. The room blurs.

Not responsive.

I'm going to be sick.

"Do the right thing, Thomas. Tell us what really happened Saturday night."

"Thomas, don't you dare open your mouth!" My father's words barely register over the earsplitting shriek in my head.

Not responsive.

Chairs squeak against the floor. Someone grabs my elbow, yanking me to my feet. "I'll have your badge for this."

Erica.

Found last night.

Not responsive.

Because of me.

"Is she dead?" I ask, but too quietly.

My father drags me from the room as the officer calls out,

"Your deposition is scheduled for Thursday morning, Thomas. Two days from now. Be ready to tell the truth then."

"Is she dead?" Louder this time, but the door is already closing.

My father leads me to his BMW, his grip like iron on my arm. Only once we're seated inside does he speak, rage lacing every word. "We're going straight home. Straight home, you hear me? And when we get there, you are going directly to your room while I make phone calls to figure out how bad this is. When I can stand to look at you, you are going to tell me every last detail. Every last detail. You hear me?"

I nod, wiping tears from my chin.

My father shakes his head, backing his car from the lot. "You fucked up big-time, Thomas. You really did."

ERICA

A SHARP PINCH PULLS ME FROM THE FOG.

A bug, biting, scuttling across my eyelids. I blink.

Too bright. I don't want to. Too hard.

But the bugs—they're everywhere—crawling all over me, millions of microscopic legs tickling, deafening high-pitched cry.

I twitch, jerk, scratching at the beetles stuck to my chest. Stuck.

Hundreds. Scampering, scuttling over me.

Everywhere. They're everywhere.

I scream, but they've crawled down my throat with the snake. I choke.

I scratch at them, but their clicking pinchers grow louder, more frantic. Hungry mouths sink in and drink my blood. A green hornet is at my elbow, stinger pumping poisonous venom into my veins.

I thrash my legs but can't break free. I thrash again. A lightning bolt of pain explodes between my legs, freezing me.

My eyes fly open in time to see large creatures zoom nearby, but the white-hot sun blinds me. Then I see.

Not outside: A dingy room.

Around me, not creatures: people in white, green, maroon rushing toward me.

Up, not the sun: too-bright bulbs blocked by heads crowding in.

In my mouth, not a snake: a wide tube out my throat, around the bed, joining a small machine on wheels.

Down, not bugs: smaller tubes, in and out of blankets, entering my elbow where a dark bruise has formed like an ink blot.

Like the words they wrote on me.

I know where I am.

Hospital. Because of the pills. Because of the words.

Mom's voice registers seconds before her face bursts into focus. Exhaustion pools under her eyes, hair a collapsing wasp's nest.

"Erica!"

It's her voice, but far away, past the lake of marbles, the shrill shriek of the bugs.

"No more, please! . . . Slept so much already!" says the muffled voice—Mom's voice—mountains and valleys and rivers away.

But it's too late. I'm falling backward, into the water. The cool spheres roll through me, and I'm sinking again, floating . . .

THOMAS

I HAVEN'T LEFT MY ROOM SINCE MY FATHER DROVE ME home.

At first, I kept my door open to see if I could catch any news of Erica. Then Mom fell into hysterics when my father sat her down in the living room, so I shut it.

But now the urge to pee takes over, and I force myself out of bed.

I'm halfway down the hall when a throat clears: my father, hand gripping the banister at the base of the stairs. "Thomas, come down. We have things we need to discuss."

I follow him to his office.

"Close the door," he says.

I don't know what's worse—the way he's looking at me, or having to step inside this prison cell of a room with him and shut myself in.

I've never liked his office, full of dark wood and shelves loaded with heavy books and a giant desk taking up most of the space. His office at work looks exactly the same. I close the door behind me, all the fresh air going with it.

When I was a little kid, I'd sit outside his door, playing on the floor with my action figures or LEGOs, and wait for him to come out. Even several years ago, I would've given anything for him to have invited me into his office for a little father-son chat, but not now. Especially not now.

My father strides around his office, pulling legal texts from shelves and manila files from drawers. "The girl's alive."

I stagger, drop to the edge of a stiff chair, not realizing until now exactly how much I needed to hear those words. *But is she okay?* I can't find the oxygen to ask.

"You lucked out big-time," my father continues, "or we'd be looking at a possible wrongful death suit on top of everything else. So, now the real work begins. I've called together a meeting with all the parents for tomorrow morning. We've got to put together a plan of action for Thursday's deposition. Nip this thing in the bud right now. I also called in a favor to get a copy of the online diary, or whatever this girl wrote, by the day's end, since they took it down. Then we're going to go through it all, dissect every word, and I'll need you to tell me your side. Everything, and I mean everything. I need to know how you met this girl, who her friends are, what her family's like, what kind of car she drives. Absolutely everything, you understand?" He waits for my nod. "Look at me," he barks.

We lock eyes. The hatred in his expression makes the hair on my arms stand on end. "What the hell were you thinking." It's not a question. He holds my gaze for an eternity until I look away. Then, with a sharp shake of his head he's back in controlled-lawyer mode. "You need to focus, Thomas. Think hard on anything we can use against her . . ."

Use against her?

". . . and call her character into question. Because two days from now, we're going to need it. If that lying little bitch wants to go after you," he continues, "then she doesn't know what's coming."

He's rifling through his desk, not looking at me, which is the only way I find the courage to say, "She's not a bitch." It comes out a whisper. I regret it immediately.

"What's that?"

"She's not a bitch." I say it just loud enough to be heard over the sound of slamming desk drawers. "I'm not using anything against her."

Only then does he glance in my direction. "Don't be an idiot, boy. This girl is accusing you of sexual assault. Do you know how much trouble you're in right now? What this bitch could do to your future, to my reputation?" He throws another file onto his towering pile. "So, you're going to cooperate and you're going to cooperate fully. I tell you to jump, you jump. I tell you to crawl, you crawl. I tell you to tell the police on

Thursday that this girl is a conniving little liar, and you say exactly that."

I hadn't realized I'd been clenching my fists until I think about using one on his face. I know without having read whatever she wrote about me that it's true. All of it. Because what could be worse than the truth?

"And what if I don't?" I'm ashamed at how quiet my voice is, though my father's expression tells me he's heard me loud and clear.

He cocks his head to the side and sets the files down. In one quick movement, he's around his desk and advancing on me, all taut muscle under his suit jacket.

I rise quickly to my feet, closed fist raising with each of his steps until a pathetic, Band-Aid-covered hand is all that stands between us. With his face six inches from mine, he seems possessed.

Part of me thinks about my raised fist, mostly ineffective this close up. Another part realizes that this is the first time my father's seen me in a long time, *really* seen me, and that we're the same height. But I know him well enough to realize that everything from how close he's standing to his broad shoulders and icy gaze are all constructed weapons of intimidation. Still, the last part of me recognizes that these weapons are working. I can smell his aftershave, his brute strength. His mouth is set in a hard line, but there's satisfaction creeping into his eyes. Victory.

Before he even says a word, I know I've already lost.

He takes his time, each word breaking with sarcasm. "How noble of you to stand up for her . . . *now*. So, tell me, son," he growls in a voice already confident of the answer, "if you respected this girl so very much, then why the hell would you and your buddies strip her naked and mark your territory? Or so I hear from your principal."

A seam tears open in me and all my hot anger gushes out. I'm deflated, knees weak with the truth.

But my father's not done yet. He has me at his mercy, and he's going to savor this moment. "If you want to hate some-one," he says, "hate yourself, boy. You're the one who got your-self into this mess."

ERICA

I THOUGHT I KNEW WHAT PAIN WAS, AND THEN THE SNAKE is wrenched from my throat, and I gag, gag, gag.

Numbers drip from the clock as I drag myself from the lake, my skin writhing in acid. It's a hurt beyond words.

Words. How can you describe pain when all you have are words? Brittle, charred bones. Veins alight. Fingers and toes popping like embers. Guts, throat, skull submerged in lava. And inside, maggots eating away at brain tissue, the crunch of their greedy mouths like tiny crackles of an old-fashioned radio—the only sound I hear aside from the ringing, ringing, ringing.

But none of it truly describes the pain—fiery sparks of singeing coals. Every part of me HURTS.

This is no hangover. This is every pain I've ever felt—every jolt, slash, tear, break—all combined into one terrible agony.

My eyes fly open.

What have I done?

THOMAS

MY FATHER SCHEDULED THE MEETING WITH EVERYONE'S
parents for tomorrow morning, so I don't have much time.

After I hear my father's car pull away, I slip downstairs to use
his office phone, looking up Forest's number on the lacrosse
roster. The police confiscated mine, even though it was demol-
ished.

"Hello?" It's Forest's mom, exactly what I was afraid of.

"Hey, Mrs. Stevens. Is Forest there?"

There's a long pause. All I can hear is a dog barking in the
background. "Thomas?"

"Yeah."

"I don't think it's a good idea for you to be calling."

"Oh, well, I was hoping that—"

"Forest can't talk right now." The line goes dead.

I hold the phone in my hand—I have to talk to Forest before
tomorrow, before everyone's watching us. I need to see if he's

heard anything else and ask what he told the police, what he plans to do.

Hanging up the phone, I make a decision. I slip into the garage and wheel my old bike out the side door, then pedal hard. It's risky enough that I'm sneaking out, and if Mom heard my truck start up, I'd be in deep shit.

By the time I get to Forest's house, I'm puffing hard but am fueled by the exertion. For a second, I'd forgotten why I've made the familiar trek to Forest's. Tossing my bike next to the neighbor's trash cans, I make my way around the side of the house, avoiding the front door. Lady greets me at the back gate, pressing her wet nose into my crotch. "Hey, girl." I pet her golden fur. "Where's Forest?"

She follows me, tail wagging as I move around back, circle the hot tub, and step into the planters. I peer through Forest's window, but his room's dark.

Lady yips.

I shush her then peek into the living room. The TV blares. Forest sits watching from the couch, leaning on his fist, a plate of sandwich crusts beside him. I'm about to tap on the glass when Mrs. Stevens enters the room. I duck, making Lady yip again. "Shh!"

I only hear pieces of what they're saying over the TV, but it's enough to tell me Forest's dad is on his way home from some sort of retreat and not happy about it.

The minutes tick by as I crouch in the flower bed, muddy

sprinkler water soaking into my Chucks. Mom'll notice I'm gone soon if my father doesn't get home first, so I've gotta get back. When I risk another glance, Mrs. Stevens has disappeared. Through the doorway leading into the kitchen, I spot Forest's little sister, Elle, bent over a textbook at the table, headphones on and legs swinging.

Holding my breath, I tap on the window, but Forest doesn't budge. I rap too hard and make him jump. Sandwich plate and crusts go flying. When he sees it's me, he glances around, but his sister hasn't noticed, and his mother must be busy because he nods toward his room. I nearly trip over Lady as I follow him.

When Forest slides open his window, even through the mesh screen I can see how wrecked he looks. Still, his voice sounds the same as he whispers, "Tommy, my man. How goes it?" He glances down, and I pull my bandaged hand from the window ledge, leaving behind a trail of dragged fingerprints in the dust. *How burglars get caught.*

"Things have been better," I say. "You?"

He nods to himself. "Things have been better. Things have definitely been better. On house arrest. How'd you find freedom?"

"I snuck out." He nods like any of this is normal as I continue. "Listen, Forest, do you know how Erica's doing? She okay?" My voice pitches, and I clear my throat.

"No idea, man."

"Do you, like, know what happened last night?"

"Her blog thing? Naw, man. Only what I heard from people this morning. Before the cops came."

"What'd you hear?"

"That she took a bunch of pills, Tommy. Tried to do herself in. She left a note online, too, saying stuff about us, I guess, but I haven't read it. Can't now that they took it down. Took my phone, too. And laptop. And now Mom's barred me from fresh air for life."

"Same. I only wish I knew, you know? How she is?"

He leans out the window, and Lady starts to whimper, wanting his attention. "Well, she was definitely acting crazy yesterday, my man. Guessing she's pretty shitty today."

I stare at a dead fly trapped behind the screen, legs up, a wing broken off. Erica's face replays in my head from yesterday when I told her to never talk to me again, every muscle falling slack.

I let his words sink in, then blurt out, "What are you gonna tell the cops on Thursday?"

Forest shakes his head. "I dunno, man. A lot's riding on this, you know? Like, our entire fucking futures for one. It was one thing to act all self-righteous when the cops weren't involved, but now? Stakes are high, Tommy. Sky-high."

"But, Forest, do you think we did this? Like, are we responsible for her trying to kill herself?"

He drops his gaze, once again looking like the wilted shark

from Zac's kitchen who's trying to hold his puke in. "I mean, I doubt it. People say she had some real problems."

"Yeah, but, like—"

"Listen, man," he cuts in. "Sure, we wrote on her. People teased her. But we didn't make her take any pills or shit. And I had the same thing happen to me last year, remember? Went around for a week with a hairy dick drawn on my face."

A long silence stretches between us.

"Yeah. Sure," I finally mutter. But the look we share says it all—that what we did to Erica is nothing like what happened to Forest, and we both know it.

"Forest?" Elle calls from somewhere inside.

"Man, I gotta go." The window slams in my face, the blast of air pushing the dead fly from sight as Forest scrambles from his room.

Giving Lady a final pet on the head, I turn to leave with even fewer answers than I had before.

ERICA

A HOSPITAL ROOM. CRISP WHITE SHEETS COVER MY LEGS. Stomach sears with pain. Limbs full of lead. Something tugs at my inner elbow. I look to find an IV entering at the crook— Ricky was here. Ice fluid fills my veins. Fresh bandages cover my cut hand. Tubes and wires crisscross me, attached to machines on either side. The heart monitor to my left records spiky green mountains. *Isn't it supposed to beep?* I can't hear it past the shriek of the bugs. . . .

But there are no bugs.

Something's wrong.

The hospital I see, but something else. My brain's trying to tell me, though I can't understand. Nausea pounds in my stomach. Throat, raw like a scraped knee.

I drag shaky fingers over the hospital gown, heart monitors stuck to my chest. I move to sit up, but my head spins, and a sharp pressure between my legs stops me. Working around wires and tubes, I pull down the fitted sheets. A thicker tube runs between my thighs—**Stallion! / Zac B. BITCHES!**

What are they doing to me? I can't take it—any of it—the tubes and wires and sheets chaining me to the bed, keeping me here, dragging me down into the lake.

I start to twist, pull. Movement catches my attention. Mom's friend Valerie, dressed in green nurse scrubs and with a haphazard ponytail, rises from a chair, watching me intently. She rushes forward and takes my hand.

There it is again—that Something Wrong. Her mouth moves, but no sound reaches me. Valerie, spirally curls the color of ravens, is an actress in a silent film, animated but mute. Trying not to pull on my IV, I jab at my ears. Nothing happens. I can't stop the screechy whine.

I fight the fog in my mind even as waves of nausea hit and a strange thought wraps itself around me. The marbles from my nightmares were actually real. And they got into my ears, blocking all outside sound. The bugs are in there too, making that shrill sound in my brain.

I shake my head to clear it. Because the marbles, bugs, lake—they *weren't* real.

Valerie leans in, face scrunched in concern. She moves her lips again, and this time a thick, muffled something penetrates the sound barrier. It's a blob of words I can't make out, but it's the first sound I've heard since waking.

What's going on? Where's Mom? Why can't I hear?

Val must see confusion on my face because she repeats her words, and this time I catch the raised end of her question: ". . . all right?" She's asking if I'm all right.

I pull my hand free from hers and slap at my ears, the dull thud I feel rather than hear. Looking back at Val, I shake my head. Panic takes over. The mold has found me here, too. *No, I'm not all right. No, this isn't happening. It's only a dream. Another nightmare.* My eyes dart around for something, anything that will help me, but it only increases my nausea.

I can't hear. I can't hear.

Did I say that aloud? Did I not?

Val taps me hard on the shoulder until I focus on her. Her hands fly. Her mouth overexaggerates. As though from underwater, each of her words comes at me: "YOU. HAV-ING TROUBLE. HEARING?" Muffled noises, squished consonants.

I nod hard, pressing my shaking hands into my lap, and add a tiny "Yes."

I can't hear. I can't hear.

What have I done?

Val raises a single finger—*gimme a sec*—then calls out something to the hallway. I feel so very far away, watching all this from my nearly silent island of flashing machines and a single shrill note.

A male doctor strides into the room, rail-thin and taller than

Valerie by a foot. Val stands back, hands on hips, giving him room. He glances from my chart to me with slate-gray eyes. His rigid posture and the upright way he holds the clipboard leaves no doubt that he's the brusque, "all-business" type.

As he leans in, I shrink back. His thin lips move, probably asking if I can hear him. I guess my nonresponse gives him the answer he's looking for because he tucks the clipboard under one arm and moves beside me. I catch a glimpse of shiny metal and plastic before he presses something cold into my ear. Closing my eyes, I try not to move, try not to vomit, as I feel his hot breath on my face, so close.

My eyes fly open as something presses against my foot. It's Val settling in at the edge of the bed. She holds a small whiteboard. Her pen loops across it before she holds it up: *You okay? Doc is checking your ears now.*

My nod is the smallest I can manage.

The doctor withdraws, moving around to check my other ear, and the breath I've been holding rushes out. I'm reaching for the whiteboard when I realize Val can hear me perfectly. "Where's Mom?" I think I say out loud. The question brings tears to my eyes.

Val scribbles. I want to lean forward to read, but the doctor pushes the instrument into my other ear, and it's taking all I have not to vomit. After a bit, she holds up: *Asleep down the hall. Been awake for 24 hours, which is how long you've been out.*

Twenty-four hours.

Val runs the side of her fist across the board to clear it, looking up as the doctor pulls the instrument from my ear. Val nods at whatever he's saying, lips pursed, then returns to her writing: There's nothing blocking your hearing, but aspirin can damage the inner ear. Likely in this case with how much you took. Just not something we can physically see or test for.

I grip the sheets with shaking fists. A clammy sweat breaks out across my skin as Valerie and the doctor talk. The doctor keeps gesturing at me, and Val's hand holding the pen flies as she responds, though not a single word reaches me. Long minutes stretch by as I look between Val and the doctor, then around me for some place to throw up. I find a used coffee cup—Mom's?—and pop the lid off, ready. Finally the doctor moves to go. As he nears the door, he turns and points his pen at me, saying one last thing to Val. Her shoulders rise then fall as she takes another deep breath. She sits by me again, scooting closer. Bad news. It's bad news.

"What did he say?" I ask, unsure if I'm too loud or even making the right sounds but knowing my raw throat hurts when I speak. My nausea swells. "Will it come back, my hearing? Can't they give me anything for it?"

Val's pained expression asks, *"Don't you think you've taken enough?"* But she's writing again. And before she even finishes, I know I won't like it.

We can't know for sure. Will have to wait and see.

She squeezes my foot as I stare at her words, trying to make them sink in. Then I jerk the cup to my mouth and vomit violently, insides burning hot as Val's words whirl through my mind:

Wait and see. Wait and see. Will I hear again? Wait and see.

THOMAS

MY FATHER HASN'T COME OUT OF HIS OFFICE SINCE HE returned earlier. No doubt he'd rather stare at stacks of old case files than have to look at me. And lying on my bed staring at the ceiling, I doubt I'll leave this room again before the deposition.

Mom's the opposite, trying to worm her way into my space all afternoon. So, when there's another knock at my bedroom door, I ignore it. I don't feel much like talking or responding to her schemes of "just checking on you," or "just checking for dirty laundry," or "just checking to see if you've seen my keys."

The knock comes again, more insistent this time, but it also comes with a voice. "Tommy, open the door." Not Mom's voice—male. I know that voice. The knob twists but doesn't open.

It's Michael, home from college in the middle of his semester. Which can only mean Mom holstered her lipstick gun and pulled out a bazooka. I can't blow off my brother like I can Mom, and both of them know it.

I can't think of anyone I'd be more afraid or more relieved to see right now.

"Thomas Patrick, if you don't unlock this door right now, so help me . . ."

I leap up and yank the door open, catching a glimpse of maroon shirt before flopping back on the bed. As he enters the room, I don't know what to do with myself. I consider grabbing the book off my nightstand, an autobiography on Muse's lead singer, to pretend like I've been reading. But I haven't lived with Michael most of my life without learning that delay tactics won't work on him.

"So," he says, bringing in a wave of cologne. "I assume you know why I'm here." Even in the few months since Christmas break, he's gotten tougher looking, more fit. The Bruins tank top and workout pants he wears only emphasize how buff the last wrestling season made him.

I shrug then reach for the book. I need something to look at besides his glare.

Michael strides across the room, ripping the book from my hands and tossing it away. It hits the wood floor before skidding a few feet shy of the dresser. "Cut the crap, Tommy." He plops down next to me. "You know why. Why Mom's chain-smoking in the backyard. Why Dad's frantically researching with half a dozen paralegals. So, don't be an idiot. The parent meeting tomorrow morning, maybe? Your police deposition in two days?"

"It's too late for that." I rake my fingers through my hair, still not looking up.

"Too late for what?"

"Not being an idiot."

He snorts, but there's no humor in it. A pause. "Look at me, Tommy."

But I can't. I know that if I do, I'll completely lose it. I flex my knuckles against the Band-Aids.

"Okay, then listen. Dad wanted me to keep this under wraps, but I think it's something you need to see." He drops a stack of papers in my lap. Illustrations in little boxes fill the page. I know that superhero girl. And that's . . . me. It's Erica's webcomic. It has to be. What everyone's been talking about. And she'd posted drawings of us together?

"Where'd you get this?" I ask, incredulous.

"Picked it up from one of Dad's cop buddies on my way into town. Guess Dad didn't want to be seen cavorting with the opposition, so he sent me." A flash of bitterness crosses his face, like this isn't the first time my father's asked Michael for a favor he didn't like.

"Anyway, someone took screenshots before it got pulled." Michael shrugs. "I think you need to read it. All of it. There's a lot you should see."

"Do colleges run criminal background checks?" I blurt out.

Michael nods, jaw tight. "Yeah, especially in California. And pending charges do show up. Sexual assault crimes aren't . . . aren't usually overlooked."

My guts free-fall. Thornton will find out, then.

He stares at me hard. "What are you going to do?"

I shake my head, blinking fast. "I dunno yet."

"Want to talk about it?"

"Not . . . not yet."

He watches me for another minute, then nods and gets to his feet. "Well, I'll be in my room when you need me." Michael pauses, hand wrapped around the half-open door. "And by the way, I made some calls. That girl, Erica?"

My heart stops.

"She's going to be okay. Well, she'll survive. There's apparently some complications, but she's awake and talking. Thought you'd want to know."

I sit there, gripping her webcomic in my hand, too stunned to speak even though I want to ask him *What complications?*

His gaze hardens, and he points to the pile of papers. "Read those." The door closes behind him.

My chest feels ready to cave. I heave in a breath, dropping Erica's drawings at my feet. I can't read any of this after knowing she almost died, or see the pictures she drew of us before . . . before everything.

But Erica's alive. She's going to be okay.

Head in my hands, I break down. Waves of relief crash over me, but it's the crushing weight of guilt that pulls me under.

ERICA

VALERIE HAS TOSSED THE COFFEE CUP FULL OF MY VOMIT
and replaced it with a small basin and glass of water.

Now I stare at her whiteboard, watching as she resettles and
writes: I'm going to wake your mom soon—

I nod, head pounding.

—but first you need to know some things.

My eyes stay glued to the tip of her pen.

Tests came back. The pen hovers. Levels indicating
proper liver and kidney function were—

What? They were what?

—abnormal.

The air's punched from my lungs.

Meaning the drugs you took affected your organs.

"What does that mean?" My voice must be small—it's lost in the
ringing in my head—but her nodding lets me know she's heard me.

Not sure of the extent of damage just yet. Further tests are needed.

I see the written words—*extent of damage. Further tests*—but I can't understand them.

Do you remember what you took/drank? Her eyes brim with tears, and she takes a deep breath before writing: You stopped breathing on the way here.

Stopped breathing?

Because of the vodka, the pills? *56. 149. 20.*

Like a locker combination: *56-149-20.* Like a game of numbers and colors: *56 blue, 149 brown, 20 white.* A game that mutes the world, guts your body, sucks all the breath from your lungs.

Until Valerie wraps her arms around me, I don't realize I'm crying too. It's an empty crying in a hollow place. But her arms are warm and squishy and familiar around me, and I realize I would've given anything for this hug yesterday. And today, it means everything. She holds me for a long time before breaking away to write. Erica, I'm so sorry. I thought you were hungover. Not this.

It takes my sluggish brain a minute to realize she's talking about the morning after, when she saw me on the bathroom floor. Her face looks so sad now, so guilty, like any of this could possibly be her fault. Before I can think of a response, she writes: Your blog—is everything you wrote true?

My blog? She must read the question on my face.

The police have a copy, brought it by this morning.

I stare at her with dawning horror. She means my webcomic. They found my webcomic. The illustrations. The posts to Caylee. The good-bye letter. But how?

She knows.

Everyone knows.

I'm still here and they all know.

They know everything.

Everything they did to me.

My breath catches mid-inhale. Valerie's brown face hovers in front of mine.

They know.

I can't breathe.

Dizzy, I try to pull air into my lungs—it won't come. I tear at the heart monitors, try to rip them from my chest. I am back in my room at home, airless, helpless, choking, falling.

I can't breathe. I can't breathe.

Heart monitor stickers pop loose. My chest rises in quick spurts, but no air comes.

I can't breathe I can't breathe I can't breathe.

Ican'tbreathe Ican'tbreathe Ican'tbreathe

Valerie's at my side, eyes wide, grabbing my hands and pulling them away. *Breathe*, she mouths. *Breathe.*

I shake my head furiously, nausea returning and spots of light popping in my vision. *I can't. I can't.* She exaggerates a huge inhale and exhale, eyes locked on mine.

It's in this moment of zero oxygen that realization hits. I finally understand what's been living inside me alongside the mold, like a dark, cancerous growth—the feeling that's hovered over me ever since I woke in Zac's room, my skirt missing, underwear inside out. Since hearing Ricky and Zac talk about my breasts while Thomas just listened. It's how I feel for failing to realize earlier that there were Zacs and Rickys and Stallions and Forests and Thomases in the world who would do that to someone. Or Tinas who'd joyfully record the whole thing. For having to endure every snicker or shitty rumor or evil comment on my posts. For poisoning myself. For making my mom stay up for longer than a body can stand, trying to watch over me, making sure I didn't leave her alone in this world so she wouldn't have to bury her only daughter. For being in this hospital. For pushing away people like Valerie, who care, and trusting people like Thomas, who don't.

The emotion burns white-hot through me:

O shame!

I am ashamed, so ashamed.

A blur of blue. A nurse rushing in.

Mom.

Her face is frantic, scrubs wrinkled, hair frazzled.

Valerie has stepped back, and Mom's hugging me tight. She smells of stale sweat and cheap strawberry shampoo. My head spins, but I can't breathe her in enough.

It's a hug I know I don't deserve, but also a hug that breaks loose the piece of shame lodged deep in my chest so that I can finally breathe. Then I'm coughing and choking and spitting, dry heaving into the basin. My chest rises and falls as Mom holds on to me. Her tears mix into mine. And we cry together. For everything.

I cry and cry until there's nothing left in me but a raw, empty space—a hollow that remains.

NNNGGG!

WEDNESDAY

THOMAS

"FIRST OFF, I WANT TO THANK EVERYONE FOR COMING. I can't stress how important this meeting is." My father stands at the head of the table, hands gripping the chair in front of him. The wall behind him is emblazoned with MCMURRAY AND ASSOCIATES in giant gold letters. Always the lawyer, he scans the table, pausing on each face like we're members of his jury instead of everyone implicated by Erica's posts—Forest, Stallion, Zac, Ricky, Tina, and Caylee—sitting next to their parents. We're a chair short of filling the twenty-person table.

Seated next to my father is Zac's dad, a balding man in jeans and a neon orange Syracuse windbreaker—by far the most underdressed person in the room. Beside him sits his new wife, who's probably closer to my age than his and looks more Barbie than human. On her other side sits Ricky's father, a widow, his tanned skin and hair both a little too dark to be natural. Ricky just looks nervous, burrowed into his blazer like a scared rabbit.

An empty chair separates them from Tina's mom. I've never heard mention of Tina's dad, but Mrs. Marcus would give my father a run for his money when it comes to business attire with her stiff suit and mini briefcase. Tina looks near tears, arms crossed, the face of someone who's suffered a serious injustice. No doubt that's how she views this whole thing. I can see her split lip from here, but she's pointedly not looking at me. Beside them, Forest's hippie parents keep tossing disappointed looks at their son. His head is bowed, this subdued version the complete opposite of Saturday's pool-jumping shark.

Mom's not here. My father told her not to come even though she'd asked to, so Michael's to my right, wearing an expression I can't read.

Stallion's parents are to my left, by far the richest parents in the room with stakes in some foreign resource or another. They peer around them with disapproval and something bordering on disgust in their eyes. Stallion sits perfectly upright next to them in a button-up and new haircut. His eyes are bloodshot like he's been crying. I heard he and Jasmine are truly done for good, even though he begged her to take him back.

Sitting beside her dazed parents, Caylee's white as a ghost, clinging to Zac's good arm like she'll fall off her chair if she lets go. Zac tries his best to look unfazed, but I can tell he's shaken too. He catches me looking and stares me down over a swollen nose the color of raspberry jam. I turn away, remembering the blood in his teeth from two days back.

My father's gaze skips past me and lands on Michael as he continues. "We all need to have the same story going into tomorrow's deposition to shut this thing down." He paces up front like it's his stage. "I'll present you with questions that the police will be sure to ask, and you'll want to write them down. We'll go over them, one by one, then you can practice your answers at home. So long as we're all on the same page, tomorrow should go smoothly. We're playing along, voluntarily, but I can't stress enough the importance of adhering to our collective narrative."

"Hold up," Ricky's dad interjects, craning around to face my father. "You mean we don't have to participate in this deposition thing? So, wouldn't that be sticking our boys' necks out further?"

My father shows no emotion, but the slight pause in his pacing tells me he's annoyed at being interrupted. "While your concern is certainly valid, Jim, what we need to do is align our stories and look cooperative to the police. Show that we're not the bad guys here. Project a cooperative yet unified front."

"With all due respect, Tyler," Ricky's dad adds, "if we're not required to do it, then no way is my son going to talk to the police tomorrow. Not if he doesn't have to. Clearly the authorities are trying to blow this thing out of proportion and turn it into something serious."

"To be frank with you, Jim," my father replies, "in the eyes of the law, the charges against these teens are very serious. These include"—he ticks them off on his fingers—"sexual assault of a minor, assault of an intoxicated person, assault of an unconscious person, distribution of child pornography—"

"Child pornography?" Forest's mom cuts in. She's thrown out a hand, wrists eaten up by bracelets and beads. "These kids aren't sixty-seven-year-old pedophiles in windowless rooms sharing naked photos of little girls." She looks around her. "Now, I know what they did was wrong. Getting drunk and taking the clothes off that poor girl. But child pornography? That's taking things too far. They're only boys. And girls," she adds with a glance in Caylee and Tina's direction.

Michael shifts in his seat, jaw tightening.

Out of nowhere, a wail silences the room. It's Tina, clutching her mother's arm. "I didn't know she was going to try to kill herself! I didn't! I just wanted her to go away!" She breaks down sobbing as her mother puts a stiff arm around her.

My father's eyes bore into Tina. "Now, I know how hard this is on everyone." To the rest of the room, his expression of sympathy must look sincere. But it's not sympathy that drives him. My father does not lose cases. "And yet emotional outbursts like this are exactly what we need to avoid during the morning's proceedings. We mustn't give the cops anything they could use against us. Guilt is the surest way to sink this ship, so we can't let them tap into our emotions. Because, if we're not careful and don't play our cards right, things could get real ugly real fast. We're talking felony convictions here. And if the—"

"But, tomorrow, surely we . . ." Ricky's dad interrupts.

A few chairs from my father, Zac's dad rises to his feet, tenting his hands on the table as Ricky's dad trails off. Even in an orange-and-blue windbreaker, Chuck Boyd commands the room. It's one of the only times I've seen him not in the Panthers' bleachers wearing one of his old jerseys with BOYD and a worn number six across the back, matching Zac's on the field. "Let me be clear to everyone in this room." Chuck speaks softly, not sharp like my father, and he doesn't look up from the center of the table, but he doesn't have to. When he talks, everyone listens. "My son can't afford to have some girl cry 'rape.' He's got a scholarship riding on all this. His whole future's at stake. So, my boy and I are going to do exactly"—he jabs the table—"what it takes to make this thing go away as quickly as possible. And if you all know what's good for you, for your sons *and* daughters, you'll get in line with Tyler and do precisely what he says tomorrow, down to the letter."

Down the hall, a phone rings and a printer whirrs as Chuck Boyd takes his seat.

My father nods appreciatively into the silence, though I can tell it irks him to have someone else win his battle for him. "Which is why we're going to take care of all this, Chuck." He gives a confident nod before turning to the room at large. "And please remember, everyone: according to statistics, the chances of this thing being pursued, let alone brought to court, are less than three percent—slim to none—so long as we play our cards right."

"So, what's our story, then?" Tina's mom asks, lips pursed and voice clipped. "The one we tell the police?"

The look on my father's face sends a chill through me, like he already tastes victory. "Only the truth: that the plaintiff is a sad, lonely girl. She's new to town, doesn't have a lot of friends."

Next to Zac, Caylee shifts uncomfortably. There's not a person in this room who doesn't know she's the reason Erica's blog got leaked. It had only taken her sharing it with Zac for it to go viral and for everyone to know where her loyalties lie, not to mention for the police to glean the whole story once they had a copy of the post—though no one's exactly sure who tipped them off to the blog's existence yet.

My father continues, "The plaintiff feels largely ignored. She's not a bad girl, per se, only . . . misguided. An attention seeker. So, one night when she gets invited to a party, she decides she's going to seek out all the attention she's longed for. She lures these boys up to Zac's room with the promise of a strip show, and what curious young man would turn that down? She strips for the boys, gets off on them writing on her. We even have a witness"—he gestures to Caylee—"who says the plaintiff went upstairs voluntarily."

Caylee shrinks into her chair, cheeks blazing.

My father's gesture swings wide, bringing my classmates

into the mix. "Everyone corroborates this, even a girl friendly with the plaintiff."

Tina's eyes brim with tears, but her mother nods in earnest.

"And everyone came down at the same time," my father continues. "No harm, no foul. The point being, we need to make it clear the plaintiff brought this on herself. Not only that, she invited it. The fact that there's no BAC report—blood alcohol content analysis—will work in our favor. I've already managed to get my hands on her blog posts, mostly a bunch of fictionalized cartoons that showcase her immaturity and insecurities."

I swallow hard, thinking of the unread copy I'd left by my bed.

"As for the photos that were circulated," my father continues, "they're not great, but they're also not too damning. Even the video we can work around, especially if we claim she was conscious and willing. We can spin it as a harmless joke. With the right attack angle, we can make this work."

A few people nod. Others look uneasy. Michael rubs his thumbs over closed fists, muttering, "Such bullshit." Michael's heard it too, then—the conviction in my father's voice when he speaks. My father really believes Erica's to blame, and his "story" of how it happened isn't what matters. Only that he arrives at his version of justice.

"I know this doesn't make us feel good." My father's gaze sweeps around the table. "But above all else, we need to make sure we're united tomorrow." The back of the chair he's hitting for emphasis slides into the table. His gaze locks on me. "We need to fully cooperate with the authorities. Keep our story straight. So long as we do that, everything will be fine." He moves on, scanning the remaining faces. "Then this will all go away, and we can get on with our lives—careers, lacrosse scholarships, even senior prom. Sound good to everyone?"

No one says anything, their faces filled with the hope that this could all just go away.

Could it?

Taking his seat, my father snaps open the file in front of him and passes papers down the row. "Great. Now, let's move on to police questions. . . ."

ERICA

"I SHOULD HAVE KNOWN."

It's the same line Mom's been repeating all day, the first words I could sort of make out through the ringing fog when my hearing returned a fraction—going from empty, shrill nothing to underwater hum. I overheard Mom say it to Valerie, to herself, but only because she was standing right next to me when she did. And it must be overwhelming her because now she won't stop saying it in front of me, mouth forming the words I almost can't hear.

"I should have known."

As she sits on the edge of my bed, staring off into the distance, shaking her head from time to time, part of me wonders what she thinks she should've known. That those guys did what they did? That Caylee dropped me as a friend? That Thomas discarded me? That the whole school saw me naked? That no matter what happens I can never go back to Bay City Prep?

I have no reason to go back. There's nothing left for me there. Most likely, there never was. Most likely I'd imagined it all—a world within those walls where I could fit in and be myself. Where a girl like Caylee Mermaid would be a real friend. Where a guy like Thomas the Rhymer would be as perfect as he seemed. Somewhere my peers would accept me—the silly girl who re-creates people with paints and rainbow pens so that she can try to understand them.

"I should have known."

Mom blames herself. *She* blames herself. She saved my life. I want to ask her what happened after I fell, but I'm too ashamed. I picture her ear pressed to my bedroom door, a hollow silence the only answer to her calls. Her kicking down the door, screaming, dragging me downstairs, or did the paramedics do that? Did she drive or will there be an ambulance bill we can't afford to pay? What is all of this costing us, costing her?

Earlier, she'd explained the pain in my veins, the weird dreams. "The antidote they gave you, to bind to the medicine. Coupled with side effects of the pills you took." Mom had tried to state all this as matter-of-factly as possible, though both her hands and voice had shaken. Then she'd repeated her mantra:

"I should have known."

What should she have known? I'm too afraid to ask.

She's been by my bed all day. When she gets too fidgety for sitting, Mom checks my vitals, straightens my blankets or readjusts my pillows, checks my IV, medications, the latest batch of lab results. She talks to the doctors and nurses about my progress or future tests to run.

She stood by when my dad called an hour ago, stuck in a snowstorm in Boston but fighting his way here. I mostly listened through the thick cotton in my ears, asking him to repeat himself when I couldn't make out what he was saying even though he was already full-on shouting into the phone to be heard. I cried as he gushed and cried, saying he was sorry, that he should've been there for me more. He told me stories about what a beautiful, chubby baby I was, that he'd bawled in the delivery room, how proud of me he is. It felt weird to have all his attention, something I've craved for so long and now have, but for all the wrong reasons.

"I should have known," Mom says. Right now she's sitting here, my hand in both of hers, thumbs caressing the back of my knuckles. It would take worlds of crisscrossing ink lines on paper to capture all her worry wrinkles.

As I look at her, it feels like through someone else's eyes, and I realize it's incredible. To be able to tell—by the way your mother's scrubs fall from her shoulders, her face all flat lines, her whole presence radiating sorrow—that she blames herself for what you've done to yourself. And you want to shake her by the shoulders and say that none of this is her fault even though you don't know whose fault it is: yours or theirs. And you're tired. More tired than you've ever been, like every crack in your body is filled with cement, and the world is asking you to keep treading quicksand, but all you're really doing is lying in a hospital bed in so much pain, falling in and out of sleep, not sure yet if you're glad you didn't die. These thoughts crush you because, even as you think them, your mother cries softly beside you, thinking you're asleep.

And you feel so many emotions at the same time that you don't know how you're ever going to find a place for them all to live. Guilt—the one in your head. Fear—the one in your chest. Shame—the one in your heart that will stay with you for a long, long time.

They tell me the police are coming to question me in an hour.

"I should have known."

What part? All of it?

I should have known too.

THOMAS

"VANB. HEY, VANB!"

My father turns to me. "Thomas, I believe someone is trying to get your attention."

I stop short of the elevators, but only because he and Michael do. Zac's the last person I want to talk to right now. Even Caylee must've felt the same way because, after watching the video again, she'd hurried away with her parents, ignoring Zac's "Babe. Babe!" as she left. Still, if the past's any indication, she'll be back with him before the day's out.

But Zac's already caught up with us, and there's no way to avoid him.

"Mr. VanBrackel. Mikey," he says, nodding at them. Up close, his face looks even worse, nose dark and ballooned in the center with matching bruises on his temple and lower jaw. His cast looks just as awful, all filthy and stained with blood.

Michael just stares at Zac, though my father gives him a quick return nod. "Zac."

"Mind if I talk to Thomas?" Zac asks.

My father waves a hand before turning away. "Be my guest."

Michael gives me a *You good?* raised-eyebrows stare till I nod, then he follows our father to the elevators.

Zac starts in, "So, I know we've had our differences . . ."

Differences. I think of Erica passed out on the bed, Zac sticking his dick in her face. "Differences" doesn't exactly cut it.

"And okay, yeah, I made some mistakes too," he adds, reading the disgust on my face. "I know I have, but so have you, though there's nothing that we can do about that now. So, we gotta keep looking forward, keep our focus on the horizon."

Like this is all just a pre-game pep talk.

"I need to know that you're in for tomorrow," he adds.

I shake my head. *"In?"*

"That you're going to tell the police what happened. Well, what we talked about today. Because like your dad said, everyone has to be on the same page. The same team."

I stare at him, incredulous. "Boyd, you and I are done being on the same team."

"Aw, c'mon, man." His smile is tight as he gestures between us. "You and I, we're like family, right? Like brothers, even. Been playing lacrosse together since we were rug rats."

I shake my head in disbelief. "You're not my brother, Zac. Never have been. So, don't pretend like you are."

Fear flashes across Zac's face. I flinch as he steps forward, grabbing my arm. "Thomas, please. I need this. I can't lose this scholarship. It's not about the money, man. They could ban me from the sport. I'd be blacklisted. No division team would want me then. None. Then who would I be?"

His voice catches, and for a second, I'm too stunned to respond. In all the years I've known him, Zac's never sounded so earnest, so desperate.

Zac releases my arm and clears his throat, attempting another smile. "And, hey, I know you wanna think you're so different from me." He slaps my chest with his good arm. "But we're a lot alike, you and me. Both of us want more out of life. You with your music. Me with lacrosse. And we'll both get it so long as you do your part."

Anger rips through me. Of course. This is just another power play, trying to get me to go along with whatever he wants. "Oh, you're so full of shit, Boyd," I spit, beyond caring that everyone passing this hall can hear. The too-friendly smile slides off his face. "What?" I scoff. "You thought you could come over here and buddy-buddy me with this 'we're the same' bullshit and I'd eat from your hand like a little lapdog? Say or do whatever you wanted? All you've ever cared about is everyone watching you. All eyes on Big-Shot Boyd! Well, guess what, you piece of shit? You've got your audience. Everyone's going to be watching you now."

For just a second, everything's completely quiet. Then Zac

gets right in my face, finger raised, all fake-nice dropped. I sense Michael approaching as Zac growls, "You think I'm the only one who's gonna lose in all this? Think Thornton is going to want you with 'rape' on your record?"

My chest squeezes. *They'll find out. They'll never take me then.*

"So, don't you forget, Music Man," Zac spits. "If I go down, you go down. I'll make damn sure of it."

"Is that so?" I sputter.

"You bet your ass it is."

Smacking Zac's hand from my face, I blow past him, nearly crashing into Michael as I make for the elevators. But then I pull up short. My father stands by the closed metal doors, having watched the whole exchange, a dark expression twisting his face.

ERICA

THE POLICE HAVE COME TO THE HOSPITAL TO SEE ME. THEY
say they've been waiting all morning to ask me questions.

Mom looks angry, though, because they're here or because
of the whole situation, I don't know.

Both cops stand tall, hands on their belts like in the movies.
Officer Rodriguez has hair pulled back in a ponytail that's as
severe as the expression on her olive face. Officer Shiva, a short,
burly white guy, holds a stack of papers that I try not to look at.

They're standing so close, which is the only reason I can hear
some of their conversation with Mom above the cottony hum
in my ears.

"Didn't you . . . classmates already?" Mom asks. ". . . tell you
all you need to know?"

". . . conduct interviews at . . . ," the female cop answers.

I cringe at the word "interviews," thinking about the cops

rounding up my classmates in groups, asking who's heard what, who's seen the video.

". . . But our jobs require . . . question all parties . . . standard protocol . . . place blame or cause undue . . . verify Erica's side of the . . . said online . . . is of the essence if . . . accountable for their actions."

My head throbs as I try to piece it all together while Mom's lips press shut, spent of excuses.

Officer Rodriguez's eyes meet mine, and she comes very close, enunciating every word. "Erica, is it okay if we sit down?"

I nod slowly, completely drained as they take their seats. Unable to meet her eyes, I study her uniform—midnight-blue collared shirt and tie; metal name tag with RODRIGUEZ above one pocket, silver badge above the other; gold Police Academy pins on either side of her collar; American flag patch on one shoulder, Bay City Police Department patch on the other.

"We're going to need to ask you a series of questions. Try to be as . . . and detailed as you can in your answers. The more you give us to . . . the stronger your case will be."

Case.

Officer Shiva hands me a folded stack of papers, though I'm staring at the leather sheath of his gun as I take it.

". . . need you to look this over . . . confirm its accuracy," he mumbles.

I open it with fingers that haven't stopped trembling since I woke and flip through the first few pages. It's a copy of the last few posts from my website, the one where I tell Caylee everything and the one after I took the pills. The last page is a mess of misspellings. It scares me, to see what my own fingers typed, and precisely how out of it I really was. Teetering on the edge of not coming back.

A cold chill runs through me.

"Would I have to testify?" my own voice asks. Too loud?

"More than likely . . . be asked to give a statement, yes," Officer Rodriguez replies.

I imagine a trial: Thomas, Zac, Ricky, Forest, Stallion with all their expensive lawyers and rich families on one side, Mom and Valerie and me on the other. Would they call in Tina, too? Ms. Adams? And Caylee? I imagine the judge pulling everyone up one by one to question. Then it would be my turn. I'd get cross-examined, grilled about everything over and over and over again. They'd project images onto a white screen for the jury to see, images of me, naked and covered in writing. They'd play the video. Jurors would burn me with their eyes: *So that's what you look like naked*; Mom would hold back tears as Ricky fondles my breast, as Zac slaps my face with his penis. Everyone would see it: my mom and aunts and uncles, my grandparents and grandmother, and old friends, too. And perfect strangers, sitting there, silently judging me, their brains asking why I'd gotten so drunk, or why I hadn't gone to the police right away. What was I trying to hide? Why was I lying?

Maybe the boys' lives would be ruined. Maybe they'd

despise me, send me death threats. Break windows in our apartment. Light fires on our welcome rug. I'd have to face them all in court, and in school every day. We'd have to move away. Everyone would be talking about it, about me—the stupid drunk girl. And would I even be able to hear the questions they ask me in the courtroom? Would my body still be broken? Even before this hospital, I felt broken, but now? I can't take it.

I flip further into the printouts so I can buy myself some time. The images are a gut-punch. It's the illustrated spread I did of Erica Strange fighting off a horde of zombie pirates. I trace the outline of her cape, her superhero hair.

Erica Strange would tell. She'd do it. But I am not Erica Strange. I never was.

I can't do it. I can't.

I won't.

"None of it's true." I drop the papers into my lap. My hands are shaking too hard to hand them back. "None of it's true," I repeat.

"Bug . . . ," I think Mom says.

In my periphery, I can see the officers glance at each other and then back to me.

"Erica," Officer Rodriguez begins. "These are very serious allegations . . . need you to know that what you say matters."

"I know," I say, fighting my heavy limbs and fuzzy thoughts. Because they need to believe me. "I made it up. I didn't . . . I only wanted . . ." But I have no excuses, nothing that would explain what happened, where I am now.

For a second, I fool myself into thinking they do believe me, that they'll take my word at face value, chalk it up to me being a hysterical girl and go away. That this will all go away. That it can all go away.

But this is reality and that's not how it works. Things don't just go away when you want them to. Didn't I find that out the hard way, with the pills?

Officer Rodriguez looks at me. "Erica, I know you're going through a lot right now . . . need you to be honest with us about what happened to you."

When I keep shaking my head despite the head rush it gives me, she rises, her partner following, and hands a business card to Mom. "In the meantime, we'll continue the investigation . . . leaving my card. Call me when you're ready."

THOMAS

I'M IN THE KITCHEN HELPING MOM WITH THE LUNCH DISHES.
After the meeting, my father had stayed at his office, so
Michael had driven me home. Then, after sitting through a
near-wordless brunch of bacon and waffles, he'd gone to his
room and closed the door.

Mom dips a plate in rinse water before placing it in the
drainer. "Thomas, I want to talk to you about tomorrow."

The dish towel freezes in my hand. "What about?" But it's
not like I've stopped thinking about tomorrow. I can't. Every
time I try to come up with my speech, Forest's face flashes in
my head. Tomorrow could change his future. Ricky's, Stallion's,
Zac's, and Tina's, too. And mine.

It's like I finally hold music school in my hands. I can feel
it, cupped in both palms, something I've worked for my whole
life. And now it's being threatened. But I won't let anyone rip

it from me. Not Zac, not the cops, not anyone. I've worked too hard.

Mom suds up another plate, choosing her words. "Well, your dad called while you and Michael were on your way home, and he mentioned that you seemed a little . . . indecisive about what you'd say tomorrow. But you have to do what's right, you know?"

"And what is that, exactly?" Michael cuts in. He stands in the doorway, leaning into the frame, hands tucked under opposite arms.

Mom turns, wiping hair from her face with the back of a soapy hand. "Well, the truth, of course. That Thomas and his friends didn't mean it how it looks. And, well, that maybe that girl is a little troubled. She does sound like she needs some help." At the look on Michael's face she adds, "But I guess that part's not for us to judge."

Michael stares at Mom long enough to make us both uncomfortable. "I seriously can't believe what I'm hearing right now."

Mom's taken aback. "Well, Thomas has a lot riding on tomorrow. They all do, and he should remember as much."

"Are you even listening to yourself?" Michael's close to yelling, hands flying. "You're talking about this girl like it's her fault."

I run my thumb over the little duck on the dish towel. Does he think it's my fault, then? Does he blame me?

"I didn't mean it like that," Mom says. "I don't think it's her fault exactly . . ."

"Well, that's what you implied. But what if this had happened to Chelsea or Chrissy, or even Barbara? Would you feel differently then?"

Chelsea and Chrissy, our eighth-grade twin cousins. Or Barbara, Michael's girlfriend. But I would never do anything like that to them.

And you thought you'd do it to Erica?

Michael wheels on me, and I nearly drop the towel. "And I love you, Tommy," he says, "but you are so in the wrong. You all are. What you do tomorrow won't only matter for a day. It'll matter for the rest of your life. And no, I'm not talking about you getting in trouble. I'm talking about being a decent human being because I sure expected better from you. From all of you." Michael storms out, leaving a stunned silence in his wake.

Mom stares after him until his footsteps fade before picking up her sponge. "Tommy, why don't you go find your clothes for tomorrow. I'll get the rest of these. Your father said to wear the gray slacks and blue button-down. I'll iron them after I clean up."

I hesitate then toss the towel in the dish rack, still stinging from Michael's words. *Decent human being.* When I pass by his old room, the door's closed, though a bar of light shines underneath. I approach, knuckles raised to knock, when I hear him muttering into his phone.

". . . unbelievable, Barbs. Seriously . . . it's tomorrow . . . not sure what he'll do . . . They're all nuts, my father especially. . . . I know, I know. . . ." He's talking to his girlfriend about me.

I let my hand fall and turn away, trying to summon the energy to find my clothes.

In my room, the first thing I see is the spray of pages from Erica's webcomic held together by a binder clip, the ones I stepped around this morning trying to ignore. I throw myself onto my bed and away from the pages, wishing with all my might that they didn't exist so I wouldn't have to read them.

ERICA

IN THE WILD, SHARKS HAVE BEEN KNOWN TO CIRCLE THEIR prey for hours. Circling, circling, feigning indecision, and right when you think they aren't interested, that they won't actually attack, they move in for the kill.

At least, that's what I saw on Animal Planet once. And it's what I'm thinking about as I stare at the scrubs Psychiatrist Austin is wearing as he sits by my bedside—tiny gray and green smiley sharks printed randomly across the cloth. White-haired and Asian with a kind smile, Austin's watching me with all the patience in the world, waiting for me to answer his question, insisting I call him by his first name like that makes us friends. He's the mental health provider assigned to my case, and his presence should bring comfort.

It doesn't. He's here to figure out why I tried to kill myself, why I wouldn't talk to the police. But I can't talk about that.

The walls of this hospital have become a safe haven, a massive machine holding me in its steel belly, and I never want to leave. Its steady rhythm, its routine order, and the sameness of every hour bring me comfort. Life's not complicated here. Leaving is what's complicated—clawing your way out of the steel fortress only to be met with blinding sunlight and a feeling of nakedness that won't go away.

Well, technically, I guess I may not be going straight home after this hospital stay, or so I found out from Mom this morning. There are talks of sending me to some residential treatment center for "further evaluation and care" that's supposed to help teens with my "level of anxiety." Like it's all my anxiety's fault I'm in here right now.

And clearly Psychiatrist Austin is just *dying* to talk about this right now, judging by the way he's leaning forward in his chair. But honestly? All the sympathy and expectation oozing from him makes me want to jump out of this bed and take off down the hall in this stupid, paper-thin gown of humiliation. This is wishful thinking, of course. I can't do anything with these machines looming over me like they're feeding on me as they *meep* and groan. Their wires snake through the sheets and into my skin, dripping liquid into my veins and monitoring every output. The hospital gown twists around my body, smothering me. My long hair catches between my back and the pillow, yanking my neck.

Austin already visited once, last night after I woke. Mom

had held my hand, trembling as badly as I was while he asked me a million questions using Valerie's whiteboard, bothering to write my name with each question like it somehow gave more weight to everything he said. Or maybe so he wouldn't forget it in his massive caseload.

How are you feeling, Erica?

Do you know why you are here, Erica?

Erica, are you having any more thoughts of hurting yourself or others?

And on and on and on.

Last night, above the never-ending whine in my ears, I'd given him the answers I was supposed to, the "should" answers, though it took all my brainpower to form the thoughts. I should feel this way. I should comfort Mom and say this. Nod your head here. Shake your head there. Meanwhile I was wondering what Austin's fail rate was, how many people passed his test only to go home and off themselves for real. Not that I wanted to be one of those people. Still, I'd be lying if I said there wasn't a small part of me that wished I'd succeeded with the pills. Then my mother had squeezed my hand, and instantly, I'd felt ashamed. She looked more exhausted than I'd ever seen her, a bird that had braved a storm, stripped of half its feathers. And yesterday, when Austin had gotten to "So why did you try to hurt yourself, Erica?" that's when I'd shut down. He had a copy of my online posts. He knew. He just wanted me to say it. Tell him why I'd lied to the police about the website being mine.

"You told a lie, an odious, damned lie." Or so says Emilia to Iago in *Othello* and my mind to me now.

And now here he is again, sitting too close so that I can hear him, asking the same questions that I don't want to answer while my stomach aches, my head aches, my body and heart ache.

"Sharks can circle for hours before they attack," I tell Austin.

"What's that?" I've caught him off-guard.

"Sharks," I repeat. "They can circle their prey for hours before attacking." When he still looks confused, I add, "You asked me what I was thinking."

And I'm sure *he's* thinking about the zillion things he has to do on his rounds that don't involve getting lectured on shark behavior.

"Oh," he finally says. "I didn't know that, Erica." But I can tell what he's really thinking. *What do sharks have to do with anything? With why you're here? Why you won't talk to the police?*

And if he would've asked this question aloud, maybe I would have answered: *Everything.* Sharks have everything to do with why I'm lying in this hospital bed. Because that's what one single memory is doing in my head: relentlessly circling my groggy thoughts, then attacking, attacking, again and again until my mind is a bloody mass in the water, being ripped to shreds from all directions.

The scene that circles, haunts, attacks, is from Sunday morning, the worst day of my life, the scene I can't replay aloud even though this is what Austin really wants to hear. I should tell him all this, explain my shark metaphor so that he'd understand, so he'd jot down the right notes in that folder of his instead of words I'm sure are in there like "uncooperative" or "troubled" or "deeply anxious." But I can't. Instead, I sit back and watch as the shark that is the worse memory of the worst day of my life moves in for the kill. And when it has completed its circle, it loops back to the beginning. Back to the nausea, gray walls, words carved in Sharpie. Back to the laughter, male voices, and frantic escape. Again and again and again.

Inside, I burn with agitation, but I can only do what I've done for days. Cry.

"I'm sorry," I manage, because it's what I'm supposed to say. What I'd like to say to—no, *scream* at—Austin is to go away and leave me the hell alone. Everyone wants something from me, tries to wring a few more drops of my energy, but I'm like the Giving Tree in that book, cut down to a stump with nothing left to offer.

Austin's answer comes back relaxed, like the rest of him. "Take all the time you need, Erica . . . right here when you're ready." He leans forward, chair squeaking beneath him, and places a large hand on the sheet near my elbow. I try not to flinch, turning my eyes to the clear, nearly spring day happening outside the filmy window.

"It's just . . . I don't even know where to begin." My voice chokes off as another wave of tears spills over my cheeks.

"How about . . . very beginning?" he asks.

A Kleenex makes its way into my hand. I rub at my wet face then count backward. Was Saturday night really only four days ago? Four days of nightmares, sharks, and losing best friends and crushes and whole worlds.

Erica Strange, she'd tell, my mind says.

Yeah, well, the sharks got her, too, I say back.

Tears dot the tissue as I smooth it out against the gray-white sheets with hands that seem like they'll never stop shaking. I fold the tissue in half, then half again, and again until I hold a tiny square in my hand. Pressing it into my palm, I clench it with everything I have.

All the while, Austin watches me from behind a web of crow's-feet. I wonder how he could enjoy talking to sick people day after day. People who would rather kill themselves than talk to you. Still, this is his job. He does this all the time. And he's waiting for me to speak.

But where do I start? How do I start?

How about from the very beginning?

The beginning. How far back should I search when the past few days alone feel like months on end? But I know the answer to that. I know exactly when it started: when I transferred to Bay City Prep. When I first saw Thomas.

Thomas.

I can recall exactly what the sun smells like on Thomas's skin, feel the warmth of his breath against my neck, taste the lemony oil of his ChapStick.

His name in my mind sends a thrill through my body, followed immediately by shame snarling its disgust. Because there's no coming back from what he did. What they all did.

But that part's not a secret anymore since my plea to Caylee and good-bye post went public. Since being admitted here, I have no more secrets. But what Austin wants to know—what they all want to know—is if it's true, if any of it is true. And I want it to be not true so very badly, but I can still feel the names. Every last one of them, though all traces of Sharpie have faded.

"My anxiety didn't do this, okay?" I snap and surprise even myself. "Everyone's saying I'm too anxious, like me being anxious is the only reason I'm here and not what they did to me."

If Austin is alarmed by my outburst, he doesn't show it. He responds slowly, carefully, "You're right, Erica. Neither you nor your anxiety caused this, and an extreme reaction was certainly warranted here."

His words have caught me off-guard. But he's not done, adding in a measured tone, "What I think they're trying to get at is that the extreme reaction needed to come in service of yourself, not against you. Does that make sense?"

"But they didn't rape me. It wasn't like that." The words geyser up from deep inside me, and I know my thoughts are all over the map right now. But I need Austin to know that it's not as bad as he thinks, as bad as everyone thinks. As bad as it maybe could've been.

"Okay," Austin responds, and even my damaged ears can make out the intensity in his voice. "But perhaps a . . . we should ask ourselves is, what is rape? The Department of Justice defines rape widely for a reason, as most any sex act without the consent of the victim, so what happened to you could very . . . fit under that categorization. And at the same time, we must also ask ourselves, does a devastating event require a certain definition for it to be considered world-altering to the person it happened to?"

My eyes refuse to meet his, and I realize that my brain is trying to both scream that what they did to me is a big fucking deal while, at the same time, downplay everything, telling me even now that I'm overreacting and that others have had it worse. I have to ask Austin to repeat his next question.

"What *did* they . . . Erica? . . . Ready to talk about that?"

I take a deep breath, knowing he wants me to speak. To tell him if it's all true so he can write it down in that fancy notebook of his, maybe even report it to the police. But doesn't he know I'd have to take a running leap into shark-infested waters to do that, praying I can keep treading water before the sharks snag a foot, an elbow, and pull me down into a watery grave?

I shake my head, lost for words. *Not ready. Not ready. Not ready!* Because there's too much to say, to explain, to feel and relive. Because ready could never exist when you're taking on a shiver of sharks.

THOMAS

I LEAP FROM MY BED, SNATCHING ERICA'S COMICS OFF THE floor and rolling them into a tube. All afternoon, I've stared at them from my pillow, fanned out below me, wondering how to make myself read them. Now, in the rapidly fading light, I grip them like a baton and pace around my room.

How did it come to this? Erica in the hospital, a restraining order against me, the police deposition tomorrow . . . And I'm supposed to tell the cops what my dad told me to say or no one will ever speak to me again. I could get in major trouble. Life-changing trouble. But if I say what we rehearsed, that'll mean that Erica . . . she'll be on her own. Again.

My brain slams on the brakes. I can't do this.

I'm halfway down the stairs before I realize I've thrown on my hoodie still smelling of Erica and my Chucks. My hands squeeze truck keys and Erica's comics because I'm leaving.

Because there's no right answer for tomorrow. I'm screwed any way I turn.

The house is silent, growing darker, and I don't see anyone. Good. I grab the doorknob.

"Going somewhere?" a voice calls out from the corner.

I spin.

Michael sits on the couch, laptop in his lap, textbook open beside him.

"Jesus, Mikey. You scared the shit out of me."

"Planning on skipping town, then?"

I don't bother asking how he knows. "Don't worry about me. I'll be fine."

He gives me his *Really, Thomas?* look, scanning me over. "Didn't bother packing a bag, I see. So, enlighten me. What do you plan to do for money? Can't use credit cards. Too traceable. And with no money for clothes, food, and, what, eighteen miles to the gallon in that beast of a truck, you'd make it, what, a hundred miles—two, maybe—before they caught up to you?"

"I'll figure something out."

"Sure you will." He closes his textbook and laptop, then pats the couch cushion next to him. "Come. Sit."

My fist squeezes the knob. "Mikey, you don't understand. I can't talk to the cops tomorrow. I can't. . . ."

"Actually it's you who doesn't understand, so shut your mouth already."

His serious tone pulls me up short. So does the expression on his face. Heavy. Sad.

"I'm going to tell you something, and I need you to listen," he continues. "Tomorrow is not about Zac or Forest or any of your buddies. And it's not about Dad, especially not him. It's about you and who you want to be on the other side of this. And it's about Erica. I've read her posts. You've taken a lot from her, agreed? Or maybe you don't know that, and that's what this is about. But even if you can't fully understand, surely you realize that you at least owe her the truth about what happened and your part in it. So, go to the deposition tomorrow, Tommy. Tell the truth. You owe her that. You owe yourself that."

The whole time he's talking, my anger grows. My whole body shakes. "Like you know anything about this. What it feels like to be me right now." The keys cut into my injured hand, papers crunching in my fist. I snatch his phone from the end table and am out the door.

He's off the couch in an instant and chasing me down the porch, calling my name. I try to pull open my truck door, but he blocks me. "Tommy, stop for a sec. Listen."

I dodge his waving arms and run. He's bigger than me, but I've always been faster. At a full sprint, it takes me three blocks to lose him, but finally I do. I run and I run, pumping my hands that are full of keys, and a stolen phone, and a dying girl's final thoughts. A strange girl that I liked so much.

I sprint—five minutes, ten minutes, fifteen, past trees and

fire hydrants and green lawns—until my muscles start to seize and my lungs feel like they're sucking in splinters instead of air. In the middle of the sidewalk, I stop and double over, fists on knees, prepared to lose whatever stomach contents I have. Meanwhile the phone in my hand buzzes and buzzes: HOME. I don't answer.

Minutes pass. Birds sing from the trees. Cars whiz by.

Finally, I look around me at a quiet street in a quiet neighborhood I've never seen before.

There's a park with a playground full of colorful plastic tubes.

I make my way toward it like I'm swimming and the plastic tubes are the rescue boat.

Rubber bark squishes under my shoes, but my eyes are on the purple slide. Erica's favorite color. I sit at the scooped-out base, the one that helps kids not fly out too fast, and look down at my hands, one bandaged, one not. Several Band-Aids have worked their way off, exposing wrinkly skin. Deep scratches run across Michael's phone where the keys gouged it during my run. It buzzes again: HOME. I sit and watch it vibrate.

Dropping the phone and keys, I unroll the pages of Erica's drawings. Flipping through them, I start to see an order, from when she transferred to Bay City till she took the pills, then I return to the first page. The title blares: "Bay City Day Two: A Wild Whimsical Success Involving Too Hot a Boy and Too Little Caffeine!"

There she is, exactly as I would've drawn her if I had any art skills. Beautiful green eyes. Warm, the way a fire is unless you get too close, wearing purple pants Prince would've been proud of, and that smile like burning embers that knocked me on my ass the first time I saw it. And she had been looking—*really* looking—at the dorky guy leaning against the picnic table, listening to music, and staring back at her like he saw her, *really* saw her. Like she mattered.

Blinking hard, I take a deep breath and start to read.

ERICA

I SLEEP WELL INTO THE DAY, INTERRUPTED EVERY FEW hours by either Mom or another nurse checking in or taking more blood for labs. At some point, Mom prods me awake, holding a cup of broth, the only "food" I'm allowed since my stomach definitely couldn't handle anything else. Not that I'm hungry anyway. My guts still hurt like I drank bleach, and part of me wonders if they'll ever be normal again.

"Drink up, Bug," Mom says, handing me the lukewarm broth. Though not crystal clear, they are the first words since I arrived here that don't sound like they were said completely underwater, and I realize the steady whine has quieted a bit too. Then the doctor who comes in later to do a sound test tells me my hearing has improved and may continue to do so, though only time will tell. And even though it's still a far cry from normal, my relief overwhelms me.

Around two I can't sleep anymore, so Mom and I start a Scrabble game balanced on my tray table. Valerie brought it from home along with my favorite illustrated novels—*The Graveyard Book*, *Anya's Ghost*, and *A Monster Calls*—though, without a word to me, Mom tucked those away in her purse. Apparently murder and death aren't things Mom wants me reading about right now.

I'm playing "jest" for fifty-four points when Nurse Sabaa walks in, hovering in the door and saying something I don't catch. Both turn to me. Mom repeats loudly, face full of concern, "You have a visitor."

"Who?" I ask.

Mom and Sabaa exchange words. "One of your girlfriends from school."

Caylee?

"You up for it, Bug?" Mom asks.

Even though I'm not sure, I nod. Mom passes the nod to Sabaa, who leaves.

I pull the sheets up farther, disrupting the Scrabble board on the tray. It nearly topples, though Mom saves it in time.

But when the door opens again, it's not Caylee who steps through.

As she comes into the room, I see a flash of red first, though Amber's hair looks almost orange under these yellowish lights.

I give her a small smile, my voice tiny. "Hi."

Amber exclaims something, then, to my enormous surprise,

beelines for the bed and gives me a tight squeeze before taking a step back. I hear almost every word because she's so close: "Sorry . . . wasn't hurting you, was I? And you must . . . Erica's mom. Hi. Amber."

Mom gives her a tired smile. "You have to speak loudly and articulate so Erica can hear you," Mom says, demonstrating. "Her ears have some damage."

Amber's eyes grow wide, though she doesn't comment. Instead, she takes in my IV drip, then drags a chair beside Mom's, a few feet from me. "How you feeling?" she asks, voice raised.

I shrug, because any time someone asks me that and I answer with actual words, tears usually follow.

"Shitty, I bet. It's a stupid question. I don't know why I . . ." Pause. "So, I would have come sooner, but they weren't letting in visitors."

To her credit, Mom doesn't bat an eye about Amber saying "shitty."

I smile through my exhaustion. "It's fine. Thanks for coming." And I mean it. Amber's the only one who's shown up, as far as I know, even though I'd kind of hoped it'd be Caylee.

There's a long pause before I get up the nerve to ask, "Where's Caylee?"

Amber's silent for a moment. She mutters something then catches herself and raises her voice. "She didn't want to come."

Maybe I already knew. Still, it cuts.

"Sorry to be so blunt," she says, and she does look sorry. "But forget about Caylee. She's not a real friend. Because no real friend would treat you like that or blame you for what her disgusting pervert boyfriend did, you know?"

When I don't say anything, she rushes on. "I mean, she and I go way back, to our Girl Scout cookie-selling days, if you can believe it. And I've always felt like a protective big sister to her, but honestly, she's changed so much since Zac entered the picture that it's like I don't even know her anymore." Amber huffs, then grows quiet, her eyes distant. "I guess I expected her to snap out of it soon, wake the hell up and see him for who he really is, you know? I didn't want to just abandon her when she clearly seems lost, so I stuck around, thinking she'd need me after Zac inevitably dumped her and moved on. But for her to still be with him after everything . . ." Amber shakes her head, then stares up at me.

When I don't speak, she continues, "Anyway, I never got to say this fully on Monday, but in case you had any doubt, I want you to know I believe you. About Zac. About all of it—all of *them*—okay?"

Tears squeeze from my eyes as I nod.

"After you left school . . . Well, Caylee and I got in a huge fight. I told her again what a pervy dick Zac is, but of course she didn't want to hear it from me, either. Surprise, surprise. Guess that means she and I are done." Standing up, Amber surprises me with another hug, carefully navigating my tubes and wires this time, and doesn't let go. I realize she's much better at handling tears, or any hard emotion for that matter, than Caylee ever was. "Plus, once I saw your blog post, I knew I had to report that also," Amber finishes.

My brain feels too numb to reply.

"I'm not sorry I did it," Amber says into my pillow before releasing me from the hug and sitting back down. "Or for telling Ms. Adams. I'd do it again. It all just . . . sucked to witness, you know? First they hurt you. Then you hurt you . . ."

Shame floods me as I relive Mom cupping my face in her hands last night, near hysterics, her scrubs crumpled and her expression a cracked desert of worry lines. *"Tell me you're okay,"* she'd pleaded. *"Tell me you're okay."*

Now, picking at the greenish lint from the sheets, I avoid looking at Mom as I tell Amber, "I'm sorry I told you I'd come with you after talking to Caylee. I'm sorry I lied."

"*And* that nothing had happened at the party *and* that Thomas wasn't involved," she ticks off on her fingers.

"That too."

She shrugs. "Well, since that's your one freebie lie in our friendship, I guess you really made it count, huh? Just . . . don't let it happen again, okay?"

I nod.

"But, Erica? There's something I have to ask you."

The seriousness of Amber's voice pulls my eyes to her.

"Why'd you do it?"

I stare at her, confused. "Do what?"

"Give away your power—to Thomas, to Caylee? Let them tell you who you were. You never needed them, you know."

I know she's talking about my posts, the desperation I'd expressed over wanting to belong.

"I . . ." I attempt to argue, find a flaw in her logic, but all I see is myself trying so hard to get them both to like me, to think I'm someone special so that I could think so too. Wouldn't Erica Strange be proud.

I'm too ashamed to say this aloud, but Amber seems to read my mind just the same. "You're already her, you know. That Erica Strange you drew on your webpage in all her glorious badassery. You just gotta find her again."

I replay two nights ago when, drunk and drugged up and hopeless, I'd tossed my sketchbook in the trash, dousing her pages with Red Bull and vodka. Ruining her. Abandoning her.

"Which brings me to this." From her purse, Amber pulls a plastic grocery bag and sets it in my lap. Inside is a packet of markers and a pad of paper. The markers are the thick Crayola ones that bleed right through pages, while the pad has that recycled brown paper with the guidelines on it that kids use when learning to write.

I blink through my tears. They're perfect.

"They didn't have real sketchpads, but hey." Amber shrugs. "I figured you could draw some more weird stuff, maybe give Erica Strange an origin story?"

I stare down at the yellow-and-green box, the row of rainbow markers, shiny like Skittles through the smile-shaped hole. And I realize I've misunderstood Amber all along. She wasn't judging me. She was watching, observing, accepting me in a way maybe Thomas and Caylee never really had. "Thank you, Amber. For coming, and for this." I gesture. "It means so much to me, I can't even tell you."

She shrugs, then stands and rights the Scrabble board. "I expect great things. But on a less sappy note? I'm a beast when it comes to Scrabble so prepare thyself."

THOMAS

BEFORE MICHAEL LEFT FOR COLLEGE, WE TOOK A FAMILY vacation to Cabo. Michael and I had somehow convinced our parents to let us go quad riding with a local guide, despite the fact I'd never done much in the way of driving quads. Soon enough, Michael and I were going Mach 1 through winding dirt roads in a desert gorge, guide leading the way. I tried really hard to keep up and did okay for a while. Then I could only catch glimpses of brake lights, choking on their dust clouds until even those disappeared.

I wasn't paying good enough attention, trying to catch up, which is why I slammed into that rock in the middle of the road, flew over my handlebars. Rolled midair. Landed on my side. Slid several yards in the dirt, helmet bouncing, quad missing my legs by inches. On impact I felt my ribs go, like steak knives in my side. I lay there trying to breathe, but the air had gushed from me.

After what'd seemed like hours, Michael and the guide returned, tires spewing rocks. By that time, I'd sat up, still trying to breathe but barely able to because of the pain. Tears rolled down my face, but I didn't care that Michael saw me crying because he was crying too.

Feeling my ribs go, the steak knives . . . that's what it feels like to sit on this hard plastic slide and take in the pages from Erica's comics, posts confirming she liked me as much as I liked her, all the while reliving my own memories of the same events. It's rough hearing her describe everything she went through from the moment she stepped foot on Bay City grounds and reading the list of insecurities I never knew she had about fitting in, or questioning herself on the way she dressed, or being the scholarship girl in "Richy McRichville." I'd never thought about it before, not from her point of view, anyway, but it must've been tough for her, even before shit got so crazy.

And then there's the post about the party, told through her letter to Caylee. My brain fills in the gaps while Erica narrates waking up. It's brutal, both reliving it and seeing it fresh through her eyes—how humiliated she felt, how hopeless.

And if I close my eyes, I can picture that night perfectly, like I'm still right there in Zac's bed, Erica beneath me.

I'm lying on top of Erica, kissing her with everything I have. The night's so full of firsts. I've dreamed about this for weeks. And now, finally, this: my hat falling off her head, her hair spilling in all directions, kissing me back with the same enthusiasm.

The door slams open. "What have we here?" Zac's voice, booming through the room.

I roll off Erica as Zac moves in. Forest, Stallion, Ricky. Tina in a yellow dress, closing the door behind her. "Told you they were up here."

Erica blinking, trying to sit up, running her hand across her mouth. Nose and chin bright red from our kiss, underwear on full display between spread legs. I'm about to pull her to her feet when three bodies lunge toward us, leaping onto the bed.

"Cannonball!" Forest, a blur of gray-and-white shark.

The mattress bucks as Zac and Ricky join, bouncing us at their mercy. From the door, Stallion and Tina look on, laughing. Zac, rocketing himself into the air, hat flying. Ricky's face blazing red as his sweatshirt. The tail of Forest's costume flapping with each hop.

"Hope we're not interrupting," says Ricky, breathless.

But the bouncing is too much for Erica. Panic flips my stomach. She slips from the bed, taking down paper and Sharpies from Zac's nightstand. What he'd used to make "21 and over" signs so cops wouldn't have probable cause to enter. Erica barely misses hitting her head on the nightstand. She lands hard on her butt. I scramble down, ready to help her up. But Zac beats me to it. He reaches down, yanking her to her feet, all grin as she falls into him. I stare as his hands wrap around her waist, hold her to him. Slide over her jean skirt.

"Hello, peach," he says.

Something touches my arm. I jerk. Tina, resting her hand on my forearm.

I glance back at Erica. Shake my head. What am I seeing? Everything, a blur of color. A windshield in the rain. Then my eyes focus, and I see.

The bottom drops out.

Erica, pressed to Zac. Him, kissing her.

Her, kissing him.

His tongue meeting hers. Hands cupping her ass.

In my head, everything goes quiet.

Erica?

In my mouth: the taste of metal. In my head, roaring: *But she's my girlfriend. We're together now.*

Panic.

In my head: lunging, knocking Zac over. Tearing Erica away.

Not with Zac. Not him.

My Erica Strange.

In reality: me, watching. Erica's lips, tongue, moving against Zac's. Where mine had just been.

He lets her go. She stumbles, plops heavily on top of spilled paper, Sharpie.

This time, I don't move to help her up.

I stare at her, anger rising. So drunk. Leaning against the nightstand, head too heavy.

With Zac?

He's in the closet. Returns. A handle of tequila, red cups. "Who needs a drink?" Glugging alcohol into each cup— enough to drown a rat. Handing them out. Zac holds a cup. My hands won't unfist. Slides it onto the dresser. Holds Erica's cup. Spilling down her front.

My Erica Strange. Mine.

"Poker, ladies?" Zac to Tina, eyes on her dress, rummaging through a drawer. A deck of cards. "I gotta warn you"— fanning cards out—"stakes are high. Loser removes all clothes." A smirk, dramatic shrug.

A sound from Erica. An almost laugh, smile—*How can she?*—legs tucked under her. Trying to say something, voice slurred.

How could she?

Forest still bouncing, oblivious. Ricky sliding to the floor beside Erica. Stallion laughing behind me. "I'm in."

"Stallion, no one wants to see . . ." Zac shuffling the cards. "Enough of that shit in the locker room."

Tina, hand on my arm, stepping forward. "Got a better idea."

Cup from the dresser, rising to my lips. Tina crawling to Erica. Erica, skirt hiked high. "Erica, want a tattoo? Look so great. . . ." Tina's fist, closing around a Sharpie.

Erica, eyes closed. Still smiling. Playing along. Them, laughing. At her. Wasted.

Crackling. Red cup in my hand. Crushed. Liquid sloshing. Cup rises, empty. Watching. Watching.

Hating them all.

Hating Erica most.

Skirt hiked. Eyes half-closed. Wasted.

Tina, a Sharpie, the cap off. Dragging the pen above Erica's shirt. Erica not moving or caring. Me, tequila boiling through my chest. Should've known better. Should've known.

Head thrumming.

Zac staring. "Having fun yet?"

Tina pulling Erica's shirt. Covering her stomach, pink bra showing. Erica, eyes closed, head drooping.

Zac yanking the pen away.

Tina—"Hey!"

Ricky scrambling. More pens. To Forest, Tina. Stallion.

Zac holding out a pen. For me.

"Write her a little message." Pen hovering midair.

". . . is stupid," I say.

"Pussy." That smirk. Leaning in. Cast pressing my spine. "Stupid bitch. Like all the rest."

Like all the rest. Like Angie. Freshman year. That other guy.

Now Ricky on Erica's arm. Forest, her foot.

Everyone turned to me.

My head spinning. Grabbing the pen. Leaning over Erica. Pen hovering.

Scanning legs, stomach . . .

"Aim high, VanB."

Chest, face. Eyes half-closed. Makeup smeared.

Me, looking away.

They're watching. Waiting.

Like all the rest.

Me, flipping her over. Moving the pen over her back—

Thomas.

I was here. I saw.

Hurling Sharpie. Hitting blinds. Disappearing.

Tina. "Hold on . . . phone."

Me, flinging open the door. Stairs, too much. Plopping down. Seething.

But I'd thought . . . Me: Thomas the Rhymer. Her . . .

Them: Laugh. Pause. Laugh.

Not my Erica Strange. Not anymore.

Later—how much later?—everyone. Stumbling out, manic. Ricky, grin wild.

Zac clapping my shoulder.

Me, rising. Tilting toward stairs. Hand shooting out. Banister.

Caylee appearing. Face glowing. "Seen Erica?"

"Could say that." Ricky. Like Zac. Tossing boots down stairs—tumbling Erica Strange.

Caylee, not hearing, seeing, knowing. "She . . . have to find . . ."

"Babe." Zac, grasping shoulders. Tequila bottle dropping. "Took care of it. Snug as a bug in a . . ."

Caylee's face, soft. ". . . the sweetest."

Zac pulling her. Down the hall. Away from Erica. Closed door.

Forest, slurpy kissy sounds. Following Stallion. Down the stairs. "Beeeeeeeeer pong!"

". . . out of beer." Ricky, scrambling, scrambling to catch up.

Me, gripping banister. Tequila. Dropping. Stumbling. Down the stairs. To drink. Calm. Sick. Anger. Darker, something darker.

Darker. . . .

Guilt.

Crushing. Choking.

Guilt.

For what I'd let him get away with. For blaming her. For what I'd done.

ERICA

MOM SHAKES ME AWAKE. "YOU HAVE ANOTHER VISITOR. . . .
Feel up for it?"

"Who is it?" I ask, voice clogged with sleep, dimly worried
Psychiatrist Austin and his shark scrubs are back for more.

"Caylee."

I sit up so fast, my guts and head protest loudly. She's here.
She came. What does she want? What will she say?

"Um, yeah. Give me a second," I say, casting around, trying
to steady myself.

". . . course. What can I get you?"

"Can you hand me that hairbrush? Do I have stuff all over
my face?"

"Yes, but honey . . . Wouldn't worry about that right now."

I yank the brush she hands me through my hair, but it's the
wrong kind of brush and frizzes my hair everywhere. Dumping

some of my water cup into my hand—onto my lap—I try to smooth it down. I blot at the blanket—there's nothing I can do—then wipe the corners of my mouth, knowing my skin's all sweaty and breath must be putrid. My armpits reek too.

"Can I brush my teeth?"

"Sweetie . . . sure you're fine . . . Not here for your breath."

I eye my tray of empty cups and straws beside me, then lift it. "Can you please take this?"

"Sure."

Smoothing down the bedsheets, I say, "Okay, I'm ready."

Mom says something to the nurse passing in the hallway, hands her the tray, then takes her seat at the edge of the room. I was kind of hoping Mom would give me a minute alone with Caylee but being without adult supervision is against the rules. I fluff my pillows and sit up as straight as I can.

Caylee comes in a minute later, wrapped in a sweater, bare legs gleaming out of short shorts. Her smile looks nervous as she steps forward, lingering a few feet from the edge of the bed, taking in the machines, my IV, the giant vase of sunflowers my dad sent.

"You can sit, if you want," I tell her, gesturing to the chairs next to me.

She hesitates for a moment then steps forward, saying something that I can't hear.

"Oh, um, you have to speak louder. I can't really hear you." I don't know which of us is more embarrassed.

She nods, over-enunciating her next words, still not looking at me. "Sorry, they warned me. I forgot already."

I nod. "It's okay."

Silence.

"So . . . how are you?" I ask, feeling like it's something she should be asking me.

"Good." She nods to confirm. "Well, not . . . Can't really compare." She glances nervously over at Mom, who sits watching us, then fidgets with the sleeves of her sweater. *Does Caylee feel guilty, blame herself at all?*

"Things have been . . . at school lately with the police and all that. Zac and I skipped today." Her eyes fly to mine. "I mean, I skipped. I don't . . . what he was doing." She tucks her hair behind her ear. "I mean, like, have you . . . to the police yet?"

"They, um, came this morning," I say carefully, "but I haven't really said much."

"Oh, well, that's good."

In my head, a strange rumbling starts, deeper than any ringing in my ears.

"Do you know, like, what you're going to do?" she continues. "What you're going to tell . . . ?"

The rumbling builds, forming a question: "Caylee, why are you here?"

The question takes her aback. She mumbles something, pulling at her sleeves and glancing back at Mom.

"Louder, Caylee," I say. "I can't hear you."

"To see you," she says, barely louder this time. Her eyes still don't meet mine as she tucks more hair behind her ear.

"Caylee, you've been here for, like, three minutes, maybe, and you haven't even asked how I am. But you're sure as hell asking about what I'm going to say to the police. So, why are you here?"

Mom rises.

Caylee's mouth moves.

"Louder, Caylee. I can't hear you."

"Why would you ask that?" she says.

"What am I supposed to think? That you're here for me? For my well-being?" Maybe Amber's right. Maybe Caylee's never really been my friend. I was just convenient to hang out with every time Zac blew her off, a shoulder to cry on. Because if it came down to choosing, him or me . . .

Full realization hits like a dropped piano. "He sent you, didn't he?" It's a question so blunt, so brave. An Erica Strange question.

Now Caylee's eyes find mine: Panic. Truth.

"To figure out what I was up to. See if I'd tell, right?" I add, and suddenly, I can see it all so clearly. Zac telling her she ruined his life when my post to her got out—even if he was the one responsible for its leak—and that she had to fix this. And still she chose to come. She chose *him*.

What would Erica Strange do? I ask, thinking of my damaged hearing, my injured liver and kidneys, my gutted stomach. I think of my mother's face when she first saw me awake, of the body I had before—before the pills, before drinking at Zac's party, before they touched me. I ache for that body, the one that could hear and move and draw and dance in capes.

I think of my mother, small and frail-looking since everything happened, since I stopped breathing and she had to save me. She rescues people for a living, and yet she almost lost me. I've hurt her. I've hurt me. I'm tired of hurting myself for what they did to me. Tired of pretty girls like Caylee who let guys like Zac tell them who they are and what to do. I'm tired of cowardly Thomases and foolish crushes and school hallways full of poison words. I'm tired. I'm so, so tired. But more than that, I'm furious. Erica Strange furious.

Mom approaches, telling Caylee, "I think it's time—"

I cut her off. What would Erica Strange do? This. "Caylee, you need to leave. Now."

"But what am I supposed to tell him?" Caylee asks, fighting tears.

The question stuns. I was right. He sent her. Zac *sent* her. But my answer is superhero swift. "Tell him that what he did to me is called assault, and he's going to pay."

THOMAS

ON THE PURPLE SLIDE, ERICA'S MESSAGE TO CAYLEE BLURS
in front of me—the pleading for Caylee to listen as she detailed
everything that people had said or done. Even me running into
her in the hallway, losing my shit. I hear her hope fade, grasping for anyone to care, but no one did. Instead, it got worse.

Sorting through her final message hurts the most. To be
able to point out exactly where the drugs started to take effect,
where she started to slip. Who had found her? How had she
been saved? Because the Erica in these pages looks beyond saving. How could I have ever thought this could blow over, that
things would magically get better? But I guess I never actually
believed that, not really.

I flip back to the illustration of us at the beach—Thomas the
Rhymer, Erica Strange, lying beneath the stars. It was a week
before I'd gotten drunk and convinced myself that she didn't

matter, that she was "like all the rest." Just because I didn't know how to tell Zac to stop. So instead, I'd blamed everything on her when she'd been wasted, not even able to protect herself.

This whole time I've managed to convince myself that what happened wasn't really my fault, that I couldn't have done anything to change how it all went down. But that's a lie. Now, reading these pages, my head buzzes with the truth of it.

Michael picks up the office phone on the first ring. "Tommy? Where are you?"

Holding his phone to my ear, I know I've screwed everything up so badly. Maybe if I'd made a different choice, Erica and I would be hanging out right now. Maybe she'd love this slide. We'd try to fit, but we'd get stuck and laugh about it. Maybe we'd date through high school and help each other through all the world suck. She'd go to CalArts and major in Animation, and I'd go to Thornton for songwriting while keeping up with guitar. We'd check out weird museums and wild concerts but always love the beach the most. We'd date for a long time. Maybe forever. And we'd both be so happy.

"Tommy?" Michael repeats into the phone.

"I dropped the glass of orange juice on purpose," I whisper, knowing he won't understand. "The morning after, when I heard her come down the stairs, I knew the guys would hear her too. Give her a hard time. So, I knocked over the glass to interrupt Zac talking about her. Distract them all so she could leave in peace. Because even then, I knew what we'd done was inexcusable. That I'd just stood there and watched them strip her and write on her. That *I* wrote on her.

"I'd been so mad, and I thought it was at *her*—I let it be at her—when I saw Zac kissing her. But she was so drunk, she didn't know what was going on. And I didn't say anything, couldn't stand up to him, just watched him put his fucking hands all over her instead of flattening him like I should've done before driving her home.

"And I should've gone after her the next morning. Said something to her. Anything. Given her a ride. Because that whole time, all she was asking for was a hand up—for me to *help* her, Mikey. For anyone to. Instead, I yelled at her and told her off. Told her I didn't want anything to do with her. I made her believe . . ." I choke. "I made her believe it was her fault. And the worst part? She *believed* me, Mikey. She believed me so much, she tried to kill herself. To not ever be here again. To not exist anymore. Because of us, because of me . . ." My voice snaps.

"Thomas," Michael says. "I need you to come home, okay? I need you to finish your crying or whatever it is you need to do. Then I need you to get your head straight and come home. Everything will be okay."

"How can you even say that?" I demand, tossing down the pages. "Nothing's ever going to be okay again."

"I promise you it will be. But, Tommy?"

The pages rustle in the wind. I press my face to my palm. "Yeah?"

"If you're looking for redemption in all this, you're not going to find it. The only thing you can do now is the right thing."

"But they'll hate me. They'll all hate me." The rubber bark at my feet blurs black.

"They might. But what's worse: Having others hate you for a while or hating yourself forever?"

"But I'll lose music school. I'll lose everything."

"You might."

I suck in a deep breath and blow it out, gathering all my courage to ask: "How? How can I do it?"

"I'll help you, kid," he says softly.

It takes a long time for me to pull myself together, to finally breathe right again, but Michael stays on the line while I do, not saying anything. I'm exhausted, can't remember ever being so tired, like I could flop back in this hard plastic tube and go to sleep for the rest of eternity.

"Mikey?" I say into the phone.

"Yeah, Tommy?"

"I wanna come home now, okay?"

He exhales into the phone. "You've made the right choice. I'm coming to get you. Just tell me where you are."

I read him the park name from the sign on the fence, then click to end the call and cover my face.

It hurts. It hurts more than anything I've ever experienced in my life. But staring down at Erica Strange fluttering in the breeze, I know now what I have to do.

ERICA

"HE SENT HER. HE *SENT* HER!" I YELL, HEAD SPINNING, THROAT aching. "And she came for him, not me!"

Caylee's just left, and fury lights my bones. A hairbrush, pillow, Scrabble tiles fly across the room. Anything I can get my hands on.

"Who sent her, Bug?" Mom asks. "Tell me what's going on." She's not understanding. She doesn't know.

"She was never on my side. Never." My legs pummel sheets, fists pound the mattress, vision darkens.

Mom's grabbing my ankles. "Erica, please calm down. Help me understand."

"She was always going to choose him, don't you see? Always!" I'm in a tunnel, a narrowing tunnel.

"Bug, please stop flailing! You're hurting yourself!"

Her agonized cry snaps me out of it. The world looms large again, blackness receding.

I look at her, breathing hard. She's flustered, face contorted with fear.

I look down. She's right. My IV's straining, close to tearing again.

I stop, still myself, breathe deeply. For a fraction of a second, I'm transported back to our apartment in the minutes before I took the pills, slamming the door in Mom's face and refusing to open up to her even after she pleaded with me to. Then I blink several times till my vision rights itself.

I've been so selfish, so very selfish. Everything I've put her through . . .

"Mom," I whisper. "I'm sorry. I won't hurt myself anymore. I promise."

And I've never meant it more. Maybe one day I can do it for me, too, but in this moment it's for Mom, for Erica Strange. I think of Austin's words, that my reactions need to come in service of myself, not against me.

But now, where to start?

How about from the very beginning?

"Something . . . something bad happened to me. Something so horrible . . ." My voice cracks, but I push through the broken. "And I really need to tell you about it."

THOMAS

"YOU READY?" MICHAEL ASKS.

He sits next to me on the bed in his old room, one hand on my shoulder, the other gripping his phone. I've told him everything, face stiff from crying so hard again.

"It won't be the same. None of it will ever be the same." I'm choking out the words because there's something in my throat that wants me to stop talking, to never open my mouth again.

Michael sighs a heavy sigh. "You're right, Tommy. It won't be."

"Music school will be over. Uncle Kurt will be so disappointed. There's no going back."

"I know," he whispers.

"God, why do I have to do this?"

He shrugs. "You already know the answer to that one, kid."

"I just didn't think I was that kind of guy, you know?

Someone who would do something so . . . unforgivable. I always thought I was one of the good guys, you know? Not like Dad or Zac. But I was both, and I betrayed her."

I picture Erica's drawings, so full of color and hope in the beginning, and compare it to the broken girl who wrote the good-bye. Heaving a shaky breath, I take the phone from Michael and dial the number he holds out. The phone rings once, then a deep male voice answers. "Bay City Police. How may I direct your call?"

"Could . . ." I clear my throat. "Could you transfer me to"— my eyes find the name on the business card—"Officer Rodriguez's line, please?"

Michael nods his encouragement, squeezing my shoulder.

"One moment."

The phone rings once, twice. "Officer Rodriguez speaking," answers a female voice.

All of a sudden, I'm freezing. My whole body shakes, knees jumping violently even when I press my feet into the floor. "Officer Rodriguez?" I say in a rush. "This is Thomas. Thomas VanBrackel. There's something . . . something I gotta say."

I think about Erica, wonder if I'll ever see her again, knowing her smile won't ever be for me again. *Thomas the Rhymer won't exist anymore.*

Over the line, Officer Rodriguez says, "I'm listening, Thomas."

On the floor between my Chucks, my eyes find the curled-up

pages of Erica's blog, catching a glimpse of a superhero cape and a small bat friend.

But there will always be an Erica Strange.

I take a deep breath, one that shudders through me. Then I open my mouth and let the truth fly free.

ERICA

AFTER TELLING MOM EVERYTHING, I MENTIONED CALLING
Officer Rodriguez. That's when Mom asked my permission to
bring Valerie in on the conversation, and together, the three of
us talked it over. It's definitely not a decision to make lightly.
Everyone knows what happens to girls in the media who speak
out. But once I made my decision, we called Officer Rodriguez
together, and she got here in no time. Maybe she thought I'd
back out. Maybe she was right. Either way, I'm glad she's here.

While waiting for Officer Rodriguez to finish talking with
Mom, I take out the markers Amber gave me. The navy pen the
color of Erica Strange's cape shakes in my fingers, and I know
my voice will too. And still . . .

I'm ready, I whisper to her—my Erica Strange—to help keep
my fear at bay. As ready as I'll ever be, anyway.

Then the officer takes a seat by my bed and begins, talking

too slowly, too loudly so that I can be sure to hear. My marker tip drags across the page in a fluid, sweeping motion as questions and names roll from the officer's tongue like an endless conveyor belt:

Zachary Boyd.

Richard Demoine.

Christopher "Stallion" Lawson.

Forest Stevens.

Thomas VanBrackel.

Tina Marcus.

Caylee Morgan. . . .

How did you meet?

How well did you know . . . ?

. . . describe your relationship?

. . . attend the game?

. . . night of the party?

. . . when you woke up?

. . . realized what happened?

. . . harassment start?

. . . describe the writing?

. . . names?

. . . messages?

. . . photos?

. . . video?

My brain is working overtime trying to focus, so the final question catches me off-guard: "What made you change your mind?"

The marker freezes in my hand, and I stare up at Officer

Rodriguez until she clarifies, "About telling the truth, I mean."

"Someone who used to be my best friend," I say.

Maybe it's not the answer she was looking for, but the officer nods. "All right, that should be all for now. We'll let you know if we have any further questions."

As she stands, pocketing her notebook, she leans over and says just loud enough for my aching ears, "You did the right thing, Erica."

Something about her parting words rubs me the wrong way, though, as if there's only one right way to handle this situation—tell the police and all will be well. Justice will be served. And maybe that's what she believes. But anyone with eyes and ears knows that's not always true. I don't even want to think about the possibility of a trial or how hard it's going to be moving forward, how brutal people's rash judgments can be. But I remind myself I have Mom, and Valerie, and Amber on my side. I even have an alter-ego supergirl with a loyal bat sidekick who will help see me through, and I have to pray that's enough.

Still, what about individuals who don't go to the police—can you really blame them? Are they any less because of it? Would *I* have been less if I'd chosen a different path, any less Erica Strange?

As I arc the marker across the page, I decide Officer Rodriguez is wrong; there is no "right." There's only learning how to survive something so horrible that living may sometimes feel impossible. There's only acknowledging that it happened and admitting—even to yourself—how greatly it affected you. In my mind, if there's any right in all this, that's it. And that's the heroic part.

Almost like she can read my thoughts, Mom pats my arm and hands me another tissue, enunciating each word: "Stay brave, Bug. It's going to be okay."

I nod, staring down at my beautifully messy Erica Strange, tear-splattered and all, knowing that so many images I haven't yet drawn need to come before this one—images of unforeseen storms and lightning-tattered capes, of mist-engulfed castles and cloaked villains made of words, of looming cliff faces and near-fatal shark attacks. But I keep drawing this final image of Erica Strange, with a crashing ocean wave emblem now burning bright where before there was none, clambering aboard a pirate ship. Because once, many moons ago, a badass superhero girl taught me that sometimes you have to write the ending you want before you can know where you need to begin. This is where we used to differ, she and I. But now, I think we might just be on the same page.

As I add in fierce, female supers surrounding Erica Strange, I realize something else, too. For the first time since I got here, since waking up Sunday, if even for just this tiny, glorious glimmer of a moment, I think I believe my mother's words:

It's going to be okay.

RESOURCES LIST

National Suicide Prevention Lifeline
https://suicidepreventionlifeline.org/
1-800-273-8255 (hotline, available 24/7)

RAINN (Rape, Abuse & Incest National Network)
https://www.rainn.org/ (live chat and hotline, available 24/7)
National Sexual Assault Hotline
1-800-656-HOPE (4673)

National Sexual Violence Resource Center
https://www.nsvrc.org/

Stomp Out Bullying
https://www.stompoutbullying.org/

The (free) Be Strong app
https://bestrong.global/

ACKNOWLEDGMENTS

Many people deserve colossal thanks for helping launch this debut, so this list is long and mighty! Profuse thanks to:

Carl for his endless love, silliness, and sense of adventure. Meeting you was the best thing that ever happened to me. Your faith in me and my writing is the reason I'm here, especially when I sometimes doubted. Your hugs are world-class, and even after all these years, you're still my favorite part of every day. (You too, Mau-town!)

My rock-star agent, Sara Crowe, who saw a glimmer in this manuscript and believed in it since Day One, well before the book was ready for the world. Thank you for your tremendous patience, for your incredible insight into all things publishing, and for finding this book the perfect home. I'm so lucky to work with you!

The whole crew at Pippin Properties for your relentless and

ACKNOWLEDGMENTS

fierce advocating of kidlit authors and their novels, and for helping bring this one to life.

My superhero editor, Liesa Abrams, who understood my exact vision for this book, who fearlessly championed its message, and whose guiding light made it shine. Meeting you over the world's best gluten-free bagels felt like the perfect kind of fate. You are exceptional in every way, Liesa!

The whole team at Simon & Schuster Books for Young Readers, whose magical touch lifted this novel to new heights, including Morgan York and Alison Velea for being the world's greatest managing editors, as well as copyeditor Crystal Velasquez and proofreader Stephanie Evans for their keen eyes. Special thanks to Sarah Creech for the gorgeous cover and her brilliant expertise in all things art; to Mara Anastas, who supported early acquisition of this book; and to Krista Vitola for so graciously stepping in and seeing this book through to the end. Y'all are the greatest!

The supremely talented Emma Vieceli for taking my weird "supergirl with bat sidekick" storyline and putting her own badass spin on it so that Erica Strange could soar off the page in a way I never dreamed possible. The illustrations are perfection, Emma. I'm forever grateful!

Ashley for navigating this publishing journey right by my side, and for being the world's greatest CP, friend, listener, and cheerer. (Long live our state-hopping escapades, white-noise debriefs, and hours on the phone with all the crunchy snacks!)

ACKNOWLEDGMENTS

We always said we could, and here we are, my debut sister! **Buy her gorgeous debut, *Amelia Unabridged*!** Thank you for everything. I'd be utterly lost without you.

Lucy for bringing such light to my life even in dark times, and for being there when I needed you most. Thank you for all the talks, tears, laughter, #wfiw!, plus all the baking and crafts a heart could hold. What would I do without you? And Jenn, we've grown so much together since meeting—thank you for always holding space for me and forever accepting me as I am. To say I'm proud of who we've become is the world's greatest understatement. You're unstoppable, friend. Endless thanks to you both for our many adventures, from Mad Hatter tea parties to roaring twenties plane rides to Buc-ee's pit stops. Team JammyPack, FTW!

Jessi and Clay, I cherish your love and kickass friendships immensely. Our weekly check-ins are a lifeline for me, as is each magical retreat spent in your company and celebrating every victory—both large and small— together. I cannot wait to return the favor and rejoice in your debuts in the very near future! And special thanks, Jessi, for the generous and insightful sensitivity read. I hope I did you proud, friend.

And to all my Hollins sisters and fierce cupcake warriors. You know who you are! Thank you for helping me create an inclusive Hogwarts built on late-night study sessions and firefly-lit campus strolls, rocking chair porches in thunderstorms and ghost stories in the graveyard, plus all the Carvin magic to fill a whole soul. Attending Hollins was one of my best life decisions because it gave me y'all. And to Hollins University herself—thank you for eternally restoring my belief in magic.

My New England homegirls, Lisl and Basia, for being the world's greatest beachcombing, antique-store-scouring, and adventure-loving ladies I could ask for. I thank my lucky stars every day that we all wound up together. Love you, babes!

My family—especially my sister, Megan; mother, Sonia; and Aunt Cathy—for their endless cheerleading. Thanks also, Megs, for being a fierce and loyal sister always, and for fighting off my childhood bullies; Mom, for always letting me check out as many library books as my small arms could hold; and Aunt Cathy, for all those magical summers, spent just the two of us, that were such a lifeline for me. I love you more than words can express!

David Gustafson for reading an early draft and calling immediately with expert feedback and an overabundance of enthusiasm. (I sure needed both—thank you!)

The Wordsmith Workshops community: Cristin Terrill for helping me brainstorm the scene that helped inform Thomas's whole arc. Beth Revis for teaching me how to make difficult characters readable when I most needed to hear it. Mama Lynn for serving up the most delicious, gluten-free gourmet while always saying this day would come. Cristin and Beth, thank you for creating a second home full of creepy documentaries, *Modelland*-level bedtime stories, and a dynamic community of writers I couldn't live without (especially you, Amy and Kim!).

My local writer kin. A profound thank you to all for the many write-ins, the sage advice, and the incredible gifts of your friendships, including Adi, Jeff, and the whole "Plague Bagels" gang; Rebekah, Karina, and Beth—love you ladies!; Erin, Lita, and the Kidlit603 New Words community.

Professor Nancy Ruth Patterson for gifting me the space in which to send those first fledgling pages and for telling me I was safe in her hands. I always knew I was, Coach. And thank you, from the bottom of my heart, for exemplifying not only what it takes to be a good writer, but also an even better person. Special thanks as well to Nancy's tutorial group and my writing comrades: Clay, Amy, Suzanne, Danielle, Caity, and Michael.

My thesis adviser, the incomparable Ellen Kushner, and her extraordinary wife, Delia Sherman, who read far too many drafts of this book, whose generous pearls of wisdom helped shape this book's very heart, and who showed me how to— quite literally—walk through a scene. Your guidance was exceptional, Ellen. Special thanks, too, to Ellen's tutorial group and my author sisters: Ash, Sarah, Courtney, Danielle, and Kelly.

Hillary Homzie, whose brilliant creative writing class inspired not only this book but another one as well, and whose encouragement let me know I had what it took to write them. Thank you, Hillary!

The BSCC: Sharon, Caitlin, and Bryan. Thank you, brave creative soldiers, for your insightful comments and endless encouragement in early drafts. Tag, you're next!

Nutschell, Alana, Angie, Maiko, and all of CBW-LA for being my original home base, kidlit writers-in-arms, and where my author journey began. You called it from Day One, Nutschell! Can't wait to celebrate your debut next!

Scott Vadala, Eddie Schumacher, and Kyle Ganson for their solid (and immensely helpful) feedback on all things medical, pharmaceutical, and psychological; Sam Harding for his singular lacrosse expertise; Jackie Harkness for her stellar advice on everything "lawyer" and for rooting me on since the early days; Cacy Duncan for her proficiency in comic books; and Scott Evans for his solid police-force knowledge. Thank you, all! (Any errors found in these pages are my own.)

Rebecca Aronson, whose gift of exceptionally insightful edits helped direct this book early on in the exact right direction, which changed everything. *(THANK YOU!)*

Stephen Chbosky, who—after I'd explained the premise for this book at a writing conference—told me to write it immediately, saying, "I can already see the movie poster in my head." Your words have carried me far, Stephen. I thank you for them!

And finally, for anyone else who has supported me throughout this Mr. Toad's Wild Writerly Ride in ways both great and small, I thank you endlessly from the bottom of my heart.